By Lauren Nicolle Taylor

Clean Teen Publishing, Inc.

Woodlands
Copyright © 2013 by: Lauren Nicolle Taylor

Clean Teen Publishing
PO Box 561326
The Colony, TX 75056

www.cleanteenpublishing.com

For more information about our content disclosure,
please utilize the QR code above with your smart phone or visit us at
www.cleanteenpublishing.com.

For my friend Chloe,
without whom The Woodlands would never have
made it out of the desk drawer.

And for my husband Michael,
you are my Joseph.

Prologue

Before

When I was eight years old, I got the distinct and unsettling impression I was unsuited to life in Pau Brazil. That my life would go off like the single firework on Signing Day. A brilliant burst of shimmering color and noise that exploded in the sky momentarily, then disappeared into the black night air.

A slip of yellow paper shot under the door in the evening, spinning across the floor like a flat top and colliding with my father's foot. It was an official notice informing everyone that Superior Grant was visiting in three days' time. He had a special announcement to make.

Citizens scrambled to make their lawns more perfect than they were before. Uniforms were pressed and cleaned. All the children were expected to line up around the edges of the center Ring and await the great man himself.

I was excited, but my excitement had an edge of terror to it—this was a Superior. My father warned me to not get my hopes up.

"He's just a man, like the rest of us," my father said as he knelt down to adjust my oversized uniform and tighten my ribbon.

My mother tsked and fussed around in the kitchen. "Pelo, don't say things like that to her. I don't want you filling her head with your ridiculous ideas."

His eyes darted to her for a second but then he locked on me.

"Ideas are never ridiculous. Ideas are just that, ideas. Putting them into practice... now that's when things get ridiculous," he smirked.

I drew my eyebrows together, confused. He patted my head and took my hand. "C'mon, let's get this farcical procession over with."

"Pelo!" My mother's angry foot stomp clacked on the tiles.

He put his hands up in the air in surrender. "All right, all right. I'll behave," he said, and then he winked at me. I beamed up at him. He was a shiny hurricane and I was happy to be swept away.

They were going to choose a child to come forward and ask Grant a question. Our nervous teachers had given each student a card with an innocuous question on it. I looked down at the printed piece of yellow cardboard. Mine said, 'Superior Grant, how does it feel to be the descendant of the brilliant founder of the Woodlands?' I frowned. I knew that Grant was descended from President Grant of the United States of Something or Other. We learned that at school. We were also taught that Grant was the initiator of the treaty; he orchestrated the signing in the last days of the Race War and negotiated peace. But this question was boring and I was sure no one would care about the answer. I would much rather have asked him what kind of food Superiors got to eat. Were they stuck with the hundred-year-old canned foods we were? The globs of vegetable that came out in one solid, gelatinous lump, identifiable only by their difference in color, as most of the labels had peeled off years ago. Green could be, but was not reserved exclusively, for peas. Orange for carrots, or maybe pumpkin. It goes on—an exciting Woodlands guessing game for ages four and up.

In my mind the Superiors must have been super-people. Beautiful, tall, and powerful.

I could barely contain my disappointment when Superior Grant stepped out of the helicopter. He was regular sized and a little overweight. He was handsome, but not like my father. It was the kind of handsomeness that required maintenance. Grey, slicked-back hair, manicured beard. He had the black military uniform on. Gold tassels swung festively in the wind created by the slowing chopper blades.

Despite this, I still wanted him to pick me. I leaned into the circle, standing on my tiptoes. My parents were a few rows behind me, heads bowed solemnly.

I kept my eyes down when Grant came close, trying my hardest not to bounce up and down like some of the other kids who were reeling with nervous energy. When the boots stopped in front of me, I stopped breathing, still staring at my feet.

A policeman tapped me on the shoulder sharply with a baton and said, "You. Ask your question." I couldn't believe it. And very suddenly didn't want to.

I rubbed my shoulder and looked up into Superior Grant's face, taking in his tight forehead and even tighter jaw. I tipped my head to the side, wondering what made him so special. When I realized I shouldn't be staring, I cast my eyes towards my shaking cardboard question, barely able to see the typed words that seemed to want to jump off the page. I opened my mouth to speak but the way he was eyeing me made me freeze, the question sitting on my lips like an un-blown bubble. It was like I had suddenly grown extra limbs or had spots all over my face because his nose scrunched up and his eyes watered like he thought I was diseased.

He took a step closer and peered into my face. I leaned away, the musty, vinegary smell of his breath overpowering. "What's wrong with her eyes?" he said in a strange drawn out twang, like 'whaat's wrawng with her eyeees?'

I felt anger rising inside me like an over-boiling pot. I glared at him. My father had taught me that my eyes were nothing to be ashamed of. It was uncommon but it didn't mean there was anything wrong with me. I had one blue eye and one brown. So did my father. Grant raised an eyebrow, unperturbed by my narrowed eyes and reddening face. He placed his hand on my eyelid and lifted it, straining my eye socket. Then he moved to the other eye and did the same. I shook my head free of him and before I knew what I was doing, I smacked his hand away.

I heard a couple of people in the crowd laugh but the rest seemed to have simultaneously stopped breathing. Behind me someone was moving through. Grant smiled down at me cruelly.

"Poor decision, child," he said smoothly. Then he turned and walked away.

I barely had time to process my mistake when a policeman grabbed me by the scruff of my neck and pulled me upwards to face the crowd. He rattled me around like a bag of apples and I could feel my inside bruising.

"See here. Here is lesson for all of you of how NOT to behave in the presence of Superior Grant."

I saw my father's wobbling figure moving towards me like a mirage.

As my brain started to whip into a milkshake in my skull, it occurred to me that I shouldn't have done what I'd just done. It also occurred to me in a dangerous revelation, that I wasn't sorry at all.

Somehow my father managed to negotiate my release. Besides, the Guardian seemed anxious to catch up to Grant, who was moving on to the next group of children. He dragged me through the crowd and we crouched behind the stone wall of Ring One, listening to the faint, quivering voice of a child asking her question. "How do you weigh your wisdom against your strength, Superior Grant?" I had the odd thought—how could wisdom weigh anything?

My father clasped his strong dark hands around my face worriedly, turning it from side to side. "Are you all right?"

I nodded, fierce tears running down my face. "I think so. I didn't like him very much."

He shook his head, but amusement twisted his face, "You want to know a secret?" I nodded and he leaned down to my ear. "I don't like him very much either," he whispered.

The crackling and whining that always preceded an announcement on the PA system started and the Superior Grant's elegant voice carried out over the sea of people.

"I am here to announce the Superiors have decided large families pose a direct threat to the security of the Woodlands. Brothers, sisters, and the bonds that result create an US versus THEM culture, which is unacceptable and in direct opposition with All Kind." He sounded bored as he talked. "Hence, we will allow each couple to house only one child at a time. This is not negotiable and any violations will be strictly dealt with."

The crowd murmured but that was the extent of their opposition.

Then he said, "Have your elder children available for collection by tomorrow morning."

The crowd hummed and then an angry voice splashed out and fell flat on the stones. "You can't take our children!" Other voices began to rustle like the crackle of shifting leaves.

I took a step up onto the ledge of the wall to get a better look. I watched as a policeman moved slowly but deliberately towards the man that shouted, with a face like horror. He took his baton and clapped the side of the man's head, hard, to show they could do whatever they wanted. As it cracked, an arc of blood sprayed onto the faces of people closest, like droplets of red rain. The crowd fell back from the man's crumpled body in a wave. A woman screamed and threw herself down beside him. The policeman joined the others, twirling his baton around in his hand and wiping the blood off on his pants. Everything went quiet, like the guardian had swished all the air out of the circle. If there were birds, even they would have ceased to breathe.

I looked to my father for his reaction. His face was white, his whole body shaking with anger, his mouth open slightly like he wanted to speak. *Don't speak*, I prayed.

He crouched down and shouted through the gaps between people's legs, "President Grant is an insane dictator!" then stood up quietly and did a brilliant impression of a normal, frightened person. The policeman's head snapped around and searched the crowd but no one was willing to point him out; they didn't want to be punished.

He pulled me to him tightly and I clung on to his leg.

"Are they going to take me away?" I asked naively.

"No beautiful girl," he whispered. "You are all we have."

When we got home my parents fought like never before. I stayed in my room with my ear pressed to the wall. I couldn't hear my mother at all but I caught my father's response to everything she said.

"No."

"Come on, it wasn't that bad. She got away, didn't she?"

"Yes, but she's a child. She'll learn to control herself."

"Yes, exactly like me. I'm still here aren't I? You're being absurd. She needs her father."

"You wouldn't do that."

Silence.

The next morning at school, my class was half-empty and half-full of red-eyed, stain-cheeked children who had lost their brothers and sisters.

In my child brain, where an hour could seem like a week and a gap of months seemed to go by in an instant, it was like my father was swapped with Paulo almost immediately. Suddenly, my mother was remarried, my father had disappeared, and where there was once warmth and laughter, there was only hardness. Looking back, I'm sure that's not quite how it happened but like I said, I was eight.

Now, at sixteen, I was amazed I had lasted as long as I had. And after the twentieth time of my mother asking me why I was like this—I started to wonder myself.

I think the answer was a combination of things. The first being that I severely lacked that healthy dose of fear most people seemed to have. Fear being healthy, because not fearing the Superiors was about as good for you as a mugful full of bleach with your morning toast. The other reason, which took me longer to work out, was that even though I hated my father for leaving, I still wanted to hold on to him somehow. His memory was slippery and I struggled to get my hands around it. But when I did something unexpected, something to raise the eyebrows and sometimes the hands of my teachers, my father's face became clearer in my mind, the edges sharpened. I could see him smiling at me crookedly and pretending to be cross even though I knew he wasn't. These memories would pull in and out of focus like flipping photos.

And ultimately, when almost everything I did was controlled by the Superiors, by my teachers and by Paulo, I took what little control I could for myself and held onto to it fiercely.

1́

Rosa

It was a slow dust of a day. The earth swirled in mini tornados, scratching up the eight meter walls and slipping back down again, because in this place there was nothing for it to cling to. It skittered across the grass, kissing the blades, and tearing around the perfectly manicured trees that sat in the front yard of every home. Here in the rings of Pau Brazil, nothing settled—nothing ever could.

I shrugged on my grey uniform. My mother was right about it being cheap and nasty. It was itchy and it seemed to beckon hot air and repel cool air. It clung to the wrong parts of me and billowed unflatteringly everywhere else. I didn't really care. Everyone looked the same so it didn't matter. I let the back of the shirt fall, wincing a little as the rough cloth brushed against my sliced-up skin. I couldn't quite see it but I could feel it lightly with my fingertips, raised ribbons of split flesh. New scabs were already forming over the old scars. I never gave it a chance to heal. Soon there would be fresh cuts to add to the healing ones. I gathered up my assignment papers and shoved them in my bag, placing my mother's treasured mascara into my pencil case. She would kill me if she knew I had it. It was given as payment about ten years ago and she only used it sparingly and on very special occasions. *Well, this was a special occasion,* I thought as I smiled to myself. My lips fell quickly as I remembered today was Friday. Friday was the worst day.

I tried to get out before she saw me, edging along the faded carpet, the door just in my sights, but a hand grabbed the back of my shirt and gently halted my stride. I thought maybe she knew, but her face only showed the same exhausted apathy it always did.

"Rosa, please eat something before you go." My mother sighed, her hand falling to her side. She looked tired, ill, a hazy shade of green sitting just beneath a layer of dark brown skin like she was being diluted. I rolled my eyes at her.

"You don't need to whisper, Mother. I'm sure Paulo approves of you feeding me. It's the rules, remember?"

She nodded, her hand trembling a little as she put the kettle on and started the ridiculously particular process of making tea for her husband so it was just right.

I listened for sounds of Paulo and heard the shower running. I nodded and picked up some toast. As I was spreading a very thin layer of jam on the bread with my mother eyeing my every move, I saw the billow of steam push out into the hall. He was out, and so was I. I slammed two pieces together and made a toast sandwich. Half walking/half running out the door, I yelled out, "Have fun sorting apples, Paulo. I hope you don't end up in the off bin with the rest of the rotten ones!"

I turned around and saw my stepfather's expression as the door rebounded open from me slamming it too hard. His dark face was a wrinkled mask of pure wrath. Good.

Satisfied, I walked to school following the curve of Ring Two until I reached the first gate. It was chilly and I cursed myself for not bringing a jacket. I sought out a sunny patch on the wall and stood with my back against it, stalling. The wall was warm where the sun touched it, yet it always gave me shivers. At least eight meters tall above ground and four meters under, I felt that trapped rat feeling and kept moving. I know not everyone felt this way but I couldn't help it. We were trapped, even if they said it was for our own protection.

I scanned my wrist tattoo at the Ring gate. It opened reluctantly, groaning like it had just woken up. I passed through it, my eyes holding contact with the camera that was following my movements. Quietly laughing, I stepped backwards, then forwards, the small black eye zipping as it tried to follow my sporadic movements. When I was done teasing, it closed behind me only to be forced to creak open for someone else a second later. I wasn't the only one who was running late. The difference being, when the gate opened, the other kids ran through it and sprinted to the school like their life depended on it. I took my time. Being tardy would result in a detention. I needed a detention.

I peered through the iron bars to see the older kids hanging around outside one of the classrooms, their backs against the grey-green rendered walls. This would have to be their last day. The five students exuded the stagnant combination of nervousness and hope—prisoners about to receive parole. I snorted to myself. There was no hope, just change. They were going off to the Classes in a few weeks' time.

I arrived at the school gate and scanned my wrist again. The double gates opened and I fell in to line with the stragglers. The neat rows of concrete classrooms looked dull and uninviting like the rest of the town. As I passed the older kids I heard a boy say, "Yeah, I'm hoping for Teaching or maybe Carpentry." His voice sounded confident, but with an edge of resignation tacked on, making his voice sound strong at the start only to peter out by the time he got to the end of his sentence.

The girl standing next to him bumped his shoulder affectionately, her red-brown ponytail swinging and brushing his arm lightly. He flinched and pulled away like it bit him. "Maybe we'll get in together. Wouldn't it be great to be allocated the same Class?"

The boy shrugged. "Doesn't much matter, we'll be separated anyway, you know that."

Smart, I thought, the girl needed to be shot down now. There was no future for anyone from the same town. The great claw of the Superiors would make sure of that. I imagined it like a sorting machine, kind of like what Paulo did, but instead of apples, the Superiors sorted races and Classes. These kids were going to be plucked from Pau Brazil, thrown into the Classes, and separated out into Uppers, Middles, and Lowers. The boy was right, at the end of training at the Classes, they would certainly be separated. Kids from the same town were not allowed to marry.

As I rounded the corner and made my way into my first lesson, I snatched a glimpse of the hopeful girl's face. It offended me. Her eyes were wide and brimming with moisture. I had little sympathy. This was the way things were. She needed to accept it. And really, she was lucky. I envied her. At least she was getting out of here soon.

First class. The teacher stood in front of us and asked us the same five questions she asked us every day. Pacing back and forth in her sensible shoes and friction-causing nylon stockings, she nodded as the class answered in unison. I scrunched up my nose; a woman that large shouldn't pipe herself into stockings that tight. The way her thighs were rubbing together, I thought she might spontaneously combust.

A while ago, I started formulating my own answers in my head. Different every time to beat the monotony. Today I went with a root vegetable theme.

"Who are we?" she barked in a low, almost manly voice.

"Citizens of the Woodlands," a chorus of bored teenagers replied.

I mouthed the words, 'Various vegetative states of potatoes'.

"What do we see?"

"All kind," we sung out loudly. The meaning lost on some but other eyes burned fiercely with belief. *As a potato,* I thought, and having no eyes. I am not qualified to answer that question.

"What don't we see?"

"Own kind," we said finitely.

I muttered under my breath, "Everything, geez, I'm a potato." I laughed to myself just at the wrong time, when the whole class was silent. The teacher gave me a sharp look, her black, olive-pit eyes narrowed.

"Our parents are?" she snapped, whipping her head to the front.

"Caretakers."

"Our allegiance is to?"

"The Superiors. We defer to their judgment. Our war was our fault.

The Superiors will correct our faults." Our faults being that we had not yet developed into the super race that was to prevent all future wars.

I looked around the classroom. Most were dark skinned or tanned, dark hair and dark eyes. One girl had conspicuously fair hair compared to her caramel skin; she was favored in the class since she looked like the ideal Woodland citizen. Her parents must have 'mixed appropriately'. Kids like me were too dark, too short, and my eyes were undesirable to say the least. I shrugged; I would have had better luck currying favor if I really was a potato.

I peered down at my skinny, dark fingers, the cracks in my palms darker than the skin surrounding them. Two hundred and fifty years on, despite the purposeful splitting up of families and distribution of races amongst the towns, you could still tell where a person came from. You could tell that my mother was Indian, as you could tell that I was half Indian, half Hispanic. The whole, All Kind and Own Kind thing hadn't worked the way they wanted it to. People didn't choose their mates because of their race but they didn't *not* choose someone because of their race either. I guess you can't just mix everyone up and assume they'll make the choice you want them to.

My father used to say, 'You can't help who you fall for,' but then he also said he thought the Superiors were about to change everything and start forcing us to mate with someone of their choosing. That was eight years ago and nothing had happened yet. I massaged my temples, feeling a slicing headache coming on. I hated him popping up in my mind without prompting and besides, my father was wrong about a lot of things.

The teacher smacked the table with the flat of her palm. "Good. Let's begin."

The first few classes went by as they always did. No one sat next to me, not that I cared. I was used to being treated like I radiated some awful smell. Sometimes I used to sniff my armpits and then look around the class. It got a couple of laughs, but didn't endear me enough for anyone to sit next to me. I got into trouble, a lot. And it wasn't because I was being treated unfairly or the teacher had a grudge. Trouble just found me. If there was a bad choice, I just had to make it, regardless of what would happen. I couldn't stop myself.

I felt preoccupied, barely able to pretend I was listening to my teachers. I sat up straight, holding onto the edge of my old wooden desk like I was riding a wave, nervous excitement about my final class blowing imaginary wind through my hair.

Lunch, bell.

As the bell shrilled out across the pathetic yard, I watched a child get dragged by her hair across the plastic lawn. Her little legs struggling to find a foothold so she could stand but just sliding uselessly across the dampness. My stale sandwich stuck in my throat. Tears were streaming down the poor girl's face. She couldn't have been more than nine. One of the policemen wrenched her head violently, trying to pull her to standing. Blood appeared at the nape of her neck as the hair pulled out of her skin. I saw her face contort and her small pink mouth form an O as she tried not to scream.

"I think she's had enough, don't you? You'll pull her hair right out of her head," I shouted. I had the students' attention but it was morbid curiosity—no one would help me. In fact, I saw a couple of kids take a few steps back. Both policemen turned their heads my way. One of them sneered at me, his olive skin scrunched around a bulbous nose that twisted at me in disgust. He closed the gap between us in a few long strides. His eyes had that familiar hardness to them that most of the policeman had. His were a stiff set blue, with flecks in them like chipped paint.

He laughed as he spoke, looking me up and down. "Are you talking to me, girl?" Meeting my eyes, he seemed confused as to which one to look at.

Don't say it, I thought. If only that voice in my head was louder. "I don't see anyone else trying to scalp a child, do you?"

His expression showed that was exactly what he had been hoping I would say. He retracted his elbow like he was loading an arrow to a bow and gave me a sharp punch to the stomach, hard enough to hurt but not hard enough to cause any permanent damage. Trained well. Part of my sandwich flew out of my mouth and I doubled over, winded. Feeling the pain spread like a stain soaking into cloth.

The policeman didn't look back, but I could see his head swinging around, taking in the witnesses as he stormed back to his partner. Satisfied that no one of importance was watching, they continued dragging the young girl. Finally, she fainted from the pain and he scooped her up. Thankfully. Most likely her parents had done something. Probably something minor. The Superiors loved to make an example. I crossed my fingers I wasn't going to be summoned to the center circle to watch another horrific punishment this week.

I drummed my fingers on the table in Mathematics, rubbing my sore stomach and seeing whether I could do both at once without messing it up by drumming my stomach and rubbing the desk. When I stuffed it up and started rubbing my hands across the small, wooden table, I took a pencil out and started tapping a rhythm instead. The kids around me leaned away, afraid to be sharing the same air as me. I looked up and teacher number five, whose name I couldn't remember, was staring down at me. She snatched the pencil from my hands.

"Rosa!" she said, like it was a swear word. "Go stand at the back of the class with your face to the wall. I've had enough of your distracting behavior."

I smiled at her sweetly. "Yes, Miss…um…" The teacher stared at me incredulously. Her thin tweezed eyebrows arched, her face creased in frustration. *Damn, what was her name?*

She put her hands on my shoulders and squeezed, digging her fingernails into my skin. "Mrs. Nwoso," she said angrily. Blinking once slowly, I considered it.

"Oh yeah, Miss Knowitall," I said, feeling her fingernails trying to touch each other through my flesh, burrowing a painful hole. She released me quite suddenly, shaking her head and showing her white teeth, which looked especially bright against her ebony skin.

"That's not going to work on me today, Rosa. Stand facing the wall," she pointed.

I shrugged and did what I was told, the eyes of my fellow classmates following me as I trudged between the neat rows of desks. I walked to the wall and leaned my forehead against a laminated poster about pi. Staring at it until my vision blurred and all I could see was the red of the circle, the numbers fading away with the monotonous tone of the teacher. The rings of Pau started to push to the front of my mind. I knew the rings were supposed to resemble a tree trunk but to me, the eight rings had always reminded me of the ripples in a puddle. And I was a stone, always trying to disrupt the order. Sending my own set of circles radiating out that didn't match and didn't line up with the ordered concrete.

I turned my cheek to the wall and stared out the window, watching the wind pick up leaves and bits of rubbish, hypnotizing myself and forgetting about my pain for a while. Sometimes I felt like the dust. Relentlessly banging my head against the walls, never getting anywhere. Always ending up in a pile somewhere, never in a corner though. There are no corners in a round world. Sleeting across the path, searching, settling for a second then pushed along, again and again.

I was startled out my reverie when the door started opening and closing, sending vibrations through my jaw. I quickly grabbed my things and ran out. Miss Knowitall was yelling after me, but I pretended I didn't hear her.

Last class, History.

I hung my bag outside and retrieved the mascara, shoving it in my pocket. I pulled out my scrunched-up assignment and smoothed it out on my legs until it at least resembled a rectangle. I grinned and strode inside, ignoring the cramping in my stomach.

Everyone sat down and Mr. Singh read the roll.

"Last week, I asked each of you to write about an incident from Woodland history or select your favorite Superior and detail how the incident or person had inspired or influenced your life. I ask that you read your assignment to the class and hand in the written part for me to mark later. Who would like to go first?"

No hands went up, so he picked someone. I rolled the mascara between my palms, rolling my eyes at the student's extremely boring presentation, clearly plagiarized from the textbook.

"…So the Superiors developed the Classes—a brilliant way to train the youth of the Woodlands, give them a purpose and a sense of fulfillment…" Ugh! Blah, blah, blah. It was a brilliant way to force children to work in jobs they would probably hate and blame it on a test. It was a brilliant way to take children away from their families, brainwash them, and fill them with Superior-loving rubbish. My brain shut me down before I yelled something out in class. Besides, thinking this way was pointless. I would have to go to the Classes too when I turned eighteen. I had no say in the matter.

"Excellent work, Miguel. Next please."

I had to sit through a few more rambling presentations, each more sleep-inducing than the last, before Mr. Singh called out my name.

"Rosa Bianca?" he said with a note of anticipatory fear in his voice.

I took a deep breath and walked to the front of the class.

2.

The Assignment

I stood before the class and held my paper in front of my face, my hands shaking a little; I patted my pocket for reassurance. Someone sneezed and I waited until the fit had ended before I started. I had the insane thought that maybe I really was dust and the corner of my mouth turned up in a suppressed smile.

"Get on with it, child," Mr. Singh said impatiently.

"Superior Grant is the lawmaker of the Woodlands. His carefully weighted and wise decisions have brought prosperity to the Woodlands," I said, rolling back on my heels, hands clasped behind my back. Trying my hardest to look like the model student.

I went on to describe several of Grant's laws. The one about people from the same town not being permitted to marry, the one about children not being allowed into certain Rings to preserve their innocence and maintain their safety. I also mentioned Grant's failed law, when he stated that people with the same eye color couldn't marry. This had turned out to be a huge mistake as almost everyone, in our town anyway, had brown eyes. This law was reversed after one year when the birth rate plummeted and the poor, blue-eyed people in our town were being harassed. Singh's face pinched at my use of the word failed but I quickly covered it by saying that Grant was not so proud that he couldn't admit a mistake and correct it. By this time, I had Singh slightly less unimpressed and the rest of the class was half asleep.

"The one-child law was Grant's most recent law. The law was made to protect the philosophy of All Kind on which our society is based. It has also raised the level of competence in schools and at the Classes five-fold due to the focused attention on one child rather than several and has therefore been a successful endeavor."

I looked to Singh. He was nodding along encouragingly.

It was so boring I was almost putting myself to sleep. And it was entirely false. The Woodlands had suffered due to his latest law—with fewer children, there were fewer workers, and of course, fewer marriages. I crossed my arms, pausing for a second. It didn't make much sense when one of the main objectives of the Woodlands was interracial breeding.

My heart started beating faster and I could feel my cheeks redden as I started into the last part of my speech, "Grant came to our town to announce the law when I was eight years old." I deliberately dropped my piece of paper. It floated down to the ground slowly, like a feather caught in the wind. I crouched down with my back to the class to get it and quickly whipped out the mascara to smear it over my top lip and chin.

I stood to face the class and stroked my chin, winking at the front row, "Hi y'all," I drawled, remembering Grant's strange accent. Someone snickered and a few pairs of eyes looked brighter. At least I'd woken them up. A girl in the front row had her jacket on her desk so I snatched it quickly and shoved it under my shirt. Parading around the room with my shoulders back I said, "As you can see—" I hefted my bulging stomach up with both hands and let it fall, "I'm waaasting away...yer children are eatin' all ma food," I slurred, slipping into more of a drunk tone than I had intended. "And," I pointed my finger to the sky, "And..." I thought Singh would have stopped me by now, but he was just staring at me with his mouth open, his fat cheeks wobbling in disbelief.

My time was running out and my courage started to diminish as I realized how very far over the line I had gone. I ran my hand through my hair and shook my belly at the class. I had to keep going. "So I'm takin' yer kids so they can make me and my gigantic wife more...more of that delicious creamed spinach you kids seem to love so much."

The whole class erupted into laughter for a second. I grinned at them sheepishly, leaning forward for a bow. My stomach fell out which caused another round of laughter.

Bang! Singh slammed a book down on his desk, rounded it, and caught a hold of my shirt, balling it up in his fist. He flung me to the floor, my elbows jarring as I tried to break my fall. Everyone went quiet.

He hovered over me like a dark storm cloud, breathing quickly, hands on his hips. "Rosa!" he said cuttingly, slapping the smile off my face with his tone. "You are making a mockery of my class and a fool of yourself. What do you have to say?" He was furious but I saw his eyes darting from window to doorway. If someone reported that he had no control over his students, then he would be the one in trouble. I knew that.

"My point is..." I started, looking up to him from my lowly position, breathless from running around and the pain in my stomach, "Grant could say anything he wanted and we would have to go along with it, wouldn't we? My reasons are probably just as true as the ones they passed out on the day they announced the law. It's rubbish. Why don't they just say each family can only have one child every eighteen years and if you disobey us, we will torture you in front the whole town? It's short, it's sweet..." That was the last straw. Singh pushed me with the tip of his shoe like he didn't want to get contaminated and told me to get out of his class.

"And wipe your face," he said, pushing a bunch of tissues into my palm and turning his back to me.

I was sent straight to detention, which was cleaning a week's worth of filth off the toilets, readying them for next week's filth.

I hadn't expected those words to come out of my mouth. I wiped the black from my mouth as I walked to the cleaning supplies room. I picked up my usual bucket, mop, and rubber gloves, and wondered why I had said it. I was just trying to get a decent detention, not make a political point. But I knew that I really believed what I had said and it worried me. My father may have been long gone but parts of him still lived and breathed in me without me realizing. I didn't want to end up on the center podium, having my eyes poked out or my fingers chopped off for being a dissident. The Superiors were all about creative forms of punishment, the worst being the punishment for violating the one-child law.

As I filled my wheeled bucket with hot water, letting it scald the tips of my fingers, I remembered the one violation that was forever seared into my memory. It was a young couple who'd had a seven-year-old boy. They lived a few houses down from me. One night, I remember waking up to police sirens and hearing a woman screaming. A heart-breaking scream carrying with it some unknown trauma. My mother had come into my room—it was rare for her to do this—and sat with me until the screaming had ceased. I still recall her cool hand stroking my hair, my tiny body curled up in her lap as she rocked me back to sleep.

The next day, they announced over the croaking old PA system that everyone was to meet in Ring One at noon. As we all gathered around, they dragged a man and woman onto the center podium, their hands tied behind their backs. People exchanged worried glances. No one wanted to be here but we were all glued to the ground. The man looked like he had been crying all night and had been badly beaten. The sun was beating down on his bowed head; sweat dripping from his glossy black hair. The woman wore the expression of one who knows her fate. Solemn, resigned, and stony. The police brought two boys to the front; they looked so similar they had to be brothers and could not be more than one or two years apart. The policeman announced that they had been hiding the younger boy for five years. We all knew what was coming next. Parents buried their children's faces in their chests and covered their ears. I wanted to look away, I tried to, but I felt the strong arms of Paulo pushing down on my shoulders and holding my head still.

The father fainted quickly. He was so badly beaten, I think he was half dead anyway. But the mother looked her boys in the eyes and locked on to them as the knife was buried in her chest. I remember thinking the odd thought that the heart didn't look quite right; it was misshapen, too big on one side. See, they carved the shape of a heart into the victim's chest. It was a reminder, a painful one. A scar they could never escape that would remind them what you got if you broke the rules and broke the hearts of the Superiors. This policeman looked like it was too much for him today. His eyes squinted and his teeth gritted as he continued his gory work.

The Woodlands

"Look into my eyes darlings, Mama will be ok," the mother said calmly, trying to soothe her terrified children.

The pain must have been excruciating but she only cried out once during the initial stab, letting out a strangled moan as it punctured her skin and sliced a gash across her lung. The policeman swore at his mistake. Like air escaping a balloon slowly, the cry had not enough air to produce much of a noise, but it was enough to make me want to scream myself. Blood pooled at her feet and dripped over the edges of the podium like a paint tin tipped over, thick red coloring the sandstone pavers and soaking into the stone. People were moving back to get away from it, blood reaching out to touch the tips of their shoes.

The mother looked up at the sky as her life left her body, her sweat-soaked, light brown hair falling back from her face in streams as she whispered, "I love you,"" to her boys. The brothers were screaming and holding each other, beyond hysterical. They were bundled into a van and driven away. It was over. Two crumpled bodies lay in the center of the circle, grotesque, misshaped love hearts carved into their chests. Everyone walked away. Mother took me to buy shoes that day.

I doubted that memory would ever leave me. It was carved into my chest like those love hearts. I felt it sitting there, a cut-in scar. I held my hand across my chest and dragged my bucket down the hall to start my work. Water sloshed carelessly over the side, sending steaming splats of strong smelling chemicals in my wake.

It would take me at least three hours, maybe more. I hoped I would be late enough that I could sneak into the house, grab a warm dinner, and go to my room. Paulo was insistent on dinner being served at seven sharp. I imagined my mother carefully laying out the meal, glancing at the clock anxiously. I felt guilty, but cleaning filthy toilets was preferable to eating with them. Paulo would bait me and I would surely say something I shouldn't. This way I was occupied, they could eat in peace, and no one ended up in an argument.

I finished one toilet block and moved to the juniors' section, nodding my head in greeting to the cleaner who was sweeping the hallway. I tried not to think about going home, about the weekend that stretched before me like a desert. I had to cross it, and Paulo was always there, dangling the ice cold water right in front my face, sneering at me and pouring it out on the cracked earth as I watched it sizzle and turn to vapor. The stupid thing was all that waited for me on the other side was more school. The Classes couldn't come soon enough. I poured out the cleaning water, almost black with things I didn't want to think about, and wrung out the mop.

The halls were peaceful. The grey walls and green linoleum was not quite so oppressive under the dim glow of the emergency lights. Without the scared, scurrying children, I could pretend I came here to learn, not kill time.

I placed the cleaning gear back in the cupboard, ready for next Friday, and noted the time—eight. If I really took my time, I could get home just as they went to bed. I made my way to the principal's office.

He was staring down at a piece of paper in his hands, reading and then putting his finger to certain words and reading again. When I tapped gently on the door he jumped, his glasses falling off his face. He fumbled around on the floor, found them, and turned his face to mine, giving me his best icy stare. I swallowed my want to mock him. He was about as intimidating as a puff of wheat.

"I'm finished with the bathrooms. Can you sign this so I can go home?" I said, trying to sound repentant.

He was irritated by my interruption, nothing new there. He held out his hand and I placed the detention slip in his palm. He scribbled on it and held it up, waving it slowly in front of my face, teasing.

I narrowed my eyes, wanting to snatch it from his stubby fingers. "You know, I don't know why they would bother sending you to the Classes," he said with a look of self-satisfaction, like he'd just solved some great mystery "We all know this is exactly what you'll be doing when you get out."

I took the slip from his fingers, managing to whisper pathetically, "You don't know that."

I exited his office quickly, but not before I heard him snort. He had me pegged. Menial, meaningless labor for Rosa.

The Woodlands

I ran out the door, dragging my bag along the ground, listening to it scrape and pick up the loose dirt. After I scanned my wrist, the gates opened, uttering my name in a computerized drone. Stepping outside the school grounds, I dropped my bag on the pavement. I closed my eyes and held my face to the sky. Opening them, I stared at the stars appearing, each one twinkling with scornful liberty. I pretended just for a second that I wasn't surrounded by walls and locked gates, that where I stood was as open as the sky overhead, then I returned my eyes to reality and dragged my sorry existence back to my so-called home.

❧3

Giving In

I managed to sneak in just as they were getting ready for bed. Mother looked to me quickly out of the corner of her eyes, concern brimming over her black lashes before Paulo snapped at her to come to bed, joyfully adding that he had thrown out my dinner. The appearance of concern was about all I was going to get from her. Actions required confidence, and maybe bravery. She had neither of those. Did she think that a sorrowful look was enough to convey some sort of feeling for me? What a joke.

"If you're not going to get here on time, then we are not going to save dinner for you. Rosa, you need to learn respect," the bedroom doorway stated.

My stomach grumbled and I put my hand to it, quickly reminded of how tender it was from the punch earlier. I made a point of poking my head in the door, flipping my hair back, and smiling at him. "It's fine, Paulo. I'm not hungry anyway." I strolled deliberately to my bedroom.

I stripped off quickly, not even wanting to look at the bruise I knew was blossoming over the dark brown skin of my stomach. I was like an ill-adorned Signing Day tree. Blue and purple blobs decorated my skin in a grotesque pattern; lash marks ran across my back, linking like plastic tinsel. I sighed. Was the principal right? Was I bound for a life of mopping toilets or emptying garbage cans? Had I given up? It seemed to me to give up you first had to give in to something. I had no ambitions, no idea what I wanted out of my life, only that I uncontrollably tumbled from one bad event to another.

I pulled on my nightdress and climbed into my rickety old bed, pulling the thin yellow covers up to my chin. Maybe things could be different. I could try harder at school. I could stop getting into trouble. It wasn't too late for me. I giggled humorlessly as I realized what a ridiculous thought that was. And I gave in to it. To the fact that I was a troublemaker and tomorrow I would most likely do it all over again, in another way, in another place, but it would always be the same. Nothing changes.

4

The News

When I woke up the next morning, the greyness still offended my eyes as it had the day before. I wondered if other people ever got used to it. Did they crave difference the way I did? I peeked out my door to see if my parents were still having breakfast and was startled when Paulo rapped on it, sending it banging into my nose.

"We need to speak with you," he said, his chest puffed up like he was so proud he could burst. I knew this couldn't be good. I rubbed my nose and said I would be out in a second. "Don't dawdle, this is important," he snapped impatiently.

My nose was searching for phantom smells of the cooked breakfast we usually had on weekends but there was no eggs or ham sizzling. So I took as much time as I could, literally dragging my toes backwards on the carpet as I walked, enjoying the itchy burn it created across my feet. When I finally got to the kitchen Paulo was tapping his foot agitatedly and frowning.

"You should sit down," Paulo said with a criminal smile. I was irked at his tone and did the opposite. I stood, leaning my folded arms across the old, wooden chair, rocking it back and forth, enjoying the creaks and the irritated look on his face as he twitched every time it made a noise.

I eyed the odd assortment of furniture, no chair matched. Everything was clean but used. We never knew where it came from. When they moved us the first time, we were told to leave everything behind and that our new home would already have the furniture we needed. I stared down at the chair and wondered who used to sit here. Did they have these parental meetings? Did they sit around the table with their child eating meals in silence?

I was pretty sure I knew what this was about. My latest string of detentions had to come up eventually. It made Paulo look bad to have such a disobedient stepdaughter.

He stared down at me as he paced around the kitchen; his slick, dark hair combed back to reveal his wrinkled brow and strained eyes. I tried to look at him objectively. Maybe he was handsome once. Now he just looked cruel, his whole face twisted into a dark, unreadable smile.

Whilst Paulo was itching to get my attention, my mother could barely look me in the eye. Her frail, dark hand traced the lid of the jam jar over and over like she would wear a hole in the rim. She would let him do the talking. She was afraid of him. I was not. Her whole demeanor curled away from Paulo and from me. Like a leaf dried up in the sun, you just had to step on it lightly for it to disintegrate to nothing and Paulo's foot was always hovering over her, ready to come down.

The table was spread with a bizarre assortment of food: pickles, jam, olives, and bread. Like Mother had just grabbed an armful of pantry, distractedly, and thrown it on the table. It didn't matter. No one was eating. I looked at the food questionably and then at Paulo. "What's this about? I have homework to do and I'm sure you have important tasks on the agenda for today, like sorting through your clothes to see which shirt stinks less." Giving him attitude would certainly result in a harsher punishment.

Paulo smiled and a shiver ran through me. He locked eyes with mine, making me feel like something someone had scraped off the bottom of their shoe.

"We are moving house in a few weeks. So yes, I do have some important jobs to do today." He smiled and twisted a stray hair back into the oily, black scrape on his head.

My mother gave him the slightest look of annoyance—like he had said the wrong thing—but covered it quickly.

"Where are we going?" I said with an edge of panic in my voice. I tried to push it down. I didn't want Paulo to see me struggling—whatever was going on.

"WE are going to Ring Two. You? Well, I don't know where you're going yet," Paulo said through straight teeth set in a sickening smile.

My heart sunk and surged and I started to panic. Panic, which quickly flipped to anger as I sifted through the possibilities that would separate our uncomfortable little family. Was I going to the Classes? No, I was too young. I was sixteen; they couldn't take me until I was eighteen, unless...

Then it dawned on me. The obvious answer.

"You're pregnant," I said dully. "But you promised to wait until I was eighteen." I was in a soundless vacuum. I was unsurprised and completely disappointed that it had come to this.

Mother didn't respond, her head bowed, ashamed or maybe too tired to bother explaining to me how she could do such a thing.

"We couldn't wait any longer," Paulo said in a voice that fit him as well as a tutu would. Happy.

"No, I suppose not," I said bitterly. "You're a medical miracle as it is," I exclaimed, walking around the kitchen, throwing my arms in the air. "Pregnant at the ripe old age of thirty-eight, that never happens."

Paulo grabbed my arm, squeezing it harder than necessary, and spoke in his irritatingly controlled voice, "Don't speak to your mother that way. This is not her fault." The chirp was gone from his voice like I had imagined it.

"I bet," I said meeting his gaze as I shook my arm free.

"I know it's how you operate but getting angry isn't going to get you anywhere, Rosa," Paulo said, in an unnervingly calm voice. "You need to decide whether to go now or when the baby comes," then he gave Mother a sideways growl, "although I don't know why we are letting you decide."

I looked at my mother, who was still avoiding my gaze. I wanted to scream at her, to try and shake some sense into that tiny body. But it was pointless. It wouldn't change anything. She'd made her choice a long time ago and it wasn't me.

"So I could go to the Classes now?" I said, thinking out loud.

My mother placed her hand on my arm as I rounded her side of the table and tried to still my nervous pacing. "I'd like you to stay," she said weakly, the shadow of a question mark hanging on the end of her statement, her eyes looking vacantly through me and out the window, like she wasn't sure she really meant it. I looked down at her loose grip on my shirt. Her thin fingers were calloused from pinpricks and running her hands back and forth through her ancient sewing machine. They worked her so hard. I shook my head; sympathy for her had no place in my mind right now. She was giving me up. Whether it was now or nine months from now, she was abandoning me.

I could feel hot tears rising and threatening to spill over but I didn't want Paulo to see me cry. "I need to think it over," I said in my calmest voice. It sounded wooden, forced out with shock.

I brushed Mother's hand off violently, like she was a bee who would sting me, and went to my room to grab my jacket.

"Take your time," Paulo called after me, his voice lacquered with dark intentions. "It won't change anything." And he was right. My fate was already decided, but at least I could have some say in the timing of it.

I walked out the door feeling like my life was being upturned and dug up all around me. Now I had to be filter through the dirt and decide which crappy future I wanted and when.

As I stood on the front step, a cool wind hit me and I felt my body tense with anger. Anger at the difference between us—the always unfulfilled wish that she would be stronger and tell him no. But I also felt a misplaced prick of protectiveness over her that urged me to consider staying. She might need my help.

A baby. Paulo, the stickler for rules, had broken the big one and they were having a baby. I wondered how he talked her into it; I shuddered at the thought of the two of them together and pulled the blind down on that visual nightmare.

This 'happy' news gave me an instant headache and I wasn't going to come to any answer right away. I stomped down the steps and strolled down our garden path, thick slabs of concrete teetering as I stepped on them at the wrong end. The word garden was laughable. Every yard was the same in Pau Brasil—one square of lawn, a concrete path, and one Pau Brasil tree in the center of every lawn, which had to be maintained meticulously.

I looked back at our dreary accommodation. The grey-green render was peeling around the doorway. The low roof hung out over the window of our modest lounge, the gutter sagging at one end. Every house looked the same. The only difference between the neighbors' and ours was the painfully cheery curtains Mother had sewn out of scraps from her workplace. The patchwork of yellow and purple looked ridiculously out of place amid all the grey.

My steps took me past three rows of houses, each a carbon copy of the next. Nervous faces peered out of windows, or over letterboxes. People stalking the morning, seeing whether the coast was clear to go for a walk without bumping into police. They needn't have worried so much. I knew police would be packing the shopping district this morning; that's where most citizens were and more people meant more chances for catching someone out.

I slapped the letterboxes as I went, chalky green residue coming off on my fingers. Inspecting them, I rubbed the wearing paint between my fingers. I could leave this green-grey world behind but for what? I was sixteen and would be two years younger than everyone else. I wasn't as prepared. And the next intake was only a few weeks away. It was so soon. I think I always thought I would straighten up as I got older and then I'd have a chance at a good Allocation. I snorted to myself. These things didn't just happen on their own and I was about as crooked and curly as could be. Maybe there was no straightening out for me. Chances are I would tangle back up again anyway.

The Superiors assessed you for your natural skill and allocated your Class based on that. I wondered if there was a Class for being a smart mouth. Probably not. They probably had a special Class for people like me. I shuddered.

I imagined a Class of troublemakers. All I could picture was a room with a man at the front pointing to the blackboard saying, 'Now what you need to do is rub the pencil all along the edges of the binoculars then get them to press it to their eyes...'

I was looking down at my feet, shaking my head at my own silliness, a prank class, yeah, that would be the dream, when I slammed straight into the gate of Ring Three, a metallic vibration pulsing through the air. Rust stains rubbed off onto my grey, wool jacket.

"Watch it! You'll break it and then we'll all be in trouble," someone shouted. I looked up to see a smirking face staring down at me. He was sitting on one of the concrete posts that supported the gates, legs dangling casually.

I tried to dust the stains off my jacket, only managing to rub them in further. I sighed. I would be in more trouble when I returned home.

I stood at the gate for a good two minutes, staring blankly, rubbing my elbows, lost in thought. I held out my wrist to scan my tattoo so the gate would open, but the rusty piece of junk didn't budge. Had I been denied access? I should be able to get all the way through to Ring Six without too much trouble. I realized that if I left at sixteen, I would never be granted access through gate Seven or Eight.

"Allow me," the smirking boy said, as he jumped agilely from the concrete post, landing with a thump. He sidled up to me, a big smile on his face. He rattled the scanner and adjusted the beam. He grabbed my wrist, without asking, and put it at a funny angle until I heard the familiar, long beep and the latch of the gate retracting.

"Rosa Bianca," the electronic voice spoke.

"Um, thanks," I said. His warm hand was still clutched around my skinny wrist. I looked up at him coolly, "Can I have my hand back now?"

"Sure," he said as he shook my stiff hand enthusiastically. I pulled back my arm sharply and pushed through the gate. I was not in the mood for company. I had a lot of searching through pointless options to do before I slunk home, just after dinner, so I didn't have to talk to my mother about what I was thinking.

"Joseph Sulle," the voice announced. I heard the gate shut and I quickened my pace towards the only place I knew I could really be alone. Loud, thumping footsteps followed behind me.

5

Break Down

"Bianca? I know that name. Where are you from?" he asked, catching up to me with Big, thumping strides.

"Same as you, same as everyone," I snarled, "Ring Three, Pau Brasil." As I walked, I tied my hair back from my face, pulling it into a low ponytail.

"No, what's your family background?" he laughed, infuriatingly. He didn't seem to be getting my tone or he was ignoring it. This boy seemed glib and I didn't appreciate his condescending question. I understood what he meant—I just didn't want to talk to him.

"I don't have a family," I lied unconvincingly, quickening my pace. What did he care?

He matched my steps.

I spun around to look at him, my ponytail whipping me in the face, a mouthful of hair momentarily derailing my anger. I took his large frame in. He seemed much taller and broader than most of the boys in Ring Three. He stood a good foot and a half over me and he was big. Not fat, just tall and well-muscled. His face was strong and older looking, with a sharp, chiseled jaw and a slightly crooked nose. His long, light eyelashes framed green, staring eyes that had no compunction about continuing to stare.

His hair and skin was lighter than most people in Pau. He didn't even have a hint of a tan and his hair, which was falling in his eyes, was blonde and curly. Not tight, ringlet curls, just a gentle, golden wave of thick shiny hair that made its way over his ears, and stopped above his neck. When he looked up, the curls linked into each other, like the weave of a basket across his brows. When he disturbed those gentle links, loose curls would fall in his eyes. He probably attracted a lot of attention, with his pretty eyes and incessant smiling. He was handsome, but irritatingly so, and I wished he would divert his attention away from me.

"You mean, you don't have a family anymore," he said in a more serious tone. "I'm sure you had one, maybe you just lost it." His eyes showed a winking concern. Or maybe pity? This made me even more furious. I wasn't sure what he meant by that—I knew where my family was. I hadn't lost them like a misplaced library book. I just knew I needed to start letting them go and also, it was none of his business.

"What's your father's name?"

I looked at him suspiciously, narrowing my eyes, wishing I had a weapon of some kind. Why was he asking me so many questions?

"Whoa!" He put his hands up in mock surrender. "Don't worry, Miss, I am not the secret police or anything, just curious. You look very familiar to me. Something about those beautiful eyes…"

Ugh! My eyes. The topic of much discussion. The source of much unwanted attention. I hated them. My mother had brown eyes, brown hair, and dark skin. I looked just like her, dark and slight, but with different eyes. They were my father's eyes. Every time I looked in the mirror, I was reminded of the man who left us. The man I had few memories of, but who was kind enough to leave his eyes. A genetic oddity I could never escape. I hated my father and I hated my eyes. He was to blame for bringing Paulo into our lives. He was to blame for what was happening to me now. I could feel tears rising. I wiped my face with my sleeve, tasting rust, and glared at the boy.

"Look, leave me alone, I'm not who you think I am. I am…" And that was it. I ran a few meters away from the confused boy and collapsed on the ground. Who cared if he saw me crying? I had every right to be upset. But I was ashamed at myself for being so emotional. My mother would never behave like this, which only made it worse. My life was about to change forever and this boy was harassing me about my eyes. I buried my face in my hands and sobbed. I could barely breathe for how hard I was crying. My whole body shook in jerky movements, like I couldn't calm my limbs down or make them do what I wanted them to do.

I felt a warm, heavy hand on my back, patting me softly, awkwardly. I let it sit there. I felt drained, no more fight left in me. I let it all out and, thankfully, he didn't say a word.

6

Joseph

Over the next couple of weeks, I skipped school. I went through the motions, which seemed to satisfy my mother. If she had any idea I was ditching, she certainly didn't let on. I packed my bag, took my lunch off the kitchen table, and walked to the school. I scanned my wrist and the large, ornate, wrought-iron school gate swung open slowly. The carved picture of the Pau Brasil tree rattled in the center as the gate came to a halt. I just stood there and waited for it to close again without walking through, watching other students running to class as the bell rang out. I doubted whether my teachers' cared if I was there or not. Being the class troublemaker, I'm sure my absence was welcome. Instead, I had been walking to the factory every day.

After registering my presence at the school, I always made my way to the gate of Ring Three, hiding behind bushes if I saw anyone I knew, which was few. Everyone worked or cared for children. Most preferred to work. It was unusual for people to be wandering the streets after nine AM. It was exhilarating not being at school, having some measure of freedom, and it was definitely fun knowing I was doing something I wasn't supposed to.

Joseph was always there, sitting on the concrete pole, waiting, ready to help me through the gate. He didn't ask about what had happened at our first meeting and I never volunteered to tell him.

The first few times he just helped me through, smiling and always holding my wrist a little too long. I always thanked him, bowed my head, and walked on through—trying not to blush at the extended contact.

After a few days, he announced that he was going to walk with me. I shrugged and let him follow in silence. I could tell he was bursting to speak but he kept quiet. I appreciated his restraint. I wasn't ready yet.

We walked until we came to the next wall. Menacingly high and straight as an arrow, the giant concrete structure towered over us. It showed no signs of wear although I knew it had stood there for at least two hundred years. We followed the curve along for a while. I let my hand trail along the cool, hard surface, sanding my fingertips, until we got to the next gate through to Ring Five. I knew he wanted to follow me, I knew he wanted to ask me a hundred questions—so I stopped him.

"Thanks for the company." I tried to smile, but my face felt awkward and hot.

He stifled a laugh at my pathetic attempt. "Anytime!" And he sauntered off in the other direction, his hand in a backwards wave like he was indifferent. It shouldn't have bothered me, but it did.

His attitude infuriated and fascinated me. I couldn't quite work out why I was even letting him be so close. Part of it was he was so different to what I was used to. In my life, in my home, everything was so serious. For whatever reason, Joseph was able to see the lighter side of things and, reluctantly, I gravitated towards him, just a little.

He kept meeting me at the gate to Ring Three and accompanying me. We started to talk.

"Yeah, I live in Ring Five," he said chirpily, looking at me from under a curtain of hair.

"That's funny, I don't remember asking you that," I said, pursing my lips.

He bumped my shoulder, sending me flying into the wall.

"Ouch, was that really necessary?" I grimaced, rubbing my shoulder. I looked at the grey concrete—if only my impact would damage it. I would like to have seen a small crumble, some evidence that it was made by humans and didn't grow out of the earth an unbreakable, natural force.

"Sorry," he grinned. He wasn't sorry.

I narrowed my eyes at him playfully. "Yeah well, watch it, you're huge. Much bigger and stronger than me. I don't think you know your own strength." I watched him loping ahead of me. This was stupid; Joseph was eighteen and would be shipped off to the Classes pretty soon. Soon he would be gone and even if I went with him, we would be separated. Flirting or whatever this was would have a nasty end.

I shook my head and kept walking. I didn't like thinking about the future. Mostly because I knew I didn't have much of one, unlike Joseph, who went to the bigger, nicer high school in Four where everyone was being groomed for places in the Middles or Uppers of the Classes. My school had every kid from ages five-eighteen crammed into the one building. We were not groomed for places in Technology or Medical. We didn't even have a computer in our school. We were going to be the janitors, the rubbish collectors. I sighed, as I knew there would be no place for me in the Uppers with Joseph. I would aim for Middles.

"What's wrong?" Joseph was leaning against the wall, his knee up and his hands behind his head. Looking like the cowboy printed on one of the very, very old cans of corn that routinely showed up in our pantry. All he needed was a twig of wheat sticking out of his mouth.

I was standing still for a long time, my head cocked to the side as I likened this boy to the label on the creamed corn—he had the strong arms, the golden hair. I wonder if we could find him a hat? Joseph snapped his fingers in front of my face. "Rosa, hello? What are you thinking?"

My face flushed red and I waved him away. "Nothing. You're just such a poser," I snorted. I wasn't about to tell him I was pondering on how beautiful he was.

Joseph shifted his weight self-consciously and waited for me to catch up. I realized I was being a bit rude. So of course I continued to be ruder still.

"Why are you so pale? I mean, you look like you haven't seen the sun in years," I said mockingly.

He held his arm in front of his face, studying his own skin.

"My parents are from Birchton and Radiata," he said frowning, His strong brows pulled towards each other like he was focusing on a speck on the ground. Made sense, those towns were renowned for being full of beautiful, blonde people.

"Ooh," I said mockingly. "Are they both blonde like you? If so, that's quite the scandal."

He raised his eyebrows at me and ran his hand through his hair. He seemed uncomfortable talking about them and he quickly turned the conversation on me. "Why are you so dark? You look like you've been dipped in chocolate," he said mischievously, then added, "Although I wouldn't mind that!" His lips curled as he kept some joke I didn't understand to himself.

"What's that?"

"What's what?"

Ugh! "What's chocolate?" I asked impatiently. I think he enjoyed irritating me.

He slapped his thigh and chuckled. "Oh my God, Rosa, you really are deprived."

I scowled at him and crossed my arms across my chest. My mouth snapped shut like a trap and I kept it that way, letting him chatter endlessly about himself. Until he turned around, intent on rattling a response out of me.

"And I hate fish and I my favorite color is blue," he said, grinning. "Now I want to know something about you." He pointed his index finger at my chest, stopping short of touching me.

"You hate fish! Here I thought you loved everything; you're always so damn happy all the time!" I snorted. He just looked at me with his soft green eyes. Being under his gaze felt like being in a spotlight, the rest of the world becoming dark and unfocused.

I avoided his eyes, looking at my hands and picking at a cracked fingernail. I wondered what I could tell him. I wanted it be something real. "Umm, I'm terrible at sewing. My mother's always trying to teach me but I am god awful at it."

"You're bad at sewing? Ha! Well, that was unexpected."

"What do you mean?"

"I was expecting you to repeat your Ring Three, Pau Brazil spiel."

I was upset that he thought he could predict what I was going to say. He didn't know me.

"You don't know me, what makes you think you can…." He cut me off.

"It's fine, Rosa, you don't have to get angry. I was just trying to say… Good, thank you for telling me something real about yourself."

"Don't cut me off!" I had forgotten what I was going to say. "What do you care anyway?" I was on the offensive, the impulsive, bubbling side of me pushing through.

"I don't know. I just do. I thought maybe you could use a friend. And for some unknown reason I like you." He confessed it like it was a crime. I suppose it was unlikely. Every other kid in my school was afraid of me. No one wanted to know me because I caused so much trouble. My attitude towards the Superiors was barely hidden. I made a lot of jokes that they laughed at but that was all. People always kept me at a distance, never wanting to get closer, in case they got included in the punishments that always followed my behavior.

I just glared at him for a while, my shoulders hunched and tensed. Recognizing my terrible posture, I relaxed a little. "Yeah, I guess I am pretty hard to like," I said, rolling my eyes.

"You're just hard to know," Joseph sighed.

"It's not like you've told me anything real about yourself."

"What do you want to know? Ask me anything." Open and honest, as I expected.

"Umm, why aren't you at school?" I knew why I was avoiding it but it seemed unlikely that he was just waiting around to see me.

"I'm in the waiting period." Of course, he was eighteen. He was leaving soon. The Superiors would give him and his parents eighteen days to spend with each other. A token amount of time to say their goodbyes and prepare themselves.

"So why aren't you with them now?"

"It's too sad—they're too sad." He breathed in deeply and considered his response. "Who wants to be around all that weeping and fussing anyway!" he said, attempting to cover his obvious pain.

"At least they will miss you; mine just want me out of the house."

"They won't miss me, Rosa, they will grieve me. I am never coming back. Your parents will grieve you too when you go. But you've got some time. You could talk to them." He nudged me with his elbow.

"I don't have time. I'll be gone soon too," I said. I thought about eighteen days stuck at home with my mother and Paulo—what a joke! We'd kill each other.

"What?" he sounded half-surprised, reacting less than I would have expected. This kind of thing was a scandal. Maybe he already knew.

I started to retell what had happened to me. Joseph listened intently and waited until I had finished before speaking.

"Wow, so you have a big decision to make." His eyes looked down kindly at me as he reached over to touch my face. I moved away. My heart was jumping around in my chest. I could see that maybe we could be friends. That we could talk. It felt nice to have someone in my life who didn't want me to be somebody else, who wasn't afraid or critical of me. Anything more than that was impossible. He was leaving soon and even if I left with him, we would certainly be separated, eventually. So it needed to be left there.

But what I wanted was confused. I pushed the 'want' side of me down, like compressing the rubbish so you can fit more in the bin, the sides of the bag starting to split a little.

He didn't seem upset or offended. He just took a step back, his strong arms by his sides, and looked at me intently. "So, aren't you going to ask me about your father? I brought it up when we first met and you've never said anything else about it."

"You don't know my father. So why would I ask?" I shrugged. There was no way he knew my father. I was not even sure he was alive. Mother said he had disappeared. It seemed unlikely that he was just living somewhere in the Rings.

"Sure I do, his name is Lenos Bianca. He teaches at my school. History."

I felt a balloon of interest floating up. "How do you know he's related to me?" I asked. My father's name was Pelo. It was not him. It couldn't be.

"One brown eye, one blue eye, right?" Joseph looked at me questioningly, leaning away. He looked like he was ready to take a few more steps back. Waiting for me to explode.

"That could be him, I guess." I popped the balloon in front of me. Whatever I was feeling, I ignored it. If it was him, I would be furious. How could he have been living so close and never come find me? And if it wasn't him, that anger would shatter into sharp splinters of disappointment. The point was nothing could be gained from following this path. Nothing at all.

There was this saying that people used many years ago before the wars—'curiosity killed the cat'—then the Superiors turned it into one of their warnings. I can't remember exactly how it went, their words were always so archaic and long-winded, but the local translation of it was 'curiosity killed the cat, and its family and its neighbors'. In other words, keep your head down and mind your own business.

"Yeah, he seems like a good guy, easy. He always…"

"Stop," I said, my hand in front of his mouth, "I don't want to hear any more."

"Ok, but I think you'll change your mind. I'll wait for you to ask next time." He smiled at me again. He made it so hard for me to be angry with him.

We walked in silence for a while. Past the grocery shops in Ring Four. The pitiful displays of limp vegetables and out of date canned goods were depressing. Their curved walls looking like a reflection in a glass ball. Living in a round environment had proved interesting for the architecture in the shopping district, where the walls of Ring Four and Ring Five were claustrophobically close.

Back at home things were much harder in comparison. With Joseph it was fun and exciting and I found myself racing out the door to meet him. My mother took my happier attitude to mean I had accepted things and was excited about my new life. She tried to spend more time with me but it was painful. The most affection she could summon up was a light pat on the shoulder. She cooked my favorite meals and made me some new clothes. This was her way of caring for me. It just made me feel worse.

I helped her pack up their things. It was a meager amount of possessions, filling only five small boxes. We had to leave most of it behind. I wondered if she was going to take the hideous curtains. Paulo was triumphant. He took every opportunity he could to rub my situation in my face. His wicked face darkened with delight as he talked about the new baby and what he was going to do with my room when I was gone.

I taunted him, "You better watch out, Paulo. If you want to be anywhere near your baby, the room better have good ventilation. You know, to get rid of the cider stink." That was the nerve I loved to tread on. Paulo always came home smelling like sour apples and vinegar. It permeated his clothes and his hair—a smell that complimented the sourness of his personality. He scrubbed and showered twice a day but it never left him.

Paulo stiffened at my words and I could see his hand digging into his thigh. *Just do it*, I willed. *Hit me.* I stood a foot away from him, my face upturned, glaring. I knew it took everything in him not to strike me. I wished he would. He would be out of here so fast. The Superiors took child abuse very seriously. They were the only ones allowed to dish out the violence. What I was trying to do must have occurred to him. He relaxed, an evil smile creeping across his thin lips.

"You'll be gone soon, so that's one stink we can clear out of this house before the new owners get here." He walked towards the kitchen. My mother was standing over a saucepan. He slipped his hands around her waist and she jumped.

She made me sick. She didn't love him. She loved me but she wouldn't stand up to him.

I stormed to my room shouting, "Forget about dinner, I'm not hungry," as I slammed the door. I could still hear him laughing at me.

I threw myself on the bed and waited for morning. Trying not to examine this new feeling I had too closely. The feeling where morning couldn't come quick enough because then I could see that warm, smiling face again.

Warming

Every day our walks became longer. I let Joseph in just a little and he just didn't stop talking. He would meet me at the gate for Ring Three and we would walk to Ring Five. He prattled on about school and the Superiors, even what he had for breakfast. Anything to fill the silence my tightly shut mouth provided. He always kept a respectful distance, after the last time he tried to touch me. I was glad he did but he didn't need keep a two-meter radius around me like I was going to infect him or strike him.

"What's it like at home for you at the moment?" he asked, solemnly.

I shrugged. "Paulo almost hit me last night."

Josephs green eyes were wide with surprise. "He wouldn't be that stupid, would he?"

"I wish he would. I tried to get him to but he just stood there, smiling at me, cruel and controlled like always." I was already plotting new ways to bait Paulo, to draw the anger out of him into action.

He shook his head, his hands balled up in fists. "Don't say that, Rosa. I can't stand the idea of…um... he could really hurt you."

"It's all right, Joseph, I can take a beating," I said, nervously un-tucking my shirt. I turned my back to him and lifted the loose cotton up a couple of inches, "See." I revealed the criss-cross lattice of little straight scars I had accumulated over my schooling. I half-expected him to reach out and touch them. Disappointed when he didn't, I turned around to see him avoiding my gaze and wincing.

"Don't worry about me; I can take care of myself," I said, trying to lighten the mood. I put my fists up to my face, dancing around him, punching the air.

He shook his head, smiled at me, and put his palms up. "Come on then, give me your best shot."

I lined them up and gave his hands two sharp punches. The impact vibrated back through my thin arms but his hands didn't move an inch.

"Weak!" he said, challenging me. I punched his hands three more times and then pretended to go for his face. He put his hands up to block me and left his stomach unprotected. I slammed him hard in the guts. "Ouch!" He doubled over and stumbled backwards. I reached out to help him, worried for a second that I had actually hurt him. He grabbed my arm and pulled me down to the ground with him. We were both laughing.

"Sorry," I said between giggles. I rested my head on his shoulder, feeling warm and breathless. "Didn't think you'd go down so easy!"

He coughed, holding his stomach and putting his other arm around my shoulder, pulling me closer, my body fitting neatly into the crook of his arm. "Nah, I let you have that one."

I could feel strength coming from somewhere inside me, a new sense of warmth wrapping me up in ribbons and rags. I also felt a need to be closer that I didn't trust. I wiggled out of his arms and stood, my hands up to my face again. "Wanna go again?"

His disappointment was clear but he shrugged it off. "Sure," he groaned as he pulled himself to his feet.

We tousled for a while until I got sick of him dodging me and I sat down again. He sat next to me but left a foot of air between us.

I sighed and leaned back against the concrete wall. Looking straight up, it appeared to almost meld with the sky. Grey into grey, melting into light blue and white.

"What's it like in the outer rings? I may never get to see them you know," I asked.

Joseph propped his elbows on his knees and stared down at the ground.

"It's not very interesting. Sad. Ring Seven is mostly fields, cows, and sheep. Ring Eight is full of old people. I don't really like going out there.

It feels like everyone is just waiting to die."

"Oh," I said, wishing I hadn't asked. "I guess that's just another way they keep us separated from each other. Those poor people."

"You shouldn't talk like that, Rosa, someone will report you."

I prickled. "Don't you start. I'll say what I want." I was being overly harsh but I hated anyone telling me what to do.

"I'm sorry; I'm just worried about you. I don't want you to get in trouble." He skimmed his hand down my arm, leaving his warmth behind like a delightful burn.

"I'm always in trouble. I'm used to it."

"I love that it doesn't bother you. You're fearless."

That couldn't be further from the truth, but I liked that he thought that about me. It made me feel strong. I was very afraid. Afraid of being close to him and equally afraid to not be.

I stood up and started walking again. *Just keep moving,* I thought.

8

The Kiss

The decision I had to make was simple. Leave now or wait a few months and leave then. So why hadn't I got there yet? Why was it so hard?

I sat in the abandoned factory, my refuge. It used to be a thriving shoe factory, employing over a hundred workers, until they shut it down. Funny now, when I think about it, that this was where everything went wrong for me. This was Paulo's factory. He became so successful, so quickly, that they took it away. The Superiors ordered him to triple his workload so the shoes could be issued to Police and Guardians. He refused. He had many loyal employees and what the Superiors were asking would mean they would have to work twenty-hour shifts to get it done in time. So maybe he was a good man, once. Of course, his arrogance at thinking he had any control over what happened in his own business was his downfall. They quickly shut it down, dispersed the workers to another town that had a similar factory, and sent him to work at a distillery that made exclusive alcohol for the Superiors.

When I was old enough to make it to Ring Five, I wanted to go there. I wanted to stand in the place that broke him. Revel in his failure. Instead, what I found was a beautiful old building, a castle. It was falling down around the edges but the structure was stunning. The windows were imposing, carved wooden arches. The big double doors were heavy wood with big, ornate, iron hinges. I climbed through a broken window and found riches for a fourteen year old—pieces of colored leather, wooden feet, old sewing machines, and colored buttons. I made myself a small space to sit or sleep, pulling together some large pieces of leather and some fleece lining. It was comfortable and warm. I felt more at peace there than anywhere else. It wasn't a home but it was the closest thing I had ever experienced.

I said he could come in this time but I was already regretting my decision. My once quiet space was filled with his booming voice. Joseph hadn't come into the factory before. He had asked but I told him he couldn't. He didn't worry about it too much, other than to tease me about what I was doing in there.

"I know, you've made a life-sized Joseph doll and you're trying to figure out how to tell me that you're choosing him over me!"

"You are ridiculous," I yelled at him as I closed the door behind me. And he was. He was too happy. He was too trusting. He pried and made statements like he knew me really well. I did like him. But I couldn't let go of the fact that he was leaving, and I was leaving. It made no sense to be making new friends, or to have any friends at all.

"So two days 'til the big day." He sounded nervous, his voice higher and crackly. It was unlike him.

"Don't worry; I'm sure you will get into Intelligence."

"Yeah maybe, probably, oh I don't know. I'm not too worried about that." He was leaning on the door, his head so close I could feel his warm breath on my face.

He hovered over me, the heat coming off his body invited me to come closer, so I took a step back. "Do you want to come in?" I said, sweeping my arm open like a servant.

"You sure?" he asked. I shot him an eye roll. "Ok, ok, in I go!" he said, stepping through the door and into my private world. I bowed and shut the door behind him.

"So this is it? It's just dust and old bits of leather." He winked at me, a flutter in my chest made me feel like I was choking. I gave him a tour, showing him the old sewing machines, the rusty old conveyor belts. He seemed bored but he suffered on until we got to the place where I spent most of my time. We sat down on the seat I had made all those years ago.

"So what are you going to do?" His voice was a loud echo, out of place amongst the dust and stillness.

"I don't know," I confessed. All this soul searching and I had come no closer to a solution. Distracted by how close he was sitting, I was startled when he put his arm around me. It reminded me of the first time we met; I sighed and tried not to cry. Despite his annoying behavior, his loud voice, and disarming attitude, I was going to miss him. He was my first and only friend. I put my head on his shoulder.

"It's ok; I know you're going to miss me. You don't have to say it. I know you can't. I am going to miss you too. More than I want to," he admitted, words pouring out of his mouth, each one floating down, nestling in my lap, behind my ears. His arms were so warm around me. Right here I felt safe, if only for a second. Who knew what might happen in the next few days? I let myself be in the moment, just this once. I leaned into the warmth and absorbed it. He leaned over and kissed me on the cheek. I pulled my face back and stared at him blankly. I hadn't realized up until now, but I was expecting something else. My whole body was agitated, buzzing. I was craving more of his touch.

He smiled at me sweetly, but there was a sad edge to it. I looked at his face, studying the line of his brow, the wonky line of his nose. I put my finger to his lip and pulled it down a little, turning my head sideways, squinting. He shook his head and I let go.

"What? What are you looking at?" he said, confused. His normally cool face looked flushed, bothered.

"What happened to your tooth?"

Joseph had a perfect smile, shiny white teeth, straight and lined up in a row, but on the bottom row, just to the side of the middle, one tooth was cracked and grey.

"Oh, nothing really. It was my dad…"

I felt an odd sense of protectiveness. It flaked off my skin, revealing a red-hot anger at the idea that someone would hurt him.

"What? Did he hit you?" My voice sounded shrill. I told myself to take a breath. I was getting too worked up.

"No," he laughed, "nothing like that. One day we were playing in the backyard. He was getting me to catch a ball. I wasn't watching what I was doing and I ran straight into the fence. I broke my nose," he touched it lightly, "here. And I broke my tooth. The nerve is dead inside it."

I laughed too. The idea of Joseph being uncoordinated enough to run into a fence was hilarious to me. He was so physically capable and athletic. I laughed until I realized how different we were. I mean, I knew we were different in personality and looks, but we also came from such different places. He had parents who loved him, who actually played with him. What a different life that must have been. I felt an overwhelming sadness for what he was going to lose.

It was stupid, but I took his head in my hands impulsively and kissed him. He didn't move at first, but then he pulled me closer and kissed me back. He held me so tight I felt like I couldn't breathe, but I didn't care. If I could have got closer to him, I would have. My body flooded with warmth, liquid gold running from the tips of my toes to the ends of my fingers. His chest pressed up against me, my heart punching through mine. But it only lasted for a moment before he pulled away.

"You don't want this, Rosa," he said, sensibly shuffling away from me subtly. I let out a short sigh. I was surprised that he was being the voice of reason here. The roles were reversed.

"I don't understand, I thought..." I don't know what I thought. I knew he was right. This was only going to create more heartache for the both us. But a big part of me didn't care at all. It was too late. That kiss was going to derail me. I felt it changing me from the inside out, causing pain and warmth at the same time.

His blonde hair flopped in his face as he bowed his head and exhaled deeply, like he was sorting through something in his head. He lifted both his hands in exasperation, pulling his hair back and looking at me with searching eyes. I bit my lip and held my breath. I knew I wasn't going to like what he said.

"I think you should stay. Spend some time with your mother. Talk to your stepfather. It's painful, I know, but it's good to have a family. It's good to have people in your life that care about you."

"You care about me. That can be enough," I said, sounding like a spoiled child.

"I'll be gone soon; I don't want you to be alone." His anguish was clear but his words made no sense. Whatever he did, whatever I chose to do, we would both be alone. Be apart. That was certain.

"I'm sorry," he said. He turned and walked away, crashing into things in his haste to escape me. I stood there like an idiot waiting for him to turn around, for him to change his mind. But he never did. He walked out, closing the door behind him.

Kissing Joseph was by far the stupidest thing I had ever done. Worse than gluing the teacher's butt to her chair. Stupider than putting laxatives in the teacher's lounge coffee machine. I just wish that I could have stopped myself from taking it too far. But I never could. I resolved to talk to him the next day. He was right. Being friends was best. I could hold the memory of a friend in my heart without it tearing in two.

It was a naive thought that things could so simply go back to the way they were.

The next day I went to the gate, same as always. I waited, but Joseph never showed.

He was gone.

I went back to the factory hoping he would be there, which was ridiculous, but in the back of my mind a little spark kept flashing. He kissed me back, even if it was only for a second, he definitely kissed me back.

I sat there waiting all day, feeling frantic. Disliking myself more and more. I didn't want to feel this way.

I started to get angry, imagining somehow Joseph had tricked me into feeling like this. It wasn't like me and I tried to pull it out of me like a choked-on strand of spaghetti. I went to bed thinking—*I'll find him. I'll yell at him. I'll push him into the gate and tell him exactly what I think of him.*

I don't know what I was expecting. I waited at the gate the next morning, fuming, but he was a no show again.

I went straight home and slammed the papers on the kitchen table in front my mother, disturbing her pile of mending.

"I want to go now. Today."

.9

Leaving Pau

She was rattled, skittish, big brown eyes blinking repeatedly like she didn't believe what she was hearing. Bobbing her head as if she could shake the news out of her brain like loose wax. I didn't realize she was so certain I would stay. I didn't realize it mattered to her one way or the other.

Due to the tight control in Pau Brasil, our wrist tattoos contained almost all the pertinent information needed to send me off. I looked down at the neatly printed barcode. I was canned goods. Scan me and you knew my value. I remember being held down on my twelfth birthday as they put it on—the burning pain of the needle and the foreign buzzing sound. My mother was holding my arms down but I was flailing and screaming. She told me it was a good thing; it meant I would have more freedom. I remember thinking quite the opposite. I was being branded. The frustrated tattooist gruffly gestured with his hairy, bare arm for Paulo to hold me still. He stormed over and held down my legs, telling me not embarrass myself. 'Be stronger' he had said. He wasn't quick enough to stop me from kicking him in the face, a small drip of blood appearing on his lower lip. I remember him smiling, licking it away with his tongue, and squeezing my legs so tight I couldn't budge. Disgusting. And exactly the kind of thing he would do. When I got home and changed for bed, I had finger-shaped bruises on both my calves.

To leave Pau all that was needed from Mother was a signature and a small bag containing a change of clothes and letter writing materials, but she was panicking. Her fragile state gave me a pang of guilt for making her do this but she was the one who was forcing me to leave eventually anyway. What difference was a few months going to make?

"I can't find a pen, Rosa. Where are all the pens?" She sounded out of her mind with worry, her voice taking on a high-pitched, hysterical edge.

"Mother, come here and sit down." I was going to have to be the calm one. Words came back to me, but not in Paulo's voice, it was my own, level and heavy. 'Be stronger'.

"It's ok, I'm sure they will give me one if I ask."

She followed me into the kitchen, back to place where all this started. She looked so frail, her tiny, dark frame teetering on the edge of the chair.

"I know you're upset but I think it's best to go now. If I stayed, I think I would only start to resent you and that baby." As the words came out, I knew they were true. "I love you. I don't want that to change. Just promise me you'll look after yourself."

I reached across the table to hold her hand. She withdrew, always a thin, cold pane of glass between us. She regarded me for a second, tears in her eyes. Then she stood up.

"There's probably a pen in Paulo's office," she muttered, mostly to herself. That was it. She walked off talking to herself and I went to my room to change.

I stood in the doorway for a while. Taking in the home I was leaving—the standard, grey-green walls that were in every home, my small bed and yellow bedspread. I wasn't really going to miss this place. To miss it, I would have had to have some enjoyable moments here. There were none I could think of. Not here. Not since Paulo came to live here. I put on my school uniform, grey-green again with a silhouette of the Pau Brasil tree on the front. Its tiny trunk completely out of proportion to its vast foliage, looking like a stick with a puffy cloud jammed on top. I looked in the mirror. A calm girl stared back at me, her brown and blue eyes steeled and determined. I had to make this work. I had to make a better life for myself. Anything would better than this. I combed my long, brown hair back into a ponytail and tied the allowable silver ribbon around it. A memory of strong hands straightening my uniform and tightening my ribbon swaddled my consciousness. Not now.

I looked tired, dark circles under my eyes. I wondered if Joseph would be there, feeling a sharp punch to my chest. I decided I wouldn't care if he was there or not. Hilarious that I thought I could decide such a thing. We weren't going to be in the same class so it didn't matter. But it did. It mattered so much more than I could ever admit to myself, bringing with it a crippling, doubling-over feeling of pain. No, I wouldn't care. I couldn't.

When I walked out to the living area, my mother had composed herself. She had put on her best coat and also tied her hair back tightly into a bun, tiny slivers of silver showing through her dark brown mane. My bag sat open by the door, packed with clean clothes, with about five pens poking out of one of the pockets.

"Thank you," I said, trying to sound normal, unruffled, but my voice was quivering. I wanted to pat her arm but my hand was shaking so I left it where it was, by my side, as hers were. We stood looking at each other. Mother went to say something but the sound of the door being unlatched stopped her.

"I forgot my jacket." An oily voice slipped through the crack in the door.

Paulo arrived and surveyed the room. His eyes landed on the bag and he quickly put it together. "Well," he said, exultant. "We'd better get you to Ring One." He swiftly picked up my bag, zipped it up, and threw it over his shoulder. I put my shoes on and had to run to catch up with him as he energetically strode down the front path. He almost looked like he was skipping. I suppressed a giggle. My mother locked the door and walked briskly behind us, hugging the papers to her chest. I looked behind me at the rows of grey houses—each one identical. I wouldn't miss this bleak, nothing of a town. Our neighbor eyed us curiously as my mother and I struggled to keep up with Paulo's cracking pace, watering the pavement instead of his lawn.

We passed through the gates to Ring Two in silence. As we approached the gate for Ring One, Paulo spoke.

"Rosa, you need to line up at the Class administration building.

Esther, you can get her bags checked, and I will talk to the transports and see if they will have any room." Paulo's hatred was actually proving useful to me that day as he quickly and efficiently guided us through the steps we needed to take to get me on that transport and out of his life forever.

I don't think Paulo really needed to worry. There were two helicopters and only about ten scuttly teenagers getting ready to go. They were dressed in their school uniforms. All looked very nervous—fiddling with their jumpers, chewing on their fingernails. One girl bawled hysterically as her parents held and tried to console her. Everyone was staring at them. It was not normal to show emotion like this in public. Others were shaking hands with their fathers and giving their mothers light pecks on the cheeks. I scanned the area. There were two tables set up, one where they were checking identification and taking paperwork, and the other with twelve small bags with oversized, yellow stickers on them piled underneath. The stickers carried ID numbers. I walked to the first table and handed in my paperwork. They scanned my wrist.

"You're sixteen," the man said, raising his eyebrow dubiously as he looked me up and down.

"My mother, Esther Amos, is pregnant, so I am entitled to leave with this intake," I said, looking him straight in the eye. He was young, mid-twenties maybe, muscular and stiff, with a pudgy face that looked odd atop his fit body.

Unsettled by my attitude, he muttered, irritated, "You're not on the list. Move aside," using his arm to 'guide' me out of the way.

Changing tack, I looked down at my feet, trying to appear humble, tugging on my ponytail, saying quietly, "I'm being surrendered." It didn't work.

Paulo expertly took control of the situation. He introduced himself and shook the man's hand. Paulo called my mother over and asked the man to scan her. The Guardian called up her information on his portable reader. It would all be there—her pregnancy, her due date, everything. Our lives were a transcript, a series of dot points and dates. I felt violated that someone could reach into our lives and take little pieces, but this was life in Pau Brasil. Nothing really belonged to us, not even our pain.

The Woodlands

After staring at the reader for some time, the man stood, straightening his uniform. "Very well, here's your ID sticker," he said, not even looking up as he scrawled my number across the yellow sticker in big, black numbers. "Put it on your bag and check it with the others." He closed down his reader and left the station. I must have been the last one.

As I put my bag down and made my way to the middle where everyone was standing, Paulo stopped. "Wait!" he said to the Guardian we had just spoken to. I was confused—was he having second thoughts? I had a sudden fear that he may have changed his mind. That he was going to make me stay. A tiny part of me flickered like the blue flame on a gas burner, not warmth, just the inkling of the idea of heat. Did he actually care about me?

Paulo spoke to the man for a few seconds. I couldn't hear what they were saying but the Guardian nodded and handed him an envelope. The flame was snuffed out in an instant, leaving a blackened, cold ring. The money. He was securing his payment for my early surrender. I returned my eyes to the center circle.

There were only a few of us milling around. The circle's large, paved sandstone ground and elaborate design was so out of place amongst the rest of Pau, which was concrete, plastic, and air conditioning. The center podium was darker than the rest of the stonework. Too much blood they could never quite get rid of, no matter how hard they scrubbed. I think, now, they put plastic sheeting down to protect it. Dark and light stones alternated from the center circle, like the circle was the sun and dotted stone lines radiated out from it like rays of light.

Everyone else had taken his or her place near the helicopters. I couldn't see Joseph but I knew he must be there. No matter how hard I tried he was always there, in the back of my mind, threatening to unhinge me. I needed strength at this point, not the heart-skipping vulnerability that kept creeping into my head.

The helicopters were stationed at the rim of Ring One, just inside the low, sandy-colored wall that surrounded the center podium. They were waiting, crouching like black angels ready to lift us from this place, this hell, into an unknown world. A Guardian in black uniform with gold trim walked to the front of the choppers and signaled for us to come forward. Another one threw the bags in the cargo hold as he read from his list. Three girls and eight boys. Joseph's name was not on the list. I felt a flood of relief that was washed away by panic. I was barely holding myself together as it was, seeing him was liable to make me fall to pieces. But he was supposed to be here.

Paulo's hand was on my back, pushing me towards the helicopter like I was an uncooperative apple on the conveyor belt. I was trying so hard to muster up some courage. Today I was leaving the only home I had ever known. I would never see my mother again. I felt the anxiety rising, the crushing pain of the separation I was about to suffer. Suddenly the grey-washed town didn't look so horrible. It was home after all, I guess. I told myself it was fear that was making me feel this way. It didn't help.

My mother, who had been quietly following us around like a dazed puppy, pulled me to her in a tight embrace. She whispered, "Sorry," in my ear before stepping back, fists clenched, showing the appropriate restraint. Some other mothers were crying and holding their children as the Guardian wrenched them away and led them onto the aircraft.

My mother's face was my own, the way she moved mirrored my own movements and mannerisms, but that's where the similarities ended. Although raised by this woman, I was nothing like her. For the first time, I saw things from her perspective. Getting into trouble all the time, never showing Paulo anything other than contempt. I must have been such a frustration to her.

They called my name. Paulo put his hands firmly on my shoulders, holding me in my place. His intense stare was impossible to look away from. "Don't shame your family," he spat at me. And with that, he made it easy to leave. I could feel the blades starting to move, my hair whipping around my face. I stripped away the fear and anxiety, leaving a girl that was fierce, empowered by his hatred.

"Don't worry, Paulo, I'll stir it up, make a little noise!" I shouted through the wind. The Guardian that let me sign up was watching me, probably regretting his decision. My mother was standing rigidly, her handmade skirt billowing as the air churned around her, her hand outstretched, pleading. I could see it in her eyes—*please Rosa, don't cause more trouble.* She couldn't stop me, no one ever could. Paulo was already walking away, his back to me. Behind my mother stood a man, one blue eye, one brown, smiling. He lifted his hand to wave. I raised my hand, confused. The chopper lurched awkwardly and I was knocked back into the cargo hold.

"Sit down!" the Guardian snapped at me. I quickly found a spot and strapped myself in. The others were staring at me, eyes wide. The Guardian tapped the pilot on the shoulder. "Wait, there's one more."

He bounded in, bag in hand, and casually threw it on the pile and scanned the seats. There was plenty of room on the other side but he squeezed his bulky form between me and the boy I was sitting next to.

Suddenly we were in the air. When the Guardian wasn't looking, Joseph slipped his hand over mine. Warmth calmed the agitation I felt, like pouring gold over lead, glowing. We stayed that way the entire ride. Eyes forward. Impossibly trying to anticipate what may lie ahead.

Soon we would be at the Classes. A new life awaited us. We must sit the Test and then we would be allocated an occupation to train for. It was excitement dredged in terror. If I could get into something decent, I could change my fate, to a degree anyway, but if I messed up, the principal would be right about me. The Superiors would still decide which town I would be sent to, but what I would do, once I was there, was yet to be determined.

The air was freezing cold up here but I found it exhilarating, like plunging into ice water. The door was open and we could look down to the world below. I could tell Joseph was taking it in too. The vastness of the Woodlands was surprising. From up here, the Rings looked like beautiful ancient structures, somewhat alien given the surroundings, as though they were dropped there from outer space. I could see all eight of them. Pau Brasil, Banyan, Casuarina, Bagassa, Iroko, Palma, Birchton and Radiata. Each named after common trees from the four countries or continents from which we all originated: India, Brasil, Russia, and Africa. They were evenly spaced out with the Superiors' dwellings in their own town in the center.

I was not prepared for two things. We were always taught every citizen of the Woodlands was treated the equally, that all the towns were the same, including the Superior dwellings. What we could see from the air was that the Superiors' town had only one ring. It had hills and fields, pockets of water, and randomly scattered around this huge, open space were the compounds of the Superiors.

The other thing that came as a surprise was the Wilderness itself. I couldn't believe the sheer density of it. The forest was pressed up against the sides of every town, threatening to break down the walls and swallow it in green. It was strange, considering there was very little plant life within the walls—only one type of tree and some grass.

There were no roads, no cleared space between one town and the next. No wonder they airlifted us out. I was peering through the tiny spaces in the foliage, my eyes finding a river, white rocks glistening in the sun, when I saw a Guardian slap the helmet of the pilot, quite hard. I don't think we were supposed to see all that. The helicopter veered away from the concrete rings sharply. The Classes were located away from the towns. I took Joseph's hand in mine, curling my fingers between his, and squeezed. He squeezed back, his blonde hair sweeping back and forth in front of his eyes as he stared out across the sky. I know he didn't want to show it, but I'm sure he was as nervous as I was.

10

The Test

I t took us about two hours to arrive at our destination. I enjoyed every minute of the ride. The world seemed so big from where we were. Not being surrounded by concrete walls was a marvelous feeling. I felt like screaming or howling but I knew better than to draw any more attention to myself.

The compound of the Classes was very different to Pau. From the air it looked like there was one big ring with two small rings inside at one end, and one big ring at the opposite end. It actually seemed to resemble a face with a surprised expression—big open eyes and a wide mouth. I looked around to see if this amused anyone else. No. They all looked petrified, their knees jittering, or holding themselves tight like they thought their insides would fall out. I felt sorry for them. For them, being separated from their parents was a big deal. Joseph was looking down at it with a quizzical expression on his face. I gave his hand a squeeze. He turned and grinned at me.

Between the inner rings was mottled green, not like the disordered chaos of the Wilderness but organized, like my mother's patchwork curtains. I couldn't tell exactly what it was from up here, but it looked like there were paths poking out here and there. I was hopeful. It was certainly different and that could be a good thing. When I looked back at Joseph, his expression had changed from one of amusement to very serious. He was deep in thought when we landed with a thud. We jolted in our seats and reality hit. He released my hand. One of the Guardians was talking but we couldn't hear him until the blades of the chopper slowed, and then he was yelling at the top of his lungs, "…then go to the Centre and we'll drop off your bags in your quarters." He cleared his throat and in a softer tone said, "Off the helicopter everyone." I giggled, which got me a harsh stare from some of the kids as well as the Guardian. It was different, but not that different. My humor was not appreciated here either.

We landed inside the mouth of the face. The walls were not as high here. I could actually see over them into what looked like a garden. It was beautiful and utterly foreign. I could see so many trees I had never seen before. Some with fruit hanging from overburdened branches, also herbs and flowers. I had only seen a real flower once. It had seeded in our front lawn, blown from the outside. I saw it for only a second before a groundskeeper plucked it from the earth and threw it in his bag of clippings. It was tiny and delicate, with yellow petals and a brown center. In this garden there were colors unlike anything made or grown in Pau Brasil. I was still craning my head around, trying to get a better look, as they guided us into the first building.

The buildings were all grey concrete, just like in Pau, but this collection of structures was grander and more imposing than our modest town buildings. They were overelaborate, with hideous, carved creatures climbing up the corners or sitting on the roof staring down at us. This was where the children had come to learn their trades, their fates, for over two hundred years. You could feel it, a mixture of history and solemnness. It was creepy, imagining dusty ghosts and stifled laughter floating down the halls.

Our small line of boys and girls was merged into a larger line as teenagers filtered in from other landing bays, until there were about fifty or sixty of us. Each of us was wearing our grey uniform with our tree emblems printed on the front. A Guardian was facing us as we were guided through a large set of carved, wooden doors. "Take your place at a table and be silent." He said it about three times, repeating himself as more of us entered the room. His voice echoed around the vast hall, which, once everyone was seated, was still two-thirds empty. I guess, years ago, there must have been more bodies to fill the space.

The Guardian stomped his foot once and called attention.

"Who are we?" he barked.

"Citizens of the Woodlands." The room echoed with the combined, unsure voices of sixty or so terrified teenagers. And I joined them. For once, I didn't want to make up my own version. All my cheek had evaporated into tiny particles that clung onto the edges of my clothes like germs. I couldn't pretend I wasn't as scared as every other kid in here.

"What do we see?" he said threateningly, his eyes squinting like he was trying to sift out the troublemakers early.

"All kind."

"What don't we see?" He scanned the room, connecting with different eyes of different colors but all with the same wide bewilderment reflected in them.

"Own kind," everyone said.

Then one kid yelled out "Own kind" out of time with the others. The Guardian marched over to him and stood over his desk for the rest.

"Our parents were?" he asked the boy.

"Caretakers," the boy whimpered.

"Our allegiance is to?"

"The Superiors. We defer to their judgment. Our war was our fault. The Superiors will correct our faults," the boy muttered deeply to the top of his desk.

"What was that?" the Guardian said, leaning on the boy's hand with his baton, pressing it hard across the boy's fingers.

The boy winced but didn't cry, "The Superiors. We defer to their judgment. Our war was our fault. The Superiors will correct our faults." He yelled like the words couldn't get out quick enough.

"Right!" the Guardian said in a voice like snapping shears. He released the boy's fingers and held up his baton, scanning the desks with it. "And this is why we do the Test," he concluded. He stomped back to the front to face us and motioned to the other Guardians who were standing against the wall.

I felt like I missed something. There were a few confused faces, some shuffling in chairs, someone coughed. I turned around to find his face.

Joseph looked as puzzled as me. He shrugged his shoulders conveying his uncertainty. I didn't realize we would be doing the Test straight off. I was hoping I might have some time to prepare. This was to decide the rest of my life. I needed to get it right.

The Guardians walked through the rows of desks handing out stacks of colored paper and pencils, their heavy, black boots sending vibrations across the polished wood floor. The man at the front kept talking. Pulling his glasses over his nose when he read and pushing them into his hair when he was looking at us.

"This is the written part of your test. Answer the questions honestly. If you answer dishonestly, we will know and you will be punished. There is no time limit. You may start as soon as you receive your packet. Raise your hand when you have completed each colored sheet and a Guardian will collect your answers."

I stared down at the stack of paper. So this was it, my life in a packet. I shrugged and started. Pink first. The questions were innocuous to begin with. 'Do you like to be outdoors?' or, 'Do you enjoy a challenge?' As I worked my way through, the questions became more detailed, more specific. They asked for answers to scientific questions like 'how does the liver metabolize fat cells'. They were all multiple choice, and the answers all sounded the same to me, so I just picked one. I did try my best to answer the questions honestly. I was mindful of my habit to be sarcastic. I didn't want to end up shoveling poo in a pig farm because I joked about loving the smell of slops in the morning.

I put my hand up when I finished and the Guardian collected my last paper, perusing it carefully, making sure I had answered every question and ticked every box. He lifted his hand, indicating for me to stand. He scanned my wrist and then a barcode on the papers. I looked around and everyone was still writing, heads down, scribbling frantically. I had finished first. I was sure this couldn't be a good thing. I was very worried I had missed something important, rushed through something I shouldn't have, but it was too late. I was already being ushered out of the room and taken to the next stage of testing.

I actually enjoyed the next part. I was brought to a room full of various stations, fluorescent lights bearing down on me, giving everything a too shiny, too bright kind of glow. On each table were different puzzles to solve. There were boxes made of wood, intricately carved into different segments that we had to pull apart and then put back together. There were mazes to solve and scenes to reconstruct from memory. Again, at the end of each task they scanned my wrist and then entered information into their readers. I found I could do these easily, feeling satisfied at the end that this, at least, I could do.

The last part was harder. It was an all-encompassing physical test. It was mid-afternoon and the sun was shining down on the grass, which was so green it looked like candy. It was hard to believe that this morning I was home, staring at myself in the mirror.

We were tested on strength, agility, flexibility, speed, endurance, vision, and hearing. I did ok in most of the categories, except for flexibility. Sitting in the wet grass with my feet planted flat against a vertical plank of wood, I was told to touch my toes. I strained but I could only reach halfway down my shins. The guardian hovering over this station scowled at me and told me to try again. When I had the same result, she made me bow down while she pressed hard against my back. "Try harder," she snapped. I wanted to snap back at her and tell her I was not a tube of toothpaste she could bend and squeeze, but I let her push me until every muscle in my back was stretching and screaming at me to release. She finally stopped pushing and grunted as she wrote down my results. My body sprung back like a rubber band and I moved quickly to the next station, worried she was going to try and tie my body into a bow if I hung around for too long.

The Guardians watched our every move, scanning, ticking boxes, frowning; making us start over if they weren't satisfied it was our best effort. I watched Joseph when I could. He, of course, was excelling at everything, as I knew he would. He was strong, agile, and undertook each task with ease. I was surprised to note that he wasn't that fast though. I guess no one's perfect. He looked focused and intense as he bent down to pick up the various weights handed to him, his blond curls falling down over his brow. I don't think his head turned my way once.

When we were finished, we were told to sit on the benches bordering the large, grassed field and watched the rest complete their tests. Girls and boys separate. No talking. We all just stared out into the green, watching our companions push themselves to their limits. I wondered if I should have tried harder but I never wanted to be placed in a physical, laboring type class. All was quiet until we saw one girl throw down her weight and shout at one of the Guardians, "I can't do it! I've already tried twice, stop asking me!"

It was so fast. Blink and you would have missed it. Menacingly swift and efficient, the Guardian whipped out an extending metal bar from his belt, cracked the back of her knees so that she fell forward, and then struck her with full force on the back of her neck. I'm sure I heard it snap and she fell to the ground, lifeless. I heard sharp intakes of breath and a few hushed whispers. This was to remind us of our place. This was not to be taken lightly; this was not going to be enjoyable. The Superiors were ever-present and ever cruel. One mistake and your life could be forfeit.

"You two there," the Guardian pointed to two boys who were working close to the girl. "Pick her up and take her to infirmary, from there they will direct you to the crematorium." The boys moved towards her but hesitated, unsure of how to lift her, scared to touch the body. "Don't just stand there. She's not hurt—she's dead—just pick her up!" The boys picked her up gently and started walking towards a building at the back of the grounds that had a red cross over the door.

"Wait!" The boys paused. The Guardian walked over to them, held up the girl's limp wrist, and scanned her number. "Ana Keffi," said the computerized voice. The Guardian moved his finger this way and that until the word "deleted" was spoken by the reader. I shuddered. Their cruelty shocked me still. Even after everything I had seen, and experienced myself, I couldn't believe that human beings could act in this way. I was close to being sick. "Back to it!" he yelled. Everyone returned to their activities, more silent and more serious.

When everyone was finished they asked us to form lines, boys to one side and girls to the other. Two female Guardians dressed in black skirts and wide-shouldered jackets marched over to us. They looked very similar, light brown hair pulled back into a tight bun pinned under their hats. The only difference was the shorter woman seemed less tidy. They told us to follow them, the untidy one hitching her tights up as she walked. I watched as three male Guardians led the boys around the edge of the field, following the bend of the low wall that edged the garden until they were out of sight. I tried to catch Joseph's eye but he wouldn't look up. I watched him until he disappeared around the bend.

We followed the curve of the garden wall in the opposite direction until we reached a platform. We waited there in the line, as a whisper quiet train pulled up. Everyone still seemed on edge after what had happened, and of course, there was no talking. I walked right at the back of the line as we boarded the train and ended up in a rear carriage with only one other girl on it. The train whizzed away from the platform and rounded the bend.

I peered out the window at the garden as it rushed past. It was thickly wooded from the outside, but through the trees I could see glimpses of other beautiful plants. As we continued I caught sight of what appeared to be pens—I think I saw a goat, and some other animals that I wasn't sure of the names. We stopped suddenly and I bumped into the seat in front of me. The girl shot me a reproachful glare as I stood up to disembark the shooting bullet of a train. I didn't like it. It felt like we were going too fast with not enough time to take in the scenery, but maybe that was the point. We weren't here to sightsee.

The tidy woman turned to face the line and said, "These are your living quarters for the next two years. My name is Mischka Baron and this is Stasia Krepke. You may address us as Guardian Baron and Guardian Krepke."

She went on to read from a very long list of rules. Things we could do and things we couldn't do, mostly the latter. I was surprised to hear that we were afforded some leisure time and quite a bit of freedom to walk the grounds. I was itching to get into that garden. Visiting the boys' quarters was strictly forbidden. We were allowed to socialize, to a point, but there were curfews. We were reminded that we were always being watched and any inappropriate behavior would be dealt with severely.

The very fresh memory of the curled up, lifeless girl flashed before my eyes. I prayed there would be a list of these rules on the wall somewhere because as soon as she said we could wander around the grounds, I had only been half-listening. Looking with longing to that wooded area.

We were led through big double gates and I realized we were to be living in one of the eyes of the surprised face we had seen from the air. The walls were as a high as those in Pau, shutting everything out, keeping us contained. Guardian Baron gestured to the relevant buildings as we passed them. The sun was going down and a low chill was floating across the grass. There were bathrooms, laundry, and lounge areas. We were required to do our own laundry and there was a schedule for when we were allowed to shower. Through to the big main building there was a list on a sidewall. There were three levels and our names and numbers were printed on the list next to a level and room number. There would be girls from last year, and the last four quarterly intakes up until this one, living together in the one building. All the first years were on the top level. I felt young. Everyone else was eighteen years or older.

Once we got to the top, we were led along a hallway and through more grand, double doors. It was a vast, open room with rows of beds. The polished floorboards were scuffed and worn from the hundreds of boots that must have walked up and down these rows over the years. It smelled musty and it was freezing cold. I could see my breath as I exhaled. On each stretcher bed there was a number stuck on a pile of blankets, bedclothes, pajamas, and our new uniforms, all grey-green. We would no longer wear the tree emblem from our hometowns. We were wards of the Classes and our new uniforms bore a simple emblem of eight concentric circles embroidered in black. I used to think my room was pretty basic; this was a whole new level of simplicity. Completely devoid of privacy.

As we walked around trying to find our beds, the great metal lights hanging from the ceiling shone like spotlights, swinging slightly from the vibrations of shuffling feet on the floor. I found my bed, which was thankfully by a window. I sat down and surveyed my neighbors. Scared, nervous girls, missing their parents, and trying so hard not to end up like the girl in the yard. I felt sure that the over-reaction to her subordinance was a message, a warning to all the newcomers not to step out of line. This was going to be very hard for me.

"Change into your uniforms and be ready for dinner at six o'clock," Krepke shouted, a little too loudly. Baron stared at her disapprovingly. "I mean, errr, umm, 1800."

We changed and I noticed we had been provided with a small toiletries bag with some basics in it. I decided I would go brush my teeth and fix my hair before dinner.

When I arrived at the bathrooms, there were other girls in there. Three of them were talking about the girl, Ana.

"It's awful but she shouldn't have yelled like that. She made us all look bad," the tall, blonde one said.

"I suppose," piped a small mousy girl, "but I think the punishment was rather harsh."

"Rather harsh?" I was, as always, shocked by people's reactions to the violence. "I think that's an understatement. She's dead—that's not a punishment, that's an execution."

The blonde girl looked down her nose at me, opened her mouth to speak, and then thought better of it. Things were not going to be different for me here. I was still viewed as the troublemaker, someone you didn't want to be seen standing next to, let alone be seen speaking to. They left, chattering about allocations and what they were hoping for.

I stared at myself in the mirror, my odd eyes staring back at me. My hair was a mess from the helicopter and the physical tests. I brushed it out and left it down. I looked tired, but then so did everyone else. The clock in the bathroom said 17:55. I quickly ran upstairs, threw my bag on my bed, and flew out the door. The dining hall was back in the main circle. So I waited for the train to speed me back.

When I arrived at the dining hall, everyone was already seated. They all stared at me as I looked for somewhere to sit. I searched for Joseph. He was sitting in the back with a group of older boys, laughing and joking. Of course, he had already made friends. I tried to make eye contact but he wouldn't look my way, although I'm sure he saw me—

everyone saw me. I sat down at the end of one of the long, wooden tables next to another group of boys, avoiding the sour girls I had met in the bathroom. The boys smiled and shuffled down to make room for me. They introduced themselves. There was a tall boy with light brown hair called Serge. He was goofy looking, like his arms and legs were too long for his body. Across from me was a handsome boy with dark hair and dark skin named Rasheed. He was younger, like me.

"Wow, amazing eyes!" he said. I glared at him but he just smiled back at me. "Whoa, guess the eyes are a touchy subject then." Usually talking to me like this would make me want to slap the person, but he had such a charming manner about him that he relaxed me straight away.

"Wow," I said in mock admiration, "amazing big nose!" Serge was laughing, a little too much. Rasheed just grinned.

"I like her," he said, elbowing a boy next to him, who ignored him and continued to push his peas around his plate.

We talked all through dinner, and for a moment, I could forget about the harrowing events of the day and just enjoy someone's company. It was a welcome change. Every now and then, I would look to the end of the table, to see if my friend had noticed me. Only once, he glanced my way. He seemed unhappy. Uncomfortable.

After dinner, we were scanned out and told to make our way back to our dorms. I wanted to walk, but I thought, tonight at least, I should try and behave myself. I took the train back. I was exhausted after all. I put my new pajamas on and crawled into bed, knowing full well sleep would probably escape me tonight. All night long I could hear other girls weeping into their pillows. Tears would not find me; there was nothing left to cry about. I thought about allocations. I hoped against hope that I might get into something decent. I also gave a secret wish for Joseph to get into what he wanted also. I did not hope for us to be in the same Class. That would not happen.

11

Allocations

We were roused at 06:00 for showers and then straight to breakfast. Krepke and Baron were at the entrance to the bathroom, shouting at us to hurry up. I saw Baron strike a girl on the back while she was still in a towel, a red welt appearing across the girl's still wet skin. I was always good at getting ready fast, so for once, I was first in line.

Breakfast was a help-yourself kind of deal, with big metal dishes full of steaming food. Food I had never even seen before. I piled a little of everything on my plate. I wanted to try as much as possible. As I went to sit down, I could see Joseph sitting at the end of the table again. He looked up at me and smiled, sadly. I took a step towards him but he shook his head. His behavior was infuriating. I wanted to go and confront him but I heard 'Hey amazing eyes, over here'. Rasheed and Serge were motioning for me to sit with them and I figured, well, at least they wanted to talk to me, so I turned away from him and towards my new friends.

"You should be quiet, Rasheed, you'll get us in trouble," I winked.

"Call me Rash, and I think trouble's more fun!" He winked back, eyeing my piled-high plate with amusement.

I dug in and, to my disappointment, found that everything tasted the same. The red meat tasted the same as the noodles with soup, which tasted the same as the orange fruit. I stared at my plate, confused.

Serge spoke, "It's synthetic, made to look like food from home but tastes like grey sludge. It has all the nutrition we require. I think it's supposed to stop us from feeling homesick if it at least resembles something from home." We rolled our eyes in unison. I was grateful that dinner, at least, tasted like real food.

"Breakfast is the most important meal of the day," Rash said with a wicked grin, brandishing his spoon like a weapon. I was sure I shouldn't be associating with this boy but I couldn't help myself. He was like me; I'd never met anyone like me.

When breakfast was over, we were told to report to our town room for allocations and the Letter. I had forgotten about the Letter. Once we received our Class allocation, we would be given one hour to write a letter to our parents, informing them of what we would be doing and to say farewell. I wondered what they would do for Ana's parents. It had to be on our own paper and with our own pens so that the parents would know it was from us. The Superiors treated us like we were ignorant peasants. If they wanted to fake a letter, they could, easily. They thought of these inane ways to placate the people when all they really needed to do was maintain the fear. And they certainly did that.

Rasheed grabbed my hand and gave it a friendly squeeze. "Good luck, see you at dinner," and with that he was off to meet his group from Banyan, Serge to the Birchton group.

I followed Joseph and the others down the hall to a door with the Pau Brazil tree stenciled on the front. Upon entering I could see my place, with the five pens on the table that mother had found and our family letterhead stamped on the top of the paper. There was an envelope on the table that I knew contained my whole future. My allocation. Everyone took their places and started opening their envelopes hungrily. There were sighs of relief, looks of confusion and sheer devastation. I opened mine. It read 'Rosa Bianca has been allocated the Class of Construction'. Confused didn't even begin to cover how I was feeling. It was like getting sucked down a drain hole, gripping the edge for a moment before it pulled you down a waterslide. Joseph turned around to face me. I mouthed the words, 'construction'. He mouthed the words 'medical'. We both looked confounded by what we had read. Though Joseph was far better off than me—I was headed for a life in the Lowers.

We were barely given time to process this new information before we were told we had one hour to write our family letters. Everyone started writing frantically. I just sat there and stared at my page. What could I say? This would be a disappointment to Paulo or maybe a triumph. I didn't want to give him the satisfaction of knowing I had failed. My mother would be destroyed by it. I wanted to write something personal, tell my mother I missed or loved her, but nothing came, my hand was still but for the pen pecking dots on the paper. Joseph was scribbling away at a frenetic pace. In fact, so was everyone else. What was wrong with me? With about fifteen minutes to go, my hand selected a pen and wrote:

To Lenos Bianca,
I hope you are happy now.
Sincerely, your daughter,
Rosa Bianca

P.S. Thanks for the eyes.

I folded it up carefully, slowly, drawing out the last few remaining minutes. I put it in the envelope and wrote his name on the front. Then I just sat there and waited for them to call time.

Joseph was writing right up until they told us to stop. His broad shoulders hunched over his desk, his arm wrapped protectively around his precious letter to his beloved parents. I was so jealous of him and angry with him too. He could talk to me—he should. He owed me at least that.

"Please stand up and place your letters on the front desk." We stood and Joseph's hand shot back. He shoved a folded-up piece of paper into my hand and walked out, without turning around. I quickly stuck it in my waistband and followed. We had twenty-five minutes before we were to report to our Class rooms. I took this opportunity to walk to the gardens.

I stepped through the gate and was immediately enveloped in greenery. It was cold but my cheeks felt warm. My heart was beating so fast as I raced to find a place I could sit and read. I was hoping it was an apology or maybe even a confession. That he wasn't going to ditch me in this place. That he was still my friend. I should have left it to my imagination.

The first part was crossed out. I thought I could read the words 'your father asked'. But then the rest was illegible. The part that I could read was an apology. But it was not the apology I was hoping for. Joseph said that he was very sorry. That he had used me for comfort, as a distraction while he was in the waiting period and upset about leaving his family. He said he never should have let it go on as long as it did and that he felt terrible. He said he did care for me, but now that he was going to the Uppers and I was going to the Lowers, it was better for both of us that we spent time with people from our own Class. He asked me not to talk to him and asked forgiveness for his behavior.

I felt my insides turning to stone, my heart slowing, my breath taking longer and longer to go into my lungs and out.

If I didn't know how I felt about him before the letter, then I certainly knew my feelings now. Now, when it was too late. *So this is what it felt like to have your heart broken,* I thought. I hadn't even noticed that I was crying until the words on the page started to blur as the ink ran together. I knew I wouldn't come back from this.

I stood up and scrunched the letter into a tight ball in my fist. I let the stone turn inside me, feeling the exquisite pain of love lost—before I even had a chance to hold it. I walked to my Class, feeling heavy but empty with tears still streaming down my face.

12.

Construction

I burst into the Class on the first day. Bleary-eyed, wiping my nose with my sleeve, smearing snot across my face. I was the last one in, of course, and they all stared at me in surprise. Their wide eyes tracked me for two reasons: one, because of my disheveled and unsettling appearance, and two, because I was the only girl in the Class. I was about a foot shorter than everyone and tiny by comparison. These boys were big and burly, like Joseph, except for one. There, standing on the end of the line, was Rash. He looked concerned and motioned for me to pull my hair out of my face and wipe my eyes. I allowed myself a small measure of relief at the familiar face and stood next to him.

Our teacher slammed through the doors about two minutes after me, scanner in hand. The big, heavy doors nearly hit him in the back of the head as they hit the wall and rebounded towards him. He scanned our wrists and told us not to be late. It was so hard not to point out his hypocrisy but somehow I managed to bite my tongue. He introduced himself as Thiago Gomez. He was a strong-looking man himself, with no hair and a grimacing face. Short and stocky, I was the only person he didn't have to look up at to make eye contact with. He hid his surprise well, but he scanned my name twice before beginning the first lesson.

Mister Gomez held a two by four in his hand, clapping it into his palm as he spoke for emphasis. "In this Class you—thwack—will learn every skill required for building—thwack—fitting out and also repairing a Woodland home—thwack."

It sounded dreadfully boring and I was sure I would be terrible at it. Creating things, building things, was not my forte. I always thought I would be much better at destroying.

"This will range from concrete pouring to cabinetry. This is important and I expect you to pay attention and work hard."

I rocked back and forth on my heels, thinking of how I could get out of this Class.

"It will be back breaking, grueling, and you'll develop callouses in places you didn't even know you had, but if you boys, er, students, listen and pay attention, you can make a good career from this Class," Mister Gomez said, pacing in front of us, gripping the two by four plank and waving it around the class. "Don't disappoint me."

We all leaned back from the swaying plank as it grazed past our noses but his actions weren't threatening. He then gave each of us a hammer and a box of nails and set us to work on framework for walls. The boys all clanged and clamored around like they had done this before. I hung back and observed. Observed nails being bent and Rash making an idiot of himself. I held the hammer in my hand—it was heavy, reassuring in a way I hadn't expected. It was simple and aweing in its purpose and it was perplexing. What made them think this was for me? I stared down at it for a long time like I was waiting for it to tell me something. It didn't.

I returned to the dorms after dinner, feeling lost. This was so very far from what I had anticipated. I walked through the garden with Rash, kicking dirt and playing with my hair distractedly. I could tell he was as surprised as me.

"So... construction... who'd have thought?" he said, breaking the silence.

"What were you hoping for?" I asked.

"Um, I wasn't really hoping for anything. This is already more than I could have dreamed," he said, not joking.

"Really?" I was surprised.

He kicked some loose stones and a plume of dust clung to his grey pants. When he planted himself on a wooden barrier, near the pens I had picked out as animal housing from the air, his expression was somber. It didn't fit.

The farm animals were separated, with gold plaques screwed into the fence posts of their enclosures naming them as goats, sheep, chickens, pigs, boars. Hands in his pockets, Rash looked like he wanted to say something but it was difficult for him. I sat down close, our hipbones touching. He leaned into my shoulder. He was almost as sharp and bony as I was.

Already, I felt like we were linked. Like our similarities drew a connecting line from one to the other. I didn't look at him but said, "You can tell me. But you don't have to. We can go make comparisons between the farm animals and the Guardians. I think Gomez looks like that boar with the missing tusk." I pointed to the pen, the hairy creature snorting as if he was offended. Rash laughed half-heartedly. He took my hand and told me his story. It was cool and steady, easy to hold. And if I had been in his situation, I would find it hard to laugh about anything.

His father died when he was one and with no one willing to marry his mother at her age and with no money, she turned to servicing the local law enforcement. "If you know what I mean?" he said. I nodded. Rash was her second child and his mother was old. Sometimes she would get money, sometimes a beating. She cursed Rash for her bad fortune and he copped a fair few beatings himself. One night, after a particularly bad run in with a customer, his mother crept into his room and held a knife to his throat.

"She was crazy. I reckon she was like that because of what she had to do to survive. She used to scream for my brother." Rash looked down at our joined hand and traced our knuckles with his other fingers. "I think she wished he had survived and not me. She blamed me for everything," he said in a voice so small it was like Rash had been swallowed.

Then his mood switched, "She did it all the time. The same speech, different methods." He said like it was something altogether ordinary. Like saying, 'I like milk on my cereal.'

"You ruined my life! she would say," Rash yelled in a hag-like voice,

throwing his fist in the air. He then went on to comically demonstrate the various methods his mother had used to try and kill him. Hands around his neck trying to choke him, his tongue hanging out, making strangled noises and coughing, and fighting to breathe with a pillow over his face. He looked so funny flailing around on the ground, like a beetle on its back, that I laughed despite myself.

He got up and I dusted the dirt from his back. His face changed. No longer a smile, but a sad expression that made him look older. He shook his head, trying to dislodge the horrible memory.

"She'd never used a knife before. I wasn't ready for that. I had to fight back. I didn't want to die."

I didn't know what to say. So I didn't say anything. I just squeezed his rough hand and stared out into the trees, watched them pick up the slight wind and dance on it. Nodding their heads in agreement that no one should have to go through something so horrible. Wishing I could lift some of the burden, that I could reach into his head and pluck out those painful memories.

"I tried to save her but there was just so much blood. Too much." He wasn't crying. He talked about it almost like it was someone else's story, like he had watched it from a distance. Commented on the angle of the knife, the ineffectual method of stabbing that left the victim bleeding for hours before the release of death.

"Anyway, I buried her, under the house. Then I told the neighbors she had run away. Of course they reported me straight away and, before I knew what was happening, I was on a chopper to here."

I nodded. He was right. Anything was better than that. His expression quickly changed, his face relaxed, and he was easy-going Rash again. He let go of my hand and punched my shoulder lightly, "Farm animals?"

"Sure." I guess everyone had their own way of coping. This was his.

After time spent joking with Rash at the animal pens, we separated and I went back to my dorm. It was dark and the moonlight made the buildings look less harsh, less like they were going to rise up and devour me. But I still felt small; the eyes of the concrete creatures clinging to the drainpipes followed me, mocked me.

I lay awake thinking about what Rash had said. Realizing that things could be a lot worse for me. Construction was a surprise, yes, but there must have been a reason why they picked it, something in my tests that pointed them in that direction. I would try. I would go into Class and absorb everything I could. I fell asleep easily. Anticipating the 'hard, hard work' but kind of looking forward to it.

It didn't take me long to realize that there had been a reason. I was good at this, really good. Every week we would learn a new skill, repeat it as many times as was necessary to perfect it, and then move on to something new. Our teacher was passionate and intense, but he wasn't unkind. He had never-ending patience for the ones that struggled. For once, somehow, that wasn't me. I enjoyed making things. Taking a piece of wood and crafting it into something useful was calming and centering for me.

My classmates were all genuinely decent young men, despite the swearing. They looked out for me in the beginning, protective because I was a girl, but once they could see I was managing really well on my own, they would often come to me for help.

Daydreaming about Joseph, I was plummeting a drill bit into a piece of plasterboard, white dust flying everywhere like toxic snow. I was thinking about talking to him, imagining a confrontation that didn't end in him running away from me. A strong hand wrapped around my own and pulled the drill back.

"Uh, Soar?" My new nickname. "What the hell are you doing?"

I snapped my head around to face Nik, a tree stump of a boy whose ropey exterior resembled an even rougher and ropier interior.

"Oh, damn, sorry Nik, I wasn't concentrating."

He looked at me dumbfounded, "What yer apologizing to me for? I jest needed yer help with sumthin'." He ran his hand through his black-as-batwing hair awkwardly, "Er, that is, if ya have the time."

I let in a puff of pride at the fact that this boy needed my help. Trying not to be too girly and blush, I punched his arm, which felt exactly as I thought it would, like punching a bag of nails, and said, "Of course. What do you need?"

"Well, I can't reach that goddamn tin of oil up there." He pointed to a high shelf. I felt myself deflating. "Can I lift you up there to get it?"

"Oh, sure," I said quietly. He grabbed me by my waist and lifted me with ease. I snatched the tin and slammed it on the bench.

"Thanks," Nik muttered. "Um, Soar?"

What now, did he want me to fix the ceiling fan while I was up there?

"Yes."

"Ah crap, how freakin' long does this take fore I can put a second coat on it, and um, do ya sand in between?"

I grabbed his impossibly hard arm, steered him to his workbench, and began instructing him, Gomez looking silently over my shoulder.

As I selected a piece of fine-grit sandpaper, I asked, "Nik?"

"Yeah."

"Why Soar?"

His pale blue eyes fixed on me and he gave a crooked grin. "Aw ya know, coz yer the high flyer in the class. And, der, it's Rosa backwards."

My mouth twitched into a half-smile. I didn't correct him.

As the weeks went by, the violence faded, as did the heartache. I was surrounded by friends who respected me and it salved my heart inadvertently. The students were all working hard towards the mid-year assessment. I saw Joseph from time to time, hanging around outside the medical building, swinging from the concrete pillars, wearing his white coat. He seemed happy. I tried to be happy for him, despite the stone that twisted in my heart. He never looked at me.

At meal times I ate with the boys. Mucked around with Rash. I was the only one from Pau Brasil in my Class. Rash was from Banyan as were two of the others, the rest were from the rocky towns of Birchton and Radiata. They were big, tall boys with strong bodies and rough language.

I loved it. I loved that they treated me as their equal, never censoring themselves. They slapped me on the back just as hard as the others. I went flying, but I still appreciated it.

Occasionally Serge would sit with us. He had been allocated Intelligence, which was the most highly regarded Class. I had this sneaking suspicion he had a crush on me, which Rash teased me about mercilessly. He would sit behind us as Serge tried to make conversation with me and raise his eyebrows repeatedly while the other boys snickered. Serge was sweet and I'm sure I could do a lot worse, but no match could be made here. We still didn't know what town we were to be placed in. Romantic connections were pointless. They happened, but they were pointless.

"Your children would look like weird-eyed insects," Rash said as he galloped awkwardly, imitating Serge's long limbs and jerky movements.

"I'm not having any children," I snapped. I couldn't think of anything worse.

It was the first time in my life, apart from the short time I had spent with Joseph, that I felt like myself. Comfortable, and could it be? At home. I didn't trust it, but tried my hardest to be in the moment. I had two years of this before I had to leave. I thought I might as well do my best to enjoy it.

Coming up to assessment, we started eating together quickly and then leaving early as a group, to get back to the workshop. As we were leaving, Rash whispered to me, "Why does that beautiful blonde man keep staring at you?" as we were clearing our table before heading back to the workshop. "I mean you are very pretty but he is always looking at you with sad, longing eyes." Rash clasped his hands dramatically, swooning, making it sound like something romantic and forbidden. I felt myself constricting. I didn't like that he made reference to my looks or Joseph.

"What are you talking about?" I said, punching his arm. Rash always exaggerated.

Somewhat seriously, well, as serious as Rash could ever sound when he was in this kind of mood, he said, "He looks at you, like, I don't know, like you're the only girl in the world, or something."

I snorted. I highly doubted it. From what I had seen, Joseph could have his pick of any girl in this place. They threw themselves at him on a daily basis. I heard the other girls talking about him at the dorms. I hated it. I was tempted to make up a rumor that he had a hideous birth defect or something. Instead, I just quietly fumed.

"Maybe he's looking at you, you idiot, since you're always making a spectacle of yourself," I deflected. I didn't like thinking about Joseph and I certainly didn't want to talk about him. That was enough to distract Rash, who then went on and on about how, of course, everyone was looking at him—he was the most handsome, clever person in this place. I kicked him in the back of the legs so his knees buckled. I glanced over at Joseph while Rash was sprawled on the floor, just to check. He was talking to his medical friends. His face was concentrated like he was talking about something very important. It had been months since I had heard his voice and I realized I didn't really know him anymore—he seemed so grown up compared to us. I blushed as I realized if he had looked over this way, he probably thought we were all clowns.

I turned to Rash, who was moaning about his aching knees. "Can you be even slightly serious for a second?" I said loudly. Then more quietly, "We've got assessment to worry about."

"Oh, I'm all about being serious, sister!" Rash stood up straight and started marching out the door, kicking his legs high in the air. The rest of the boys were barreling out the door laughing and knocking each other around. One of the Birch boys shoved me into the wall. I squeaked as I banged my elbow. I turned and leaned against the dark wood paneling, facing the doorway, rubbing the graze. Joseph was standing. Our eyes met, a pull so strong it was like we were attached with a fishing line and he was reeling me in. I took one step towards him. His fists were clenched, his face drawn down. He looked like he was having an inner debate with himself. But before I could react any further, a brown arm grabbed me and pulled me away from the entrance.

"C'mon, Soar, we have work to do." I closed my eyes and tried to convince myself that I had imagined that moment. *Assessment,* I said to myself. That's all that matters.

The assessment was a big deal. It determined what stream you would go into from your Allocation. So, if you were in the medical Class and you scored well, you would go into the high stream, training you to be a surgeon or researcher. If you did poorly, you would be emptying old people's bedpans in the outer rings. For me, scoring highly meant the difference between laying bricks and crafting furniture. I desperately wanted to do well. I had found I adored working with wood and I was good at it. Mister Gomez had let us choose our own project. We just had to make something from local resources and it needed to have a specific purpose.

Most of the boys were making tables and chairs or desks with drawers. I chose something more delicate. I was aiming for the top, so I was trying to make a jewelry box for a woman in Superiors. I had to use a lot of imagination, as I had never really seen much jewelry. Only my mother's simple wedding ring and a necklace Paulo's mother had given her. I made a lockable box with a removable tray on the top that had small compartments for rings and earrings and a large compartment underneath for larger items. I needed it to be perfect. Simple but beautiful. I had carved eight concentric rings resembling the towns of the Woodlands into the lid of the box. I painstakingly inlayed the timbers from each town into the rings.

The boys all hovered around, admiring it. Nik slapped me on the back a little too hard and I braced myself against the edge of the bench. "Hell, Soar, ya did well. Ya tryin' to make us all look bad," he said with a crooked smile.

One of the boys punched Nik hard in the gut. "Don't be a dickhead, Nik. Nah, it's really good Soar, really good." I just grinned. They were so kind to me. I never felt like I was in competition with them. We all wanted each other to do well.

When I placed the last piece of wood in the rings, I felt an enormous sense of accomplishment. I had poured my heart and soul into making this and it was beautiful. The timber was warm and smooth to touch. The design was flawless. I had never created anything I was more proud of. I'd never created anything before. I was sure that this would be enough to secure me a place in the high stream.

On my way back to the dorms, Rash and I walked through the garden, which was actually called the Class Arboretum. It was my favorite place and we had come here often over the last couple of months. He would prattle on and I would pretend to listen as I walked from plant to plant reading the little plaques. Absorbing the information like a drug. If I hadn't got into Construction, I think I would have enjoyed horticulture.

I was reading the description for the Pau Brasil tree for the hundredth time when Rash sidled up to me. He was light on his feet and he startled me with his closeness. It was dark, with only the moonlight and some garden lights dotted around to illuminate the way.

"Good luck for tomorrow, Rosa," he said. He never used my real name. I frowned and bumped him sideways. "Good luck, Rash, you're going to need it." I winked at him and he grinned at me, only his white teeth shining like a low half-moon in the dark ness. If I were to have a brother, I would want it to be him. I gave him a big hug and he hugged me back. He didn't jump away, or question the feelings behind it. We were friends. We parted and I went back to the dorm.

That night I dreamed a wonderful dream. I was in my own little workshop. Making furniture, running my hands over freshly sanded timber, working hard but enjoying every minute. I was content.

13

Assessment

If I had known this was the day, I wonder if I would have done anything different. Could I have stopped the horrible events that unfolded before my eyes?

Maybe.

Probably not.

I had worked late into the night, putting coats of oil and endlessly sanding my jewelry box. I was obsessing over it, wanting to make sure every part of it was perfect. Not even admitting to myself how much it meant to me.

Now that I was back in the workshop, after a restless nights' sleep, I stepped back and tried to appraise it critically. It was certainly eye pleasing. It didn't look like something I made and I couldn't help wondering where I had pulled it from. How was I able to create something so good? It was not like me, or at least not what I thought I was like. A sense of unfamiliar pride swelled inside me. I was nervous, but satisfied that this would be good enough. The dream crept back into my mind, a shiny, haze of a picture. My own workshop, my own work.

"Don't worry, Soar, it's fantastic!" said Henri, putting his long arm around my shoulders. I took a deep breath. He smelled wonderful, like a combination of freshly sanded timber and oil. I could tell by the dark circles under his eyes that he had been here all night, his usually flawless appearance showing some cracks, a hair out of place, a crinkle in his shirt.

Henri had been the moral compass of the group. From what I had gathered, life in Birchton was even harsher than in Pau. Henri had been raised in an extremely strict environment and his appearance reflected that. His ash-blonde hair was always neatly combed back. His uniform was always impeccable. Outwardly, he looked like the perfect student, serious and dedicated. But there was such a warmth and kindness to him. He was always looking out for us, trying, to no avail, to get the group to settle down at meal times and in class. I admired the fact that despite his hard upbringing, he had managed to keep his soul intact, unlike many of the other students. He was the one that we would look to, in case we had gone too far, and he would always let us know, but in a kind and measured way. Having someone look out for me wasn't something I was very used to. In Pau, everyone looked after themselves. I only knew one other person who behaved like Henri, or at least used to.

"Thanks, I love yours," I said, thinking it was not enough but not knowing what else to say. I ran my hands over his impressive desk. Henri had constructed a strong-looking desk out of the pale orange-colored timber of his hometown. It was deceptively complicated. Upon closer inspection, you could see the craftsmanship that had gone into it. The top, lockable drawer that slid open effortlessly and the carved handles made it look extraordinary. Each one was shaped like a delicate birch leaf, curled perfectly to allow the opener to grasp it and pull with ease.

As I shut the drawer, Mister Gomez stormed in looking like a terrified mole, squinting and crashing into things. I suppose, for him, this was an assessment of his teaching skills, and for us to do poorly reflected directly on him. But when he took in the superb creations his students had produced, his shoulders, tensed and almost touching his ears, seemed to relax a little. Until his dark eyes glanced at Rash's wobbly-looking table.

"Listen up everyone. We have until twelve to finish. Rasheed, I suggest you attend to the wobbly leg on that table." He proceeded to walk around the workshop, pointing out minor issues that needed to be fixed. When he came to me, I was just about to pick it up and take it over to the sanding bench. He put his hand on my wrist. It was all sweaty, but I did my best not to pull back.

He said, "Leave it, Rosa, I don't think there's any more you can do."

I think I must have looked hurt or worried because he quickly followed it up with, "You surprised me, girl, it's excellent work," then he gruffly snatched the box out of my hands and placed it towards the end of the judgment line.

Rash winked at me and mouthed the words, "Told ya," and then started squirting way too much glue into the join between his tabletop and leg. I wished he had taken this more seriously. I highly doubted he would end up in the high stream with that table.

The other boys were all working really hard. They were focused and I didn't want to distract them. I wasn't allowed to help, so I asked Mister Gomez if I could take some free time. He waved me off, muttering something about having enough to worry about, as he snatched the hammer out of Rash's hands. Rash had given up on glue and was trying to hammer a wedge in the join between the leg and the table to even it up. *Bricklayer,* I thought.

I wandered outside and made my way back to the Arboretum. The weather was getting colder and my thin cotton uniform was failing to shield me from the chill. Soon, I thought, there would be a light blanket of snow covering most of these tree branches. It would be a beautiful sight, another I had never seen before. I could imagine trees laden with heavy snow, green contrasting against the cool white. In Pau we had snow. But snow on concrete was just snow on concrete—it was nothing special.

I welcomed winter; there would be less people outside. I could walk freely around the trees without interruption. I walked from plant to plant reading the plaques. Each time, I remembered a little more, finding I could repeat the names of at least half of the plants in here just by looking at them.

I arrived at my favorite place. The Banyan tree's limbs stretched out, beckoning for me to climb under their thick, grey branches. The hanging roots dripped down, providing a curtain under which to shelter. I pulled them apart and nestled in amongst the roots and the damp dirt. I had about one hour to wait.

I thought about what had got me here. Hate and love in equal measure. Then I thought about how I felt now. I had changed. I had let go of the hate now. The love was harder to free but maybe, in time, that too would fade. I had learned so much. Things about myself I had never known existed, what I was capable of. Somehow I had managed to make friends. Most importantly, I felt like I had a place. In this awful situation, I had found something good. I was amazed at myself and reluctantly, proud. I held one of the Banyan roots in my hand. It was dangling maybe a centimeter off the ground, stretching and straining to get to the cool, damp earth. If I had a place, maybe I could start to heal, start to grow. I let the root fall, not long now and it would find its way to the ground, be nourished and in turn nourish its mother tree.

I heard him before I saw him. One thing he never was, was quiet. Joseph stomped up the path, snapping twigs and branches as he went. I retreated further behind the curtain of grey roots and watched. He was pacing back and forth, clearly distressed. He plonked himself down against the Brasilwood, his large form looking out of place next to the tiny trunk. Sitting right in the spot where two months ago, I had read his letter. He sat with his elbows on his knees. His body was tense, like a spring trap, as he pulled his golden curls back from his face.

My heart ached for him. He was only a few meters away, but it felt like such a distance to cover. I wanted to crawl over to him and hold him, have him hold me. But remembering the letter, I froze, feeling that stone where my heart used to be, twisting and wringing out my insides.

I clutched my chest, the imagined pain starting to feel real. I couldn't breathe. The once comforting roots of the tree now felt like they were strangling me, trying to tie me down, pull me into the ground. I knew I couldn't sit there for much longer. But I didn't want to burst out of the tree, revealing that I had been watching him this whole time. I struggled to contain myself but thankfully, after about five minutes, he sat up straight, like he had remembered something important. He muttered, "I have to do it," and then he stormed off determinedly.

I parted the curtain of knobbly roots and stepped out, surveying the scene. I wished I had time to sort through these feelings, to try and understand what I had just seen. He always seemed so happy when I saw him. I wondered if it was something that had just happened—had he done poorly on his assessment? I doubted it. There was no time. There were no answers anyway. I ran back to the workshop with minutes to spare, distracted and weary.

I walked through the swinging double doors to the workshop and was confronted with a re-stressed Gomez flustering his hairy arms about. "Good, Rosa, you're here. The judges will be here any second now." He grabbed me by the shoulders and jostled me into line with the others, leaving palm-shaped wet patches on my t-shirt. I noticed that Rash had somehow managed to salvage his table and it stood straight. It was terribly simple and I didn't hold much hope that he would score well, but at least it wasn't leaning at a forty-five-degree angle anymore.

I stood between Rash and Henri, my two favorite people, and held my breath. The judges entered. One woman and one man both dressed in a red uniform with the same gold trim as the other guardians. I didn't recognize them; they must have been from outside the Classes. Readers in hand, they walked to the first piece and circled it, whispering to each other. They scanned the boy's wrist and proceeded to type things in, adding a score to his name. The woman seemed senior. She ordered the other one around, occasionally tucking her grey bob behind her ears as she spoke in a low, hissing whisper. She had a stern, nasty face that was set in a permanent frown. The man was younger and kept looking to her before typing in his notes. His small, brown face twisting like he had smelled something bad as he inspected every aspect of the pieces. He reminded me of a rat, twitching and sniffing, following the other one around waiting for crumbs to fall.

I was the second to last to be appraised and it was agonizing waiting for them to get to me. I leaned and swayed on my tiptoes, inadvertently peering at the male Guardian's screen. He scowled at me and tucked it under his arm, protecting his piece of cheese. All he needed were whiskers to complete the transformation.

When they got to Rash, they didn't take much time. The woman raised one eyebrow as she stared down at my friend. I noticed she was wearing makeup, a rare luxury. It was caked in the corner of her eyes, balled up bits of black grit that made her blink too much. Rash shifted uneasily from foot to foot under her critical gaze, smiling inappropriately at her. I had a moment of panic, thinking he might be stupid enough to wink at her. I wanted to whack him and tell him no amount of charm was going to help him today. When they moved on, I heard him sigh in relief. It was my turn.

The woman lifted the lid to my jewelry box with her little finger. It glided open gently, elegantly. She inspected every compartment with a critical eye, checking the workmanship meticulously. She closed the lid and ran her hand over the emblem on the front, tracing each individual circle of timber with her finger. I wanted to talk, explain to her the differences in the timbers, the purpose of each compartment. I bit my lip, tasting blood. She turned to her colleague and she smiled. It didn't look right on her shrewd face. But her teeth were showing through her thin lips caked in dried-up lipstick. Mister Gomez was looking very pleased as she nodded her head approvingly in his direction. She typed in her scores and moved on to Henri. I relaxed a little. Rash and the other boys were all grinning at me. A feeling of elation was creeping through me, threatening to make me do something crazy, like jump in the air or yell out. *Maybe this could work*, I thought. My love of this craft was not misplaced—I might actually succeed.

The judges both seemed quite pleased with Henri's desk as well, nodding and whispering in a painful performance that only heightened the tension in the room. We wanted it be over. When they had completed their assessments, the judges walked to Mister Gomez, their gold-embellished shoulders glinting under the fluorescence, and turned to face the class. I looked down the line—eight young men with their futures hanging in the balance. They were all strong, good boys with sawdust in their hair and oil on their calloused fingers.

"You have all performed satisfactorily in this assessment," she stated. "Your score will be prepared and provided to you tomorrow morning. Perez." She motioned for him to step forward and then she placed a hammer in his hand.

I wish I had been prepared for this. I'm not sure whether it would have changed anything but maybe it would have. There could have been a chance. I could have had a chance.

Perez's face looked devilish as he moved to the first table. Without ceremony, without hesitation, he smashed it. I watched each of my friends' devastated faces as he moved from piece to piece, destroying their work. I couldn't believe what I was seeing. What was the point to this? I felt each blow like he was striking me. My arms held up in defense, my body vibrating with every crash of the hammer. I couldn't stand it anymore. Three pieces into the destruction, I screamed.

"Stop!" Everyone stared at me. The boys were shaking their heads, pleading with their eyes for me not to continue. Henri whispered, "Soar, no," but this was me—I couldn't stop even if I wanted to. "Please," I begged, "you can't do this." I was shaking. Even as the words escaped my mouth, I knew it was futile.

Perez took three steps towards me and pounded me in the face with the flat side of the hammer. I flew sideways, knocking Henri's desk over in the process. I felt teeth from my right jaw rattling in my mouth, which filled with the metallic taste of blood and threatened to drown me. The pain was immense as it spread from my jaw up and around my head, throbbing. The torn flesh of my face was searing hot, each nerve ending screaming. I couldn't focus, vision blurred but not from tears. I stayed silent. Trying to breathe, trying really hard not to panic.

As I lay there on the floor clutching my broken face, I wondered why Mister Gomez hadn't warned us. He had always been strict but never cruel. This was cruelty. Then it came to me, as bits of wood and lacquer rained down on me from above. Shards of my proud creation were landing in my hair and sticking to the growing pool of blood around where I was lying. There were two reasons. One, we probably wouldn't have tried so hard if we knew. And two, this was part of the assessment. It was a test. And I had just failed with flying colors. In one swift move, I had ruined everything.

The noise of my beautiful jewelry box being shattered marked the end for me. I knew it, as well as everyone else in the room. Rash stepped forward, foolishly trying to diffuse the situation. "C'mon guys…" he said as he took a step towards me. The expression on his face showed me how bad I must have looked. The grey-haired woman stepped forward and touched a black device lightly to his chest. His body jolted unnaturally and he fell to the floor. I hauled myself over to him, leaving a smear of blood-sticky woodchips in my wake. He was still breathing but he was unconscious. I saw the other boys, my treasured family, moving forward, like they were about to act. I pulled myself up to sitting, a mixture of blood and teeth spilling from my lips as I spoke, "No. Help Rash." Whatever was going to happen to me, I didn't want them dragged into it.

Two men had appeared in the doorway, dressed in the black Guardian garb. They were directed to take me by the female judge, who was definitely not whispering anymore. Her harsh shouting reverberated in my swollen head. "Remove her immediately!" she barked at them, pinching the bridge of her nose like the whole thing had inconveniently given her a headache. They roughly hooked their arms under mine and pulled me to my feet. As they lugged me out the door like a sack of potatoes, I could see the boys helping Rash to his feet. I was thankful that for now, at least, he had escaped further punishment.

The Guardians were trying to make me walk. I tried but I felt dizzy and uncoordinated, like my legs were made of jelly. My shirt was soaked with blood and my eye was starting to close up. One of the men gave up and slung me into his arms. I had no strength to struggle. Besides, there was nowhere to run to.

The hall started to narrow before my eyes. I felt my body being hollowed out and filled with lead. Everything that I had tried to build was gone, forever. Any warmth I had in me was replaced with a cold dread, knowing that I would most likely be dead in a few hours. My vision was getting tighter and tighter, until all I could see was a spot of light dancing before my one good eye. I felt my body being dumped on a hard, cold surface. I exhaled, farewelling my life. Hope was gone. Death was imminent. I prayed it would be fast.

14

Climbing

It felt like I had missed something, like there was a gap in my memory. I didn't know how long I had been here and what they were asking of me. I knew that it was big. Something I was resisting. Things kept slipping and I needed to retrace my steps. I felt like it was essential I figured it out soon, before something bad happened.

There was an ominous cloud hanging over my head, pushing down on me, pushing me to look deeper. I curled around the emptiness and pulled a yellow quilt around my shaking shoulders. This was home, right? It looked like home, but there were small things that didn't quite fit—like the small crack above my bed that I used to trace with my finger when I couldn't sleep and the quilt made from scraps of fabric, sewn by my mother, the faded spot on the curtain where the sun hit in the afternoon. There was no sun here. It felt like we were underground. It was cold. My ears sought noise from the outside world but there were none. No birds, no wolves howling, no lawn mowers grumbling. All that was familiar to me was twisted or simply missing.

And somewhere at the back of all of this, there was something pushing. A fissure was appearing in the black spots of my memory, one small shaft of light. I felt like if I could get my fingers in and pry it apart, things would become clearer. Thoughts ticked over time and I came back to home. Was I even supposed to be at home?

I was tracing that imaginary crack over and over when they came in. One, two, three people, smiling unconvincingly. "How are you feeling?" one asked, patting my arm absently. She peeled back the covers and wrapped a black bandage around my arm, inflating it until it hurt while pressing her cool fingers to my wrist. Someone handed me a tray of food and a milkshake, which they told me had the extra vitamins I needed in it. I didn't register faces, voices. It seemed unimportant. Food, however, seemed extremely important and I eagerly dove into my meal and took sips of my shake, while nodding at their questions. A tall man, with a frightening smile, all giant teeth that didn't quite fit in his mouth, asked me if I'd had any nausea that day. I shook my head and touched my stomach instinctively. My milkshake stuck in my throat.

I rolled my hands over my middle, expecting loose clothing and a flat stomach, my fingers pressing down. "What the hell is this?" I screamed. I was bulging. I looked like I had swallowed a sack of rice, or had been blown up with air. My once smooth, smooth stomach had been replaced by a protrusion, a lump. Concern flickered on the blonde lady's face but it was quickly covered up, her composure a serene mask. The other, older woman, held my hand away from my stomach. She held it tightly, as if trying to stop me from touching it again. I felt her manicured nails digging into my wrist.

"Now calm down…" someone whispered as I felt my armed pulled upward violently and jabbed sharply.

A fog rose up around me. I was floating on a grey cloud, unaware and indifferent. I went back to feeling like I couldn't quite grasp what was happening to me. But somewhere, a thought was pawing at me and I got the sense this had happened before, many times more than once.

Was I dreaming or was this real? Things swirled around in my head, blood, warmth, shredding pain. I reached out and grasped at the one thing I knew was true. My name was Rosa, I was sixteen years old, and I surrendered myself to the Classes early because my mother was pregnant. But even this memory seemed wrong. Wasn't there a boy? I shook my head, trying to clear it, but his face remained a blur surrounded by a blondish halo. I hit my thighs with my fist weakly in frustration. It was like I was climbing the inside of a bowl, always slipping back down to the bottom every time I thought I had made some progress.

15

The Fog

Whoosh! The sound of air escaping from somewhere startled me. But then a calm washed over my whole body and whatever startled me didn't seem to matter anymore. Every muscle in my body relaxed and I felt myself sinking.

Whoosh! There was that sound again. I wondered where it was coming from, but at the same time I didn't care. Curiosity was a vague shape, easily shelved. I felt at ease, peaceful and sleepy. But something sharp kept pushing up inside me and telling me to fight it, drag myself out of this strange fog. This peace was false.

I pricked my ears, feeling like I hadn't used them in months. The whooshing sound had come from underneath the slim, metal-framed bed I was sitting on. I dragged my body up to sitting and rolled over and down the side of the bed. Every movement needed my full concentration and energy like I was moving through molasses. Once over the edge of the bed, I felt like I was dragging myself over the edge of a cliff, my legs dangling in the air. I gripped the cold, metal bars of the bed, feeling like I might fall miles and miles into a dark abyss. My body felt uncoordinated and unbalanced but I persisted, pulling my awkward form along the floor like a commando.

And there it was...

Underneath the bed was a tiny silver pipe with what looked like a little showerhead over it. "Whoosh!" A flush of cold, sweet smelling air hit my face and everything went dark.

16

Waking Up

I woke up back on my bed, with unfamiliar people crowded around me. Men and women in white coats, holding my arms up, pinching my toes, looking in my eyes with small, silver torches. I pursed my lips, trying to concentrate, but explanations seemed just out of reach. Were these doctors? Or perhaps scientists? In Pau, well, in the rings I had been to, there were a few people who dressed like this. They poured out of a dingy looking building in Ring Five at quitting time. They quickly shrugged off their white coats and shoved them in their packs as they walked home. Shedding their skin as they returned to their other, separate life back in the housing areas. Pau was like that—no one ever talked about what they did for a living. Pride was not a rewarded attribute.

"I think she must have rolled off, or fallen," the tall man said. "I don't think she's compromised." I tried hard not to raise an eyebrow at the word 'compromised'.

The younger female smiled at me, patting my head soothingly. "You fell, darling. Try not to move while we examine you." I felt like saying, *I'm not a wounded animal*, but at the same time, I wanted to snap at them like one.

A harsh voice barked, "Don't bother, she can't hear you. She's not even registering that we are here."

On closer inspection, I could see the kind, younger woman wore a flesh-colored facemask over her mouth and nose. This seemed important but important kept dissolving in front of me. I was trying to reach above the fog, trying to hold my breath and climb past it. Silver pipe, shower head.

A bloody taste developed in my mouth, filling it with metallic-flavored saliva. I felt dizzy. I leaned over the side of the bed, the room tipping and tilting, and vomited on the floor. The two women jumped back in unison. The tall man raised his eyebrows, displeased. He wasn't fast enough. He had vomit on his shoes and halfway up his pants.

He looked down at his shoes and frowned. "Keep an eye on her and make sure she keeps her food down over the next day or so," he muttered to the women and hurriedly exited the room, his pants making a wet, flapping sound as he walked.

I watched him go, struggling to remember why he had left so quickly. My brain was still foggy but the vomit cleared my head a little. Vomit, right. I pressed my fingers to my mouth, trying to suppress a smile. I had the feeling I shouldn't smile or even show any emotion to these strange people.

After the younger woman had cleaned up my mess, she placed a tray in front of me and left. I held the large, paper cup in both hands and twisted it around, inspecting it. Carefully, I took a small sip. The milkshake inside tasted very familiar. I opened the lid and peered inside; it was grey and sludgy, the consistency of wet cement. The food looked more normal, some meat, cooked to death, mashed potatoes and peas. The food didn't taste exactly right. It tasted more like the milkshake than mashed potatoes, and the meat taste like charred wood, but I found that I was starving. I ate a little, drank a little, very slowly. Thinking over what I thought I had worked out.

This fog I was lost in was something they were doing to me. The masks meant it could be something inhaled.

"Whoosh!" I instinctively pulled the bedclothes over my face, trying to block out the invisible poison. A silver pipe pushed up into my memory. Had I seen something or heard something? I wasn't sure but the picture in my head was clear, a silver pipe. I pulled myself over and out of the bed, realizing for the first time that I was attached to several lines and monitors. Still holding a sheet over my face, I clambered towards the wall under my bed, the shiny grey floor reflecting my face as I crawled along. I looked thin, well, thinner. My odd eyes popped out of my head, framed by purple circles. When did my hair get so long? I ducked under the metal bed and there it was, a silver pipe and a tiny showerhead attached to it. As quickly as I could, I shoved the sheet over the opening, hearing a muffled 'whoosh' as I sat back on my knees.

I wrung my hands together, thinking. I couldn't leave the sheet there. They would work it out and I wasn't sure what I was going to do yet. I needed them to think nothing had changed. I needed to find something else to seal the opening to that pipe. My eyes searched the room, really seeing it for the first time. There was nothing I could use. It was so bare. Four painted walls, a sink, a door leading to a bathroom, and shiny grey tiles climbing halfway up the wall. There were some things I recognized, items from my room. The small details were there, but enough was changed that it now felt very wrong.

I stood up too quickly, feeling very light-headed. I held myself up against the side of the bed and took it in. It was bizarre. A lot of the details were actually painted onto the walls. My dresser with the few ornaments I possessed—a bottle of perfume, a book. All two-dimensional representations of the real thing. How could I possibly have believed this was real? I pulled my fingers through my hair, snagging them on all the knots. The looming question that was now flashing in my brain like a broken streetlight was—how *long* had I believed this was real?

The perfume bottle that used to sit on my dresser in my bedroom looked so real, the green faceted glass glinted in some nonexistent sunlight. I reached out to touch it, feeling only cold, hard wall. The bottle was now reflected on my hand. I removed it sharply, like the image would somehow stain my skin, but of course it returned to the wall. I searched the ceiling and located a little camera or, I guess, projector, streaming light over this one wall. It was a photo from one corner of my bedroom at home.

I thought of the perfume bottle. It had never moved from that position, the whole time I lived in that house. It was empty, had always been empty. It was a gift my father had given my mother. When he left, she threw everything away, except that. She gave it to me one night before Paulo had come home from work, placing it carefully on my dresser. She didn't say anything except, "Here, I don't want this anymore," and stole out of the room like a thief. Thinking about Mother was strange, almost new, like I was reinventing a long-lost memory, colors and shapes swirling, mixing together in confusion. Her face faded in and out as an unseen force pushed her away from me

Scanning the room again, I realized there was one real thing on the wheeled table across my bed. The food. I scooped up some mashed potato in my fingers and crawled underneath the bed again. Dragging machines with me, their wheels squeaking and whistling painfully, I edged closer to my target. Carefully, I unscrewed the head of the pipe and shoved the potato into it, placing the showerhead back over the top. I rolled back on my heels and sighed. No more whooshing.

17

Clara

As my head cleared, memories assaulted me one by one. Joseph, warmth and love that turned twisted and hard, Rash and the boys, something to live for, a purpose, and a new family. It hurt so much. It was a real, physical pain. I breathed long and slow, trying to calm myself. I made a decision. At this moment, in this already overwhelming and frightening situation, I would push it down. I couldn't acknowledge this pain, this loss, not without falling apart. It would have to wait.

It would have to wait because that morning one thing became very apparent and, all of a sudden, glaringly obvious. I stared down at my round belly and sighed thinly with absolute exhaustion. I was pregnant, probably about four or five months. Looking back over the foggy days, it made a lot more sense. How starving-hungry I was, how uncoordinated and unbalanced I felt, and the way I was being treated by the staff. What I couldn't understand or remember was how I came to be this way.

I'd tried to hide it the first time I remembered being taken to the exercise yard, but I couldn't help a sharp suck of breath in shock. It was difficult not to reel backwards, turn to the door, and run. There, padding their socked feet over the fake grass, the projected trees not swaying in the wind, the birds frozen on the branches, were at least a hundred girls walking around the yard. All at different stages, but most were quite obviously pregnant. They were all being ushered into different circuits that were roped off with nylon tape and were mindlessly walking through them. They would bang into each other occasionally, unaware of their swollen stomachs bouncing into each other's backs. There was no sound apart from the soft swishing of padded feet on the fake grass. I looked up at the bright blue sky decorated with puffy white clouds projected on the ceiling and wished it were real. This was nightmarish.

The kinder blonde woman, whom I'd learned was named Apella, guided me to an opening in the chattel and gently pushed me through. I walked with my eyes set on the ground, trying not to attract any attention. I felt like a spy—the only one aware of what had happened to us.

After a week of the same routine, I realized Apella was always putting me behind the same girl in the yard. She had short, black springy hair and a downcast posture. Her hands looked raw, like she had been nervously scratching them. Once she tripped and I heard her whisper, "Whoops". No one ever spoke in these lines—no one really noticed they *were* in a line.

I watched her carefully. She always kept her head down, but every now and then I saw her head dash from side to side, taking in the surroundings as I had been doing. Counting the number of guards, ten, looking at the exits, only one. The other thing I noticed was she would occasionally rub her belly. It didn't appear to be by accident, it was affectionately, comfortingly. I decided she must be at least slightly aware, as I was, and decided I had to speak with her.

Back in my room, I tried to think of some way I could make this happen and came up with nothing. I could bang into her in the yard, but with the total silence how could I speak without being noticed? I could give her a note, but I had nothing to write with and no paper. It seemed hopeless—whatever was going to happen would happen. I had no control. I pushed the wheeled table away from me in frustration, quickly retrieving it, hoping no one had heard the noise. That was the first night I spent crying myself to sleep. I lost count of how many nights I let myself be this way. I was a pathetic creature with no hope and no faith.

Then I felt it. At night, after much sobbing, it moved inside me. A tiny kick, a snare on the inside of me. I felt ill. Poisoned. It had moved into my body without permission, without me knowing. I wished I could cut it out, be rid of it. Whatever this thing was, I didn't want it. I wanted my life back. I resented sharing my body with this parasite. I resolved I would hold out long enough to get it out. I would find a way to be me again.

The days started to blur. I got bigger and bigger. The routine never changed. The girl in front of me never turned around and I never spoke to her. I felt lost and so very alone. I decided I should make a run for it, but I didn't even know where we were or how far underground.

Then one day it was not Apella that led me to exercise, it was some other woman. A much older, less gentle woman, who shoved me into the line with her cracked, weathered hands, scratched and gnarled like a tree branch. I was nowhere near the springy-haired girl. I scraped my feet along the fake grass for forty-five minutes or an hour, I don't know how long, and then tree lady pulled me out of the line and shoved me back to my room.

I walked through the doors and thought she must have led me to the wrong room. It was completely different. The woman roughly led me to my bed and sat me down, chucking my legs up and raising the rail, like she was handling a sack of grain. I tried not to look around too much, but it was difficult. When she left, I let my eyes wander over the new pictures. The photos had been changed, a lot. On one side was a condensed version of my room. On the other side was a different scene. It was darker and dirtier than my side, but it had more ornaments. All handmade. Exquisite little dolls made of sticks and colorful cloth, sitting on dark, wooden shelves amongst glass jars full of buttons, ribbons, and shards of glass. I couldn't help myself. I had to look closer. I left my bed and approached. Thankfully, a few days after the falling 'incident', they had disconnected me from the machines so I was free to move around my room. Each doll had its own personality. I reached out to touch them, my hands shaky. They looked so real. One little doll had dark, springy hair and beautiful, ebony skin. Her dress was detailed with tiny glass shards, each sewn on in a swirly pattern like the dance of a wind that had blown past a tree and picked up all the leaves. I sighed. I missed the trees. The silky purple color of her dress was deep and foreign. We didn't have such colors in Pau. The face of the doll was painted on in such detail. The kindness of her face was unmistakable. Whoever made these was very talented. A lot of love had gone into these toys. I stepped back, feeling like I was intruding into someone's very personal sanctuary. I heard the door creaking and quickly climbed back into the bed, to resume staring at the wall, when they wheeled her in.

I was to share a room. The girl's stomach was much bigger than mine—perhaps she only had a few weeks left. I had memorized the back of her head so well that it was strange to see her face. It was not at all what I had pictured. I imagined a strong face, the face of someone older and wiser than me. Someone who could help me. What greeted me was the face of a child. She couldn't be more than fourteen. She was beautiful: smooth, perfect ebony skin, and kind, dark eyes that looked completely unlike mine. They were full of hope—this was not the face of someone who had given up. She looked almost happy. Her face mirrored the doll's, only younger.

I heard the staff talking to each other. "I don't know what they are thinking, ordering more. We are crowded here as it is," one woman said.

"I know, now there is only one of us to ten of them. I don't know how we are going to manage it," someone whined.

"And with the exercises and the room changes, I've barely slept in days."

"A happy mother equals a healthy baby. Right?" I heard laughing.

"Well, what choice do we have? What Este wants, Este gets," the other voice replied in a sigh.

Este. That meant we were probably near Bagassa. Superior Este had a reputation as a formidable woman, harsh and brilliant. Her assignment was the Sciences. We were part of one her experiments. I wondered what this girl had done to end up here. I knew what my crime was.

I could hear them complaining as they walked down the hall, until they passed someone who shushed them. Then the woman with the harsh voice stormed into the room. Apella was right behind her.

"Apella, can you connect, er, um..." She lifted the young girl's arm up to a portable scanning device, which responded in its monotone, "Clara Winterbell."

"Err, Clara, yes, can you connect Clara to the monitors and organize her dinner?" She crinkled her face, her straight, grey hair looking messy. Bits of it had fallen out of her tight bun and were floating wispily in front of her eyes.

Harsh Voice seemed stressed and distracted. She wiped her forehead, attempting to push back the stray hairs. Every other time I had seen her, she was businesslike, efficient and disconnected. Whatever had happened, she was obviously frazzled by it. Apella, on the other hand, who was normally nervous by comparison, was calm and seemed almost pleased. She hooked Clara up to the various machines and monitors, tucked the dopey girl into bed, and walked out. As she passed through the door, she turned and I think she smiled at us. The door shut and we were alone.

Clara sat staring at the wall for a while. Then her hand lifted to the shelves projected onto her side of the room and caressed the doll I had been looking at. I could tell this doll meant a great deal to her. I could also tell, for certain, that she was not under the fog, as her face was running through a myriad of emotions. I couldn't tell if she was happy or sad.

"This is my mother," she whispered as she turned her head, only slightly, in my direction, her eyes still on the wall. "We have been apart a long time." Her movements seemed very careful as she turned to face me. Her face was hard with resolve as she said, "I am going to see her again, and you will see your family again, Rosa Bianca."

A small spark of hope ignited inside of me. Maybe this girl knew something I didn't. "How do you know my name?" I asked, trying hard not to lose my cool. Trying to whisper and keep calm so the staff didn't notice our talking.

"Apella told me," she said nonchalantly.

"What else did she tell you? I asked.

"That I could trust you," she smiled, "that we would be friends." She patted her belly. The look on her face was so ridiculous, given our situation. She looked relaxed, like we'd just met at the grocery store. Not like a trapped, pregnant girl who had been drugged and god knows what else.

"Yeah, sure," I said, rolling my eyes. "We can be friends." Friends, a rather pointless thing to have in our current condition. Allies maybe. I wondered why Apella had spoken to her. Why she had pushed us together was also a mystery to me. So was Clara's odd demeanor. Was she crazy?

"So you worked out the gas—how long did it take you?" she asked.

"It must be about three weeks ago."

"Oh," she said as she looked down at her belly again. "I have been awake for a lot longer than that, maybe about four months, though time is hard to measure here, isn't it?" she said, giggling. I felt sorry for her. Perhaps she had been driven crazy from being down here so long, with no one to talk to. I wanted to reach over and pat her head.

I tried to keep the sarcasm out of my voice when I replied, "Yeah I guess. So how old are you, Clara?"

"Seventeen."

I guess the surprise on my face was quite evident.

"Yeah, I get that a lot. I'm just petite. Well, that's what my mother always used to say. I'm tiny but mighty!" She held her tiny, thin arms up as if showing off her muscles.

I laughed. She was as cute as a button. There was something about her that I couldn't resist. She was unhateable. Likeable. Where I was suspicious and guarded, she was warm and honest. We talked for quite a while. I asked her loads of questions. She asked me some but eased off when she worked out she was only getting one-word answers. She seemed happy to share her past with me, and it was better than staring at the wall. She talked of her love for her family. About her deep respect and admiration for her hard-working father, who worked on a large farm fixing machinery and her devotion to her mother, who taught her how to make her dolls. She explained that her mother used to make toys for the Superiors' children. When she asked about my family I kept it brief and, sensing my reluctance, she never pushed me.

Clara talked incessantly about her home. "Palma, Ring Five!" she exclaimed, holding her hand up in mock salute. She went on to describe her home, her tiny little head nodding up and down as if attached to a spring, as she spoke. Her full, dark lips talking so fast it was hard to keep up. Palma sounded identical in size and shape to Pau Brasil but the people were different. My town was consumed with fear, where everyone watched their every move and tried so hard not to draw any attention to themselves. Palma was ruled by their love for each other. They poured themselves into creative work. They had art and stories not written in the standard, supplied history books. They even had people that made and played instruments. I was shocked. I thought all the towns were the same. That we were all in the same immovable boat, entrenched in thick, binding mud we could never pull ourselves out of. These people sounded crazy or brave, I wasn't sure. I was shocked and so very jealous. So very jealous, until I heard how the people of Palma suffered.

"How can you do things like that? I mean, how can you get away with it, without being punished?" I asked eagerly.

She scrunched up her thin, pointed nose, "Oh, we've been punished." She shook her head, recalling. "Once I saw I woman beaten to death in the street for not surrendering a simple wood pipe."

I looked at her, puzzled. "You mean, for smoking?"

She shook her head, smiling, "No, an instrument. You blow on it to make music." She showed me the Y shape of it by drawing it in the air and then held the invisible pipe to her lips and blew. I nodded and pretended I knew what she was talking about. What was music? "This woman fought with a policeman. The pipe had been given to her by her son, who had just left for the Classes a month earlier. She knew she would never see him again and this was all she had to remind her of him. I remember her holding onto it so tightly as the policeman tried to twist it from her fingers. They kicked her and kicked her until there was nothing left, wrenching it from her dead hands and throwing it in the bin. Others tried to intervene and they were arrested. They just disappeared. We have lost hundreds of lives trying to protect what we love."

I recalled the heartless couple, wincing as I remembered all that blood.

I felt relieved, as stupid as it sounds, that at least one thing remained the same. They still took the children to the Classes. This, we all had in common. Still, I was quite shaken by this revelation. The people of Pau Brasil had removed their feelings. Parents were merely caretakers. I mean, I understood the reasoning behind it. What was the point of loving someone so much for eighteen years who was going to be taken away from you? I loved my mother and she loved me, but it was understood that this was always going to be temporary. So we kept each other at a distance. She'd had to say goodbye to her parents all those years ago, when she went to the Classes, and we had known my time was coming. It was foolish to care that much—it served no purpose. The way Clara's people functioned made no sense to me. The love that she felt for her parents, her friends, what she called her 'community' was self-destructive in my mind. I didn't understand it. Nor did I understand her love for that thing inside her. I didn't get it but my heart longed for it. I had lost so much because of caring about things. I touched my stomach very gently. I wasn't sure my heart could ever love that way again.

A woman arrived with dinner and we returned to our drone-like state. Clara was a pro at looking dazed and dopey. But she was still so cheeky, taking risks I never would. When the woman's back was turned, she poked out her tongue. We ate in silence, waiting until the woman returned to take our plates. She checked our milkshake cups to make sure they were empty and left.

Lights out.

"Do you know what's in those milkshakes?" I whispered in the dark. But Clara was already asleep. I could hear her soft breathing and restless movements as I tried to sleep myself. That quiet sound of air escaping her lips was the best sound in the world to me. It felt good not to be alone anymore. I excitedly made a note of all the questions I needed to ask her in the morning, knowing I would probably forget most of them

18

Premature

Clara was getting more sleepy and sluggish every day. She waddled around during our exercise as best she could, but she struggled to keep up. I had noticed that other women, who looked like Clara, were disappearing from the lines. One day they were there, straining under the weight of their giant, bulging stomachs. The next day they were gone. They didn't return. There were always new girls to take their place, though. We all wound our way through the roped-off courses like a deformed caterpillar. The line of girls compressing and expanding when one bumped into another.

Despite her exhaustion, Clara continued to radiate that aura of faith. I don't know what she was hoping for, what gave her any hope at all. I knew for certain, she wasn't going to get it. She was too sweet and trusting. I didn't want to break the bubble that she had surrounded herself with. The one that let her believe she had any claim on the child she was carrying. Well, that's not exactly true, sometimes I did. Sometimes, I wanted to take a giant, gleaming pin and pierce it, watch it explode, covering her in the dripping truth. I wanted to make her see the world the way it really was, cruel, unfair, and devoid of hope. But, knowing her, it would only strengthen her resolve.

One day they took me to exercise and left Clara alone in her room. I couldn't help but turn my head in worry as I left her. If they had taken her out of exercise, soon they would be taking her from me. Selfishly, I was concerned about being on my own.

When I returned, I relaxed in relief to see her still sitting in her bed, eyes on the wall. She winked at me, as my attendant roughly 'helped' me onto my bed. This one was old and huge, her uniform barely stopping bits and pieces of her from billowing out. The staff kept changing now. When the large woman left, Clara started rubbing her belly again, a habit that disgusted me.

"You know they won't let you keep that thing, right?" I spat. She seemed so naive sometimes. Or caught up in her own world and I felt the cruel need to dent it, since I couldn't join her there. She couldn't be as strong as she seemed.

"I know," she said and, for a moment, a small crack opened in her positive armor. But then that light appeared from within, and she beamed at me. "I've thought of a name."

I pursed my lips. A name? That was insane! I couldn't comprehend her love for this child. I couldn't stand it. Why name it? I knew the name I would give mine. Leech. This thing that had intruded into my body was as unwelcome as it was detested.

She ignored my incredulous look. "Hessa after my father, if it's a boy. Rosa if it's a girl."

"Don't name that thing after me," I snapped. I turned and looked at the wall. I felt wretched and angry. Most of the time I felt like Clara was crazy, that she floated around on a cloud that I couldn't puncture or dissipate despite my attempts. Other times, she made me feel deficient, like there was something wrong with me for not feeling affection for this thing I was carrying.

She snapped back at me, her face seeming older, worn. She slammed her fist down on her thigh. "I know you don't understand it, Rosa, but I love this baby. I am her mother. That is a strong bond. My love is MY choice, don't ruin it." Her voice ran out at the end of her sentence and she started to pant, struggling to catch her breath. Each word seemed harder and harder to expel, like she was pushing them out and they were backing up in her throat.

I was taken aback, my body stiffening from the short attack. Over the last few weeks, I had snapped at her many times, mocked her even. But she had always been this impenetrable source of hope, a light shining from inside her. She never stooped to my level, no matter how much I pushed her. I felt terrible for upsetting her, but for me, I didn't feel anything other than the need to escape this nightmare. I was about to open my mouth and say something else rude when she screamed—a scream that tore through me, rumbling and echoing throughout the room and into the hall. Something was not right. Panic penetrated me, and something else, guilt. I prayed it was not my taunting that had brought her here.

"Rosa, something's wrong, something's wrong," she said in short, expelled bursts like hiccups. "Ahhhh!" She was holding her stomach and retching. She was in so much pain I could almost feel it myself. Beads of sweat crowned her forehead, her hands searching for something to hold onto. Her face was contorted into a grimace that didn't sit well on her usually serene face. I was about to jump up when I saw the doors swing open.

The white coats were swarming around her. Completely ignoring my presence. Clara turned towards me, her eyes wide with fear and adrenalin.

Harsh Voice appeared, looking displeased but not panicked, and said, "This is not right, she's only thirty-six weeks. It won't do, we haven't prepared her yet. Take her to theatre five. I'll meet you there." She adeptly unhooked Clara from her various machines and ripped a sheet of paper from the frantic, scribbling machine they'd wrapped around her stomach. As she studied it, the other people wheeled her out of the room. Clara screamed again. "Do something about the noise," Harsh Voice called after them. Mid-scream there was silence. She stormed after them.

I felt pure terror. For my friend and for myself. The pain she was in seemed unnatural. She looked sick. Was she sick or was this normal? What were they going to do with her? What did they mean when they said she wasn't 'prepared' yet? I held the edge of the sheets tightly in my balled-up fists, as if I could pull them over my head and shut the horror out. *Clara, I prayed, please, please, please, be ok.*

I felt a hand touch my own. I snapped my head around wildly. I hadn't noticed that Apella had stayed behind. She stepped back a little and said, "It's ok, Rosa. They won't hurt her, she's too important." This was the first time Apella had spoken to me and I knew she was taking a big risk talking to me now.

"What will they do?" I asked, the pitch of my voice escalating, feeling desperate and unhinged with every passing second that I didn't know where Clara was.

"I don't know." Apella looked at her feet. She looked to be close to my mother's age. Her neat, blonde hair swung at her shoulders as she stared down at the ground, avoiding my gaze. She seemed to be bracing herself for a tirade. But I wasn't angry. She wasn't the culprit. Like me, like Clara, she was probably here against her will, recruited after the Classes and brought to this place. She had already risked too much for us.

A man popped his head in the doorway. Apella quickly withdrew her hand. If he saw it, he overlooked it.

"Semmez is asking for you."

"Ok. I'm coming." Apella left the room, her timid footsteps barely seeming to touch the floor as she padded quietly away.

So that was Harsh Voice's name. I think I preferred Harsh Voice to Semmez.

For two days I waited. Apella never came to check on me and I didn't hear what had happened to Clara. I hoped Apella hadn't been reported or discovered. Clara must have gone into labor that morning. Had she delivered the baby? What would they do with her after it was out? I started to think about the possibilities and shut myself down. These people were capable of horrible deeds. Clara could be, no. I wasn't even going to think it.

I felt the fog rising but it was a fog of my own making, a cloud of fear and hopelessness, blanketing my brain. The problem was there was too much time to think. I kept staring over at her side of the room. I was like one of her dolls, a perfect facade on the outside, wooden and dead on the inside. I wondered how Clara was feeling, if she was even alive. If they had taken the baby away from her, what grief she must be feeling right now. Her spirit seemed so tied to that thing. It nourished her in this hell of a place. Without it, I wondered what would be left of the girl I had come to love.

At night, I felt the leech writhing inside me. I came to think of it as a monster. I dreamed it was tearing its way out of me. Claws scratching at my skin, pulling me apart as I screamed in pain. I woke up in the middle of the night with someone's hand over my mouth, a hand that smelled vaguely of earth and smashed herbs. "Shhh!" the dark figure whispered. "You can't be dreaming in here. The others don't dream." I nodded my head and he removed his hand. "Who are you?" I whispered into the dark, but he was already gone.

The next morning, they wheeled her in. She was alive, drugged up to her eyeballs, but definitely alive and still very, very pregnant.

I waited eagerly for the people in white to leave so I could ask her what had happened and it seemed like forever. They were fussing over every detail, making sure everything was in order. They brought me my dinner but brought her nothing. It was then that I noticed the new tube coming out of her arm. One woman disconnected the tube and syringed a yellow-tinted liquid into it. I watched it track up the tube and into my friend. She looked so tiny, so weak lying on that bed, her head propped up with a boulder sitting on top of her, her eyes closed. Maybe that's what they did, drugged her to stop the labor. I had heard that was possible. We didn't have those kinds of facilities in Pau. Anyone who had the misfortune of going into labor early was generally in big trouble. The baby usually died.

Once everyone had left the room, I tried to wake her, to no effect. She was heavily drugged, and would only open her eyes for a second before falling back asleep. Her dark lids fluttering and closing like they were a leaden weight, too heavy to lift. I decided to let her rest and try and talk to her tonight, at lights out.

The day went by uneventfully. Although, again, the white coats looked more stressed than they had been before. They looked tired. Tired and unhappy.

When I got back from exercise, Clara was sitting up but there were people all around her again. I was led back to my bed and given dinner. Inside I was bursting to jump up and talk to Clara. I wanted to shake her awake and pepper her with questions. But I had to wait, eat my dinner slowly, and wait for the last check before bed. Looking calm and dopey on the outside but buzzing on the inside. I did what was required, and thought it was safe, until someone came in again and injected more liquid into Clara's tube. I was very worried this was more mind-altering drugs, like the gas. Clara seemed so dopey, her head lolling from side to side listlessly. She barely looked in my direction.

Lights out.

Clara's voice was crackly as she spoke, "I know what you're going to ask me but I didn't see very much." I couldn't see her face very well but it sounded like it was an effort to speak.

I wasn't going to ask her that, well, not at first anyway. I held my tongue from saying anything defensive and asked, "How are you feeling?"

She laughed. "Oh, wonderful," she said with unfamiliar sarcasm. "At least the baby is safe."

Luckily, she couldn't see me rolling my eyes in the dark. "Yeah, there's that I guess. I'm glad you're safe, Clara." I gulped and said the words that would give me away, "I was really worried about you. What happened?"

"I don't really know," she whispered. "All I remember was that horrible pain and then being rushed out of here. They took me up, Rosa. There were real windows, a real sky, not just pictures of the real thing. I don't think we are that far underground. We got in an elevator and the numbers read B6 to Ground. They covered my mouth to stop me from screaming and then jabbed me when I got to the top. When I woke up, the pain was gone and the baby was fine."

I absorbed this new information. Critical information. If we were only six levels underground maybe there was a way to get out. If there were elevators maybe there were stairs, maybe… my mind was running away with the idea of escape.

"What else? Anything else you can tell me?" I said urgently. I think she sensed my desperate tone when she replied.

"Calm down. There was something else."

"What?" I was barely keeping my nerves contained. I felt like I was jumping out of my skin.

"There were other girls up there. Most were pretty dopey. But there were two that were out of control, screaming and carrying on. One of them yelled 'how could you do this to me?' The other one was just crying hysterically. She was so scared. I wanted to run to her and hold her. Rosa, I think they were the girls that moved into my old room. Someone said that these were the crazy ones from room 112. That was my room."

I felt a shiver of dread run through me. I wasn't sure I could even ask her the next question.

"What happened to them?" I could hear Clara sniffing. She was crying, a choked, crackly sound.

"I heard two of the people in white talking while they were cleaning my room. Something about a waste." She hesitated and took a breath before imitating the conversation she had heard, "What a perfect waste of time and money, a waste of two perfectly viable fetuses and two good breeders."

I could hear her wiping her face with her arm as she uttered, "I think they killed them. No, I'm sure they're dead." For the first time, she sounded as hopeless as I felt.

I felt the need to protect her, to preserve that shining light. "Maybe they didn't, Clara. Maybe they just moved them to another place. Gave them another purpose."

"Maybe," she said breathlessly, but I don't think she really believed me. I didn't believe it myself. If life in Pau Brasil had taught me anything, it was that the Superiors were not merciful.

"You need to sleep. Shut your eyes and we'll work it out in the morning," I said, trying, unsuccessfully, to sound soothing. Trying really hard not to sound petrified. Because I was. If the girls were from Clara's room, it wouldn't be long before the white coats worked out what we'd done. And once they did, acting dopey wasn't going to save us. I was sure they would be coming for us soon.

1:9

Smoke

Iwoke up coughing, tears filling my stinging, itchy eyes. Clara was coughing too. The lights were still off, but as I watched, strips of light started illuminating the floor like miniature airstrips. It felt like my lungs were on fire. It wasn't like smoke from a fire. It was odorless but leaving a bitter taste in my mouth when I exhaled. I couldn't see where it was coming from and it was filling the room fast. I thought—*this is it*. They have finally worked out that we are aware. They were going to gas us to death. I fumbled around, trying to disconnect the leads to my machines and monitors they had reattached to me after Clara's episode. I quickly gave up and just rolled to the floor, feeling the machines towing along behind me. A convoy of sounds—metal crashing against metal, emergency beeps and blips.

I could breathe a little better, down on the cold, linoleum floor. I called to Clara, my voice raspy and hoarse, "Clara get down on the floor." I could vaguely see the shadow of her awkward form climbing carefully out of bed as the photo wall flickered images I'd never seen before, a window with grey wool curtains, a desk with a photo frame on it, stacks of Woodland textbooks dog-eared lying in the corner. An old wooden chair projected over Clara's back as she used the wall to support herself as she got down on the floor. I cursed her careful movement and wished she would move faster.

We started crawling towards the door, an oppressive cloud of smoke hovering just over our heads. The machines started disconnecting and setting off alarms. Ignoring them, I stood up and went for the door handle. I lost my balance and slipped in some kind of liquid. What was it? It was slimy and thick. "Clara, are you ok?" It felt like blood. I shuddered involuntarily. "Are you…bleeding?"

"No," she responded quickly. "I think it was my bag of fluids." Relieved, I reached for the handle. I was about to open the door when it slammed into me from the outside and knocked me to the floor. Someone strong picked me up under my arms, dragged me out the door, and then went back for Clara.

What I saw in the poorly lit hall was absolute chaos.

It was a war zone: girls coughing and screaming. Disoriented and frightened. The white coats were trying to get them into a line, but they kept wandering off, banging into walls, into each other. Each of them lost in their own foggy panic. Clara and I were pushed towards a wall that had a long bar running along its length. We held onto it and followed the strips of light. It stayed dark as we walked in line, collecting more confused, coughing girls as we went. Whatever this smoke was it had infiltrated the entire place. Some of the staff were wearing masks, but I could still hear them coughing. They pushed us through doors and upstairs, through another door, up some more stairs until I started to lose count.

Finally the darkness lifted; I could see Clara in front of me. I put my hand on her shoulder, determined not to lose her in the crowd. Now that I could see better, it was apparent the gas was a curious, dark purple. I held my breath for a minute but buckled quickly, watching the gas move into my mouth as I breathed in and seeing it, as it came out, like it was almost solid. Clara's breath was the same. Other girls were mesmerized by the same phenomenon, but when they breathed out the smoke was tinted pink.

We walked passed a window. A real window. Clara was right. We weren't that far underground. Sunlight was streaming through it like an invitation. We were on the surface. One of the people in white went to the window and tried to open it. He heaved and strained, his face showing his panic and exertion, but it didn't move. "It's no good, it's sealed," he said to the one that had a hold of my arm. "We'll have to take them outside."

I felt the grip on my arm tighten as I was strongly guided to two large, locked, security doors. One of them typed in a key code and spoke into a microphone while the other one pushed his fingertip into a jelly-like substance. There was a sharp beep and then a voice said, "Prints incomplete".

"You're too sweaty," one of them said in frustration, girls squashing him up against the wall. "Wipe your hand and try again." I could see the purple cloud thickening around us. Bubbling and pushing into the corners. Some of the girls were on the floor, survival instincts telling them they could breathe better down there. The coughing was deafeningly loud. The room kept filling with girls as more and more of them came up from below. Just when you thought no more would fit, more would come, and you were forced to compress yourself further.

"Verification complete," the computer voice said and the doors swung open. The men repeated the process again, at the second set of doors, swapping who used their fingerprints and who used their voice as verification. The second set of doors swung open but the first set of doors we had walked through was trying to close, banging against hapless girls. Continuously knocking them over, as they were carried through on a wave of bodies. I saw one of the white coats take off his shoes and shove them under one of the doors, jamming it, so the girls could get through. It creaked and groaned as it tried to pull back to closing.

I stumbled into the outside world, turning around to see purple smoke billowing out the doors and into the sky. Fighting its way into the air, like a hundred purple worms, intertwining, squirming, and pushing out in different directions. Girls were spilling out, some crawling, some being dragged, some kicked along by impatient white coats. There were hundreds of them, they just kept coming and coming.

I looked down at my feet, registering the squelchy, wet feeling between my bare toes. I inhaled deeply, enjoying my first taste of the sweet, fresh air. Delicious. Scanning the area, I could see we were in the Wilderness. From where I was standing, all that pointed to the immense dwelling below was a grassy mound with doors in it and a few windows puncturing the sides of the hill. The clearing we were pouring out into was only as big as my old school courtyard and soon, it was completely packed with coughing, panicking girls.

Heels of hands pushed us backwards, as far away from the doors as we could get, so we were right up against the rough, puzzle piece bark of towering trees. I was eased down onto a moss-covered log. The smells of damp, decomposing wood made my heart do little flips. Clara was right next to me and was guided to the ground as well but by pale, willowy arms. It was Apella. "Stay there," she said, fanning her hands and then she disappeared into a sea of girls. We sat and watched, as all the girls were planted on the ground, some not very gently, by the extremely stressed people in white.

For a moment, it was quiet. I heard birds off in the distance, a flutter, a foreign scampering sound of some unknown, forest-dwelling creature. We sat there for about an hour, pushing our toes into the mud, looking at the endless sky, the odd cough breaking the stillness. As I watched, little puffs of pink smoke were being exhaled by the girls. They floated up, carried by the breeze, dissipating into the atmosphere.

Then it started, very slowly. At first.

It began with restlessness—girls moving, shaking their heads, and touching their stomachs. Then we heard a girl shout out, then another, and then soon there was an immense chorus of wailing girls. I realized then that the purple smoke was some kind of quick working antidote to the fog. Some of them were screaming, "What have you done to me?" Some were crying, some were calling out for help. One thing was clear— these girls had woken up. The drugs were wearing off. The people in white were exchanging glances, nervously. What they had said before was true. There was only one of them to ten girls. One man was bracing himself, his fists clenched, his chest puffed out, as if ready for a charging stampede. I saw one, with a face as white as her coat, drop her gear and run for the trees. Action was necessary but they all stalled. Then the decision was made for them, as girls started to stand and run. Some pushed through, parting the bodies like they were swimming through a fleshy sea. Some just ran right over the top of the others. Most of them were trying pull themselves out of the fog still, and they were the first ones that received the needle to the arm.

It was pandemonium—girls dropping to the ground unconscious, girls fighting, girls screaming hysterically. One girl was louder than most, yelling, "It's coming, it's coming." I stood up to help, but Clara was holding my arm, not allowing me to step forward. For someone so small, she seemed immensely strong, her iron grip making an imprint on my forearm.

Soon the needles were too time-consuming and the bigger men started walking through the crowd, knocking girls out with large, rubber batons. Swiping and chocking them in the temples like they were knocking posts into the ground. There was blood and pain all around me. I felt my nerves about to fray and spark into a thousand tiny threads, each one pulling at me, hurting me—burying hundreds of shocking, violent images in my memory.

A few girls who were not far along, their stomachs showing little or no bulge, turned on one of the men. He was hitting out at them desperately as they scrambled and scratched at his face, their eyes feral. They took him down and grabbed his satchel, needles falling to the sodden ground. One of the girls picked up a needle and plunged it into the man's eye. Her reddish hair swung around her face as she whipped it from side to side quickly. She crouched over him like a deranged, wild creature protecting its prey. I have never heard a noise like that in all my life—a gurgling, strangled scream like a stuck animal. Just for good measure, the girl elbowed the man in the face, ceasing the screaming. She then sprung from her crouched position into a full sprint, her long legs carrying her gracefully to the edge of the woods and beyond.

Then I was dragged into the play. A man, badly bleeding from his leg, was limping towards me. At first, thinking he needed help, I moved towards him, not noticing the baton in his hand until it was too late. He raised it above his head, his eyes showing no mercy. He was as delirious as those girls, caught up in the craziness. I put my arm over my head and shut my eyes. Not even thinking to run or fight back, just sitting there, an easy target. I heard the deadening thwack of wood against flesh and opened my eyes to see him fall to the ground. Clara stood above me with a blood-stained branch in her hand.

"We have to go," she said as she jerked me to my feet. Where she was pulling this strength from I'll never know, but I followed her into the forest, leaving behind me a mess of panicked souls on both sides. To my left and right there were girls running, tripping, falling. Some were being chased. *Someone must be chasing us,* I thought.

Clara kept charging through, never letting go of my hand, never looking back. I, on the other hand, was fervently looking backwards, forwards, and sideways, wondering how long it would be before someone caught up with us. Anticipating rough arms grabbing my shoulders and pulling me down. Suddenly Clara stopped dead and listened, her head cocked sideways like a wolf.

"What are you doing?" I shivered as a breeze blew through my thin, cotton gown.

"Shh!" she said, pressing her tiny, dark finger to my lips.

I didn't want to stop. I could barely hear the girls anymore. I didn't want to think about why that was. I was hoping against hope that if we kept going, maybe we wouldn't get caught, that we could escape this nightmare. I started tugging on Clara's arm, figuring the horror had just hit her and she was temporarily incapacitated.

"Get down," she hissed. But it was too late. I felt the sting, and then warmth coursing through me, before I dropped to the ground.

2.0

Truth

I was getting quite tired of waking up like this. Being rendered unconscious and coming to in a strange state or a strange room. I knew they must have caught us or at least me. Maybe Clara had got away. I hoped so. I was captured, I was sure of it. I had that same groggy feeling I always had after being jabbed in the arm by the White Coats.

I opened my eyes, fluttering them suspiciously, not really wanting to see the sickly glow of the ceiling of my underground room. But what greeted me was not the glowing fluorescent lights from the room Clara and I shared, but the night sky. A million twinkling stars, against a deep, dark black. I reached my hands out to touch it. Surely it was painted on. But my fingertips were only grasping at air.

"It's real," he said. That voice. Full of sadness. Kind and regretful. I hadn't heard that voice in such a long time. I didn't want to look. I must have been dreaming. It was not just unlikely, it was impossible that he could be here. I let myself dream a little longer and continued to stare at the sky. One side of me felt cold as ice. The other side, a little too warm. I looked to my left to see flames dancing in the half-light. I counted five other bodies lying by the fire. One tucked up in a sleeping bag, with an enormous mound of a stomach illuminated by the fire, masses of black, springy hair protruding from the head end of the bag. She had her back turned to me but it was Clara. Thank God she was all right. I swept my eyes in a circle above me, the sun was gone but I could still make out shapes of tall trees looming over the top of us. Pines.

My stomach grumbled. I was starving. I pulled myself to sitting.

"Are you hungry?" he said. That voice. I turned around, ready for the dream to disintegrate. His face was the same as it had always been. Still smiling, although he looked tired and perhaps a bit thinner. His hair was a little shorter, but it was him. I hadn't imagined it.

He handed me a piece of bread and some dried meat without waiting for an answer. I had a million questions to ask him. But my stomach had other ideas. I grabbed the food and started devouring it. He waited patiently, hands collapsed casually over his knees, watching me polish the food off, licking my fingers. The leech kicked me and I moved uncomfortably, putting my hand to my stomach.

Joseph's eyes showed concern as he moved towards me just slightly. Concern and something else indiscernible. The fire casting orange light on his beautiful face, lighting his hair up like a crown of gold. Sadness swamped me. I must have looked so different to him, a swollen, pitiful teenager. Most of the time, I tried to pretend it wasn't there, but with someone from my past staring at me, it was hard to ignore.

I took a deep breath, the cool air stinging my lungs in a good way. The big question had to be asked. But I was scared of the answer. Joseph being here made no sense at all. I was never going to see him again and now he was sitting in front of me, looking worried, looking like he cared.

"What are you doing here?" I asked slowly. Wondering what possible answer he could give that would explain his presence here, my presence in the woods, the smoke, everything. What he said was beyond belief.

Casually, in his disarming manner, he said with a smile, "That's my baby in there," as he pointed to my stomach.

The bread stuck in my throat. I scrambled back, panicked, nearly putting my hands in the fire. "What?" I awkwardly heaved myself to my feet. "What are you talking about? That's insane…but…that's impossible." I stumbled over my words, searching for one shred of sense in what Joseph had just said to me. Whatever happiness I felt at seeing him again was gone and replaced with suspicion. What did he want with me? Who were these other people? What new nightmare had I been dragged into?

I had roused the others with my yelling. Drowsy eyes stared at me across the fire. Clara was looking at me confused, still half asleep. Joseph was moving towards me, clearly worried, although I didn't know if he was concerned for me or the thing inside me he thought was his. But he looked genuinely frightened, anguish showing on his face. Hands outstretched, flapping the air, he said, "Rosa, calm down, it's ok, you're safe now."

I bent my knees, ready to run, "Don't tell me to calm down, what you're saying is ridiculous. What did you do to me? Are you one of them?" I heard my voice and it sounded crazy, like something had snapped inside my throat. I was shaking. I felt sick. I wanted to run, but I had nowhere to go. Out of the corner of my eye, I saw a man with a needle in his hand approaching me. "Get back!" I screamed. This was not happening again. He kept inching closer. "Get back!" I screamed again. My voice was swallowed up in the darkness, no echo—it disappeared in the cold air. The man moved closer still. Joseph blocked him with his arm.

"Get away from her, don't touch her!" he shouted forcefully.

I didn't know what to do. A big part of me wanted to run to him. The other part of me wanted to hit him with a branch and run as fast as I could away from here. I didn't feel like I could trust any of them.

"I told you not to tell her that way," the man with the needle said. "She's not the same girl you remember. She's probably traumatized." I looked to Joseph, that pain on his face again, an agonized, tortured look; I had seen him make that face once before. The man took steps towards me, still carrying the needle, trying to distract me as he approached. "You see, he's been looking for you for a long time now…he…" he was still holding that needle. I took one step towards him and punched him in the face, as hard as I could. It hurt my hand. He over-balanced and fell backwards, nearly landing on top of one of the other people. The needle bounced into the fire.

Joseph laughed. "See. I told you she had attitude!" he said as he leaned over to pull the man up to his feet. I realized then that he was not a man. He was a boy, no older than Joseph. Tall and thin, with dark black, spiky hair and a smooth, high-boned face. I was still standing, fists up, ready to knock out the next person who came near me, feeling like a cornered animal.

"Whoa, Rosa, it's me, can't you at least let me explain?" he pleaded.

"Clara?" I looked to her for answers; she nodded, not saying a word. It was her way of saying, yes, let him talk. He held out his hand and I took it, eyeing him reproachfully. His eyes were hopeful. The moment our hands touched, memories jolted through me like electricity: His warm arms around me, hands touching as we lifted into the air, talking, smiling. Other memories appeared too, being deserted, having my heart broken. I dropped my hand.

"What can you possibly say that could explain any of this?" I gestured around me and back to my belly. I looked down to see I was back in my Class uniform, which now sat above my belly button, my cotton gown poking out from underneath the band like a curtain, hiding my disgraceful form. Someone dressed me. I was livid.

"Did someone dress me while I was asleep?" I asked, thinking, *just give me an excuse and I'll knock your lights out*. My eyes were scanning the faces accusingly.

Joseph's face flushed red. Then he grinned. "Ha! I would have offered, but someone beat me to it!"

I glared at all of them, hoping I could sear them in half with my vision. When no one confessed, I awkwardly tried to ease myself down onto a log. It was getting harder and harder to do even the simplest of things without the leech getting in the way. Joseph reached out to help me but I smacked his hand away. I felt like I needed a force field around me, no one touching me until I knew what they really wanted. Ungracefully, I levered my form to the ground and sat facing him.

Everyone was watching us. I noticed a familiar face in the group. Apella was there, and a man was sitting with her, his hand on her knee. She was leaning her head on his shoulder. Clara was leaning back on her elbows, looking as wistful as ever. Nothing ever seemed to get to her, at least, not the way it got to me. Then there was Joseph and his friend, who was nursing a cut on his left forearm courtesy of me knocking him over a rock. He didn't seem too affected either. Joseph was the only one who looked concerned, no, more than concerned. He look genuinely in pain, his face flickered back and forth between relief and anguish.

"So…?" I challenged, "Tell me! Tell me the truth."

"What do you remember?" he asked.

"I remember working at the Classes, doing well in my class. I remember…." I touched my hand to my face. "Getting in trouble. Then waking up in a room, drugged and pregnant. Oh, and I remember your letter," I replied.

"Oh. I guess it was too much to hope that had been erased from your memory. I'm sorry, Rosa, I thought it was the right thing to do. I wanted you to be happy and not hold onto something we could never have. I shouldn't have done it, but by the time I had decided to tell you the truth, you had disappeared," he confessed. I wanted it to be true, my whole being ached for it to be true, but there was so much unexplained.

"You know, he never gave up. I tried to tell him it was no use but he risked everything to find you," the boy with the needle interrupted.

I glared at him.

"Deshi, will you shut up!" Joseph sounded frustrated, his voice strained. Maybe he was hanging by the same thin thread of sanity that I was clinging to.

Deshi shut his mouth and kept it that way.

"Well, working forward from what you remember, I can tell you what I know." He took a deep breath and launched into the story. "You know I was accepted into Medical, right?" I nodded. I remembered seeing him hanging around outside the medical building with his white coat on, talking to other Uppers. "Well, Deshi and I and a few other kids were pulled into a specialist group, dealing specifically with infertility. It was all very secretive and we were required to supply a DNA sample at the start of every morning as a security clearance." I recalled the two men in white pushing their fingers into the goo when they were trying to release the security doors. "We were being allowed access to all sorts of information but were told our lives were over if we told anyone what was going on. Apella here was one of our teachers." I looked over at her. She smiled shyly. She seemed too lacking in confidence to be a teacher or a doctor. I had always assumed she was just a lackey in our situation. The deceptions were unfolding, like a tightly crumpled letter, each crease revealing a new unknown, scrawled part I thought I had read but now, no longer understood.

Joseph spoke.

"Apella had developed a way to synthesize genetic material in order to artificially impregnate a woman. She was teaching us this process and getting us to synthesize our own DNA and other kids from the Classes. We were to collect samples from every male we could. Just a strand of hair was enough. Soon we had about three hundred samples. I wish I had known what they were planning, but I didn't, I swear," he said, clearly upset, clearly trying to purvey his own innocence.

"So you did this?" I aimed my accusation at Apella. "You're responsible for what they did to me, to Clara?" I was disgusted with her. She was obviously brilliant but had no morals.

"You say it like I had a choice, Rosa," she appealed.

"You always have a choice," I said.

"Even if the choice is dying, or someone you love dying?" she said, looking to the man next to her.

"Yes." I knew what I would do. I would never have done what she did.

"That's what I love about you. You are nothing like anyone else in Pau, you do believe in a choice. You always do what you want and to hell with the consequences!" Joseph said. I was offended. I didn't think that was true, but I would like to think that I would make the right choice, if I had to.

Apella looked devastated by my response. Clara shuffled over and patted her back. It made me sick that she would even touch her after what she had done to us. I felt like I had heard enough. But Joseph continued.

"Shortly after the samples were created, we were told that they had been destroyed, that someone had left the fridge door open and they had all expired. We were moved onto another program and we were told Apella had taken a leave of absence."

"Pretty stupid to believe that," I snapped.

"I know," he admitted, "but I swear we thought it was all for practice.

We never dreamed that they were going to use them for anything."

I was starting to put it together myself, "And then I disappeared." I felt cold. Worn down to a point, a speck. Was there ever any end to it?

"Yes." He looked at the ground, tracing patterns in the dirt with a stick. "You disappeared; you stopped walking to the construction Class with your friends..." he stopped on that word, setting his mouth in a hard line, like it was difficult for him to say. "You weren't exploring the Arboretum." So he was watching me. "You were gone without a trace. Every day I snuck into the lab after hours and searched for any information that might lead me to you. Every day for about a month I would type your number in, or your name, but there was nothing."

"It's true!" Deshi chimed in. We both shot him a look.

"Then one day I typed in your number and all that came up was 'matched'. That's when Apella caught me. She found me sitting, staring at the computer. I had just about given up hope when she leaned over and typed in a password. There was your name *Rosa Bianca matched Joseph Sulle*. Apella explained it to me. Although I think she had to explain it about ten times. The Superiors had taken you and used my sample to create a baby. Our baby. She told me that they had taken her technology and were using it to begin a repopulation plan for the Woodlands. They would eliminate the need for families. They could control the genetic mix this way. So we were matched to create a particular genetic composition." He sounded like a scientist, like one of them.

I yawned, stretching my arms. The leech kicked me and I jumped, instinctively touching my belly. Joseph looked at me longingly. "Did it..." he didn't finish. "You're tired. Maybe you should sleep and we can finish tomorrow."

"No, keep going. I want to know how this fantastical story ends," I said sarcastically.

He ignored me. "Apella asked for my help. She said she would help me find you, if I helped her and Alexei escape from their life also." So that's why she was helping us. To protect her love. My opinion of her lowered further.

"I'm sorry it took so long but we had to make sure the plan was perfect before we tried. There were so many things that could go wrong and we only had one shot at it. I'm sorry for..." he said, leaving it hanging.

This was a lot. It was too much. A wave of sadness for all that I had been through, for what I was yet to experience, crashed over me. What did I do now? The question was foolish and pressing. I was exhausted. All I said was, "So a computer chose us and now you're here." It was ridiculous, but then so was everything else. I laid my head down and cried, while the others stared into the fire, orange and yellow flames dancing in their eyes. For all my bravado and 'attitude', as Joseph put it, I was still a scared sixteen-year-old girl, pregnant and confused.

He moved closer and I let him. He gently put his hand on my head and stroked my hair until I drifted off to sleep.

21

Questions

I woke up feeling uncomfortable and cold. My back was sore and I was all twisted. Noises I had never heard before punctured the morning, birdcalls, fire crackling, and wind through the massive trees that surrounded us. I had imagined these sounds before, fantasized about how it would feel to be out in the forest, but hearing the real thing was a strange experience.

I turned to the sky, realizing that I was still sitting next to him. He had fallen asleep sitting up, his hand still in my hair. I lifted my head and his hand fell with a thud, startling him awake.

"Morning," he said croakily, stretching his neck. He locked eyes with me and I saw it. That look. Somewhere in the back of my memory I heard, *'like you're the only girl in the world'*. I looked away.

Everyone else was up. Clara, Alexei, and Apella were huddled together, examining a flimsy piece of colored paper. On the side that I could see was printed 'Travel the Great Trans-Siberian Railway'. There was a picture of what looked like an antique train on the front, with the phrases, 'trip of a lifetime', and 'family friendly' written in yellow bubbles.

"What are you looking at?" I asked. Curiosity was getting the better of me, even though I really didn't want to talk to Apella.

"This is the map we are going to follow," Apella said.

"So this is your plan?" I said, hoping to God it wasn't.

Apella patted Alexei's arm lightly and turned to me. "Alexei used to work in the archives. He found a map in a folder marked 'Pass Times'.

When he noticed the railroad led all the way to Mongolia he, well we—" she gazed at him adoringly, "thought this would be the perfect plan."

"And then what?" I said, folding my arms across my chest.

She avoided my eyes, looking to the side of my face. "When we find it, if we can make it to the mountains, we might find a safe place to hide over winter."

I laughed bitterly. It sounded ludicrous. No, suicidal.

Sensing my not-very-well-hidden skepticism, Alexei added, "We can find the railway tracks and then we can follow them. Since we can't use the reader's GPS for risk of being tracked, it is the best way forward." It was the first time he had spoken and it didn't help my impression of him. His voice was wobbly like he wasn't used to speaking. He sounded unsure and defensive.

What could I say? I was their captive at this point so I went for an attack. "Yeah, well, if you two don't stop gazing at each other like that, you're all going to remember what I had for dinner last night," I spat at them. They were disgusting. I was truly fighting to keep my stomach calm. Apella blushed lightly and Alexei looked at me like I was some breed of female he had never encountered before. What was the word for him? Genteel.

Joseph chuckled. "Well, let's get some breakfast into you."

Deshi walked over and sat next to me. I shifted away from him a little. He just shrugged. He was holding a grey box. He opened a drawer, tapped a small pill from a jar he pulled from his pocket into the tray, and dripped some water into it from his flask. He replaced the tray and waited. A light on the top of the box turned from red to green. He pulled out the tray to reveal grey mush filled to the brim.

"Breakfast is served!" he said with a wink.

"What the hell is that?" I asked, staring at the gelatinous glob wobbling in front of me.

"I made it," Deshi said proudly, shaking the tray under my nose. "It's a self-sufficient, rehydration…" he twisted his lips to the side, thinking, "thing-a-ma-jig."

I raised my eyebrows. "Thing-a-ma-jig?"

Deshi smiled unsurely. "The title's a work in process. You probably recognise the grey substance from your milkshakes in the facility. It's a high-protein, highly nutritious, synthetically manufactured food. It tastes like licking a glue stick but it will keep us alive."

I shrugged. It was tasteless, but I ate it. It settled my stomach at least.

When I had finished, I was ready to fire my questions. I wiped my mouth on my sleeve and said, "So the plan is to find this track and follow it, for god knows how long, and then what? Freeze to death on the edge of a mountainside?" We had been warned at school about the dangers of the outside—the harsh terrain and the bitterly cold winters.

"It's not as stupid as it sounds, Rosa. They will be expecting us to follow the rivers or the animal tracks. This way, we may have a chance of avoiding capture." Of course, I had forgotten that people would be looking for us, especially Apella, since she was so important to the project.

"They'll find us, especially while we're with her," I pointed to Apella accusingly. If I could smack her, I would. I paused on that thought. I could... She had put us all in danger with this crazy plan. Apella held out her wrist in front of the fire. She was scarred, new flesh growing around the edges of her tattoo.

"What have you done?" Although, I knew the answer to my question. They all had the same scratchy scars on their wrists, except for Joseph. I grabbed the scanner that Deshi had been playing with and held it over Apella's wrist. "Ana Keffi," the reader stated. I wondered if there was any level this woman wouldn't stoop to. I glared at her and stood gracelessly. I wanted to leave. I picked a direction and started walking.

I could hear him following me as he noisily stomped through the forest. It was slippery, mossy grey rocks covering the ground. The trees out here were thin birches; their long white trunks spattered with grey were so close together they made me feel like I was behind bars. A natural prison. I was squinting up at the sun, trying to work out which way to go, when I lost my balance and fell. He grabbed my arm before I hit the ground, pulling me up roughly.

"You know you're walking right back to where we just got you from?"

Joseph said.

"Maybe I would be better off," I said, knowing full well that was a lie.

"Don't be so foolish, Rosa. You know…" he didn't get to finish. I made him regret every word. I turned around and pushed him hard. I wanted him to fall, but the trees were so thick he just bounced off one, rubbing his back. He didn't look surprised.

"You think I'm foolish? What the hell do you think you're doing? What exactly do you think is going to happen to us? We're going to die out here," I screamed, pulling at my hair. I was beside myself. There was no scenario I could think of where we could come out of this ok or even alive.

"Take me back," I said as I pushed him again.

"No."

"Take me back!"

"I won't take you back, so stop asking," he said with a shrug.

He let me yell, rant, and rave, smacking into trees, throwing my arms around until I had nothing left in me. I sat down panting and he sat next to me wearing that infuriating, bemused expression.

"What?" I said crankily.

"Nothing," he put his arms up in surrender. "It's just…you're beautiful."

I rolled my eyes. "Even like this?" I pointed to my ball of a stomach.

"Even more so," he said, looking at the ground. "Look, I know this is a lot, and I know you probably have a ton of questions, so ask me anything and I will tell you the truth."

I'm sure I should have had loads of questions but only two came to mind: Rash and my father. I needed to know if Rash and the boys were safe. I couldn't bear the idea that my behavior had translated into them being hurt. I hoped they were smart enough to distance themselves from their association with me.

"Is Rash alive?" I asked, shutting my eyes tightly as if that could shut out any bad news.

"If that's the kid you were always sitting with, then yes, he's alive." He sounded disappointed. "You really care about him, huh?"

"Of course, Rash, Henri, all of the boys, they were my family." I missed them so much. It hurt just to talk about them. Smells of sawdust mixed with blood permeated my senses.

"They're all fine, sadder and quieter than before, but they're ok."

I didn't really understand his attitude. He seemed upset that I had asked this question. Hurt. I was so relieved that they had survived, that I hadn't brought down some awful punishment on them. I smiled thinking about the last time I had spoken to Rash, how we hugged and he had joked about not liking me 'that way', that he preferred his girls with a bit of meat on them. A soft laugh escaped my lips. I wondered what he would think if he saw me now. Probably make some joke about me laying off the gruel. Those short months seemed like a dream to me now. I wished he were here with me.

"I'm sorry that you were taken away from them," he said.

"Don't apologize... That," I emphasized, "was not your fault."

"Can you tell me what happened?" He was searching my eyes, so troubled. I touched my hand to my jaw, remembering the devastating slam of that hammer, the way it split and shattered my delicate face. There was no scar, but I touched my tongue to the inside of my mouth, placing it in the hole where three of my teeth used to be. I shook my head. I couldn't talk to him about that. I was ashamed. I didn't want to admit to how badly I had wanted that life, and how fantastically I had destroyed it.

"Anything else, then?" Joseph raised one eyebrow. His face was so close to mine. I wanted something, but recalling those feelings was hard. They were just out of reach, buried under a thin layer of grit and rubble.

"What did my father ask you to do?" This question genuinely surprised him. He took my hand in his. I recoiled. Not ready. He smiled.

"You remember that your father was my teacher, right?"

I nodded. He hooked me with those eyes and I had to stretch my anger, remind myself that I wasn't sure about him yet. But God it was hard.

He shook his head slightly, too long a silence between us. "Your father and I were close. He was...different to the other teachers. He helped me prep for the Classes with extra tutoring." I closed my eyes and just listened to his voice. The deep rumble of it, the way it felt in my chest. I could enjoy it because he couldn't see what it was doing to me. "When word had come that your mother was pregnant, Lenos was concerned for you." I shrugged, news always traveled fast in Pau. "Especially after what Paulo had done to his brother all those years ago."

I opened my eyes, "What are you talking about?" Now I was surprised.

"I thought you knew. Everyone knows."

I narrowed my eyes at him. "Well, I guess that makes me the only clueless idiot in Pau who didn't know," I said, throwing my hands up in the air and letting them flop back down in my lap. I was regretting my question.

Joseph rubbed the back of his head. "Sorry, I didn't mean…" I rolled my eyes. His trepidation around me was as irritating as his amusement at my anger.

"Just tell me what I apparently should already know."

He gave me a look like, 'are you sure?' I just sat in silence until he continued.

"Well, about ten years ago, Paulo's brother had a child and kept it a secret. Lenos said even Paulo didn't know about it at the start. But as the child grew, it became harder and harder to keep the secret. At that point he appealed to Paulo for help. Your stepfather called the police straight away and… Well, you can guess what happened to them."

The truth was crystalizing like a mirage made real. The heartless couple. The way Paulo had cruelly forced me to watch as the police had mutilated the couples' bodies. I felt deep sadness for my mother. Why on earth had she chosen such a man? Then that too was explained. My father did not leave us—Mother left him. She couldn't cope with his constant troublemaking, his resistance to authority, and his attitudes towards the Superiors. She threatened to turn him in if he did not leave the two of us alone. So I guess she chose Paulo, because he was the opposite of my father in every way.

"Are you all right?" Joseph asked. I was staring through the trees. Thinking about my father, how I had always wondered why he left, and why he had never contacted me. It was a small comfort to know that maybe he had wanted to, but he couldn't because of my mother. A very small comfort.

Clara emerged from the clustered trees, barely fitting between the trunks as she made her way towards us. She took my hand and pulled me up.

"We need to move," she said, puffing hard but with that beautiful smile on her face. Framed by the light shining through the trunks, she was an angel. "Alexei says we only have a day's head start and we need to make the most of it." She flashed a grin at Joseph, which he returned in full. I could tell they would get along very well. "You must be Joseph," she said and curtsied. She nearly fell over but he caught her. "You're strong," she giggled as he helped her stand.

"So are you," he laughed. "You managed to move this lump over here," he said as he pointed in my direction. I scowled at him. Laughing, smiling was hard. Deshi called Joseph and he left us behind as he bounded towards the campfire.

Clara linked arms with me and kissed me on the cheek. "So that's Joseph," she said, playfully elbowing me in the side as we walked. "Finally I get to meet him."

"What do you mean, 'finally'?" I couldn't remember ever mentioning his name before.

Joseph slowed his pace at the mention of his name.

"After all those nights of you talking about him or to him in your sleep, it's nice to finally see him in the flesh."

I blushed. He was pretending not to listen, but I could see him smirking as he walked towards the others.

We reached the fire and there was a clatter of activity. There was barely time to think. Alexei threw a pack at me, and a green-grey coat. I pulled them on.

"I'm glad you decided to stay," he said, out of breath.

"I didn't say I would stay," I announced.

"Well, you have two choices," Joseph said, trying to force my hand, "follow us or go back to the facility."

"Those are not the only choices. I will come with you, but I'm not going to follow you. If you want me to stay, then you have to include me in your planning. I will have a say and so will Clara."

Joseph sighed, he knew me. He knew I wasn't going to go along with everything they had already decided. If anything, I was always good at throwing a spanner in the works. We had all stopped moving. Alexei broke the silence.

"Very well, good, we will fill you in as we walk." His voice had an academic edge to it. It didn't help that he had thinning hair and spectacles. He looked like he spent all his time indoors reading books. I had my doubts that he would be the right person to lead this ridiculous group of travelers.

"Where are we going?" I asked him.

"Into the Wilderness."

2.2.

Hunted

We walked in a southeasterly direction. Alexei had an old compass he had swiped from the archives. He held it flat in the palm of his hand and shuffled around in circles until he looked off into the distance, squinted, and said, "That way." The GPS in the reader would have been so much easier but Alexei was right, if we turned it on, it would be like a homing beacon for the Woodland soldiers to follow.

I had agreed to look for the railway line because I couldn't come up with anything better and we couldn't stay where we were. We hadn't seen any evidence that people were looking for us, but I was sure they would be. Deshi explained that the antidote smoke he had engineered was designed to stick to the inside of the ventilation shafts and continue releasing small amounts of the purple cloud for another three days. He had set it up to explode with such force that every vent and shaft, every pipe, was covered. In some cases, it probably blew the pipe covers into the rooms. I told him about my sophisticated mashed potato plug. He laughed and said that it would have shot across the room like a bullet. It would take the White Coats quite a while to clean the airshafts and get the girls back inside. So we had to make the best of the head start.

I thought about the girls we had left behind. I hoped some had got away, but we hadn't come across one yet. I wished we could have helped them. Deshi felt the same way, but our group was conspicuous enough, without adding more hysterical, pregnant girls to the mix. I felt horribly guilty about being the one that got away. But having Clara with me helped ease that guilt.

We usually walked at the back, mostly because Clara was so slow, but also because I liked to keep as much distance between Apella and myself as I could. The more I knew of her, the more I disliked her. She seemed weak and followed Alexei around, lovesick and useless. She had no skills out here in the real world, and relied entirely on him for everything. It was extremely hard to believe that she had headed up the massive, secret operation that Clara and I had been caught in. Alexei led the way, and Deshi and Joseph took turns walking behind us.

We trudged through the forest from dawn until it was nearly dark every day. There was so much to look at but we never stopped to take in the scenery. The tall pines stretched to the sky, dropping needles in our hair one minute, then we were out in a field moving through low grass and wild flowers. I loved the green, the rocks, and the flowers.

I had been underground all winter and now it was spring. I found I could recall many of the names and uses of the flowers and plants we passed. My favorite was the Campanulas, a small, delicate, purple bloom shaped like a bell. It grew in clumps in the grassier areas. I would pick them and put them in Clara's hair, making her smile, which always made me smile.

Clara was about ready to have her baby. It seemed like it could happen at any moment and I was dreading that day. I think we all were. Every time she made an uncomfortable noise, everyone jumped. They let her rest as much as they could, but we had to keep moving. Sometimes Joseph would carry her for a spell, which she loved. She would talk with him or more, at him, about her life, her baby. She pressed him to talk about me, how we met, what happened, why was I so angry all the time?

"She's always been like that," he answered as he strolled through the underbrush with Clara in his arms. She was tiny, but it must have been difficult to carry her. If it was, he hid it well. He took good care of her, which I was grateful for.

"Yes, but why?" Clara pressed. I was behind them, watching her thin fingers tapping his shoulder. The sun bounced across his golden hair and absorbed into her black hair.

"She's protecting herself. She doesn't trust people. She doesn't trust me anymore. I probably deserve it, though," he sadly admitted.

"She trusts you. I don't think she trusts herself, not yet anyway," Clara said in her singsong voice. I rolled my eyes. I wish she wouldn't say things like that.

I wanted to respond, tell her to mind her own business or defend myself, but my mouth was sewn shut with imaginary thread. I couldn't explain it well enough to even try. I didn't mean to be this way but this experience had changed me. I hoped I could get myself back. I hoped the old Rosa wasn't completely lost. When I was talking to Clara, sometimes I could forget about it, and I could laugh, smile. She was the silliest person I had ever met, bordering on insane, but despite my best efforts I adored her.

Joseph would ask her about the baby, which she was always happy to talk about. He asked her a lot of detailed questions about how it felt to be pregnant—was she tired, was she hungry, was she in any pain? I suspected this had a lot to do with the fact that whenever he asked me anything about how I was feeling, I gave him snappy, one word answers. I didn't like to think about the thing, let alone talk about it.

"I have a name," she said leadingly, "Hessa if it's a boy and Rosa if it's a girl."

Joseph laughed heartily. "You better hope it's a boy then!"

I laughed without meaning to and covered my mouth.

"Have you got names, Rosa?" he asked hopefully, turning to me. Giving me that look again.

"Yes, one, but you're not going to like it," I replied. He just looked at me imploringly, waiting. "Leech for a boy or a girl."

He considered it for a moment and then grinned. "Leech Sulle, has a nice ring to it." It was disarming. If I tried to bait him, it never worked the way I expected it to.

I held my tongue. I'd let him have that one.

After three days of walking, we still hadn't hit the railway line. According to Alexei, we were very close and needed to spread out and start searching the ground for any signs of it. It had been hundreds of years since it was last used and it was bound to be covered with dirt and plants. We were looking for anything metal sticking out of the ground. Alexei asked us to split up into teams of two; we would walk straight out from a central point for five-hundred paces and then return if we didn't find anything. If we did find the tracks, one of us would stay where we were, while the other one went back to the meeting place to fetch the rest of the group. The central point was a neat circle of Radiata pines. We dumped our packs there and teamed up. Alexei with Apella, of course, then, before Joseph could speak, I said I would go with Deshi, making up the excuse that Clara should go with the strongest, in case she couldn't walk back.

Deshi scowled at me. "I'm not carrying you."

"Never expected you to," I said as I charged off down our allocated search line.

The line we were given seemed to be uphill all the way. Deshi was puffing and panting as we pushed our way through a thicket of dead branches, intertwined with vines. He wasn't fit like Joseph, his body not built for hard, physical challenges.

"How far have we gone?" I asked. "Is it time to turn around?"

Deshi sounded confused. "I don't know. I thought you were counting."

"Great," I snorted and sat down on a log to rest for a minute.

Deshi laughed half-heartedly. "Trust me to stuff this up." I was surprised. His attitude didn't match that of before, when he was cocky and slightly aggressive. I eased myself off the log and stood, reaching my hand out to pull him up.

"C'mon, we'll go another two-hundred paces and then we'll turn around," I said, trying to sound confident. Deshi took my hand. It was cold and sweaty.

"Thanks," he said as I pulled his slight frame to its feet.

Deshi's presence here with us didn't make much sense to me. He wasn't doing it out of guilt or some misplaced family duty. He didn't have someone he had to save like Apella and Alexei. I wanted to trust him, but in order to do that, I had to know his motivation.

"Can I ask you something?"

"Sure, what?" he said suspiciously, as he tried to find a foothold on the crumbly ascent.

"Why are you here?" I asked outright. I was never good at leading into things.

He was scrambling up the incline, bits of rock and rubble sliding down the hill.

"That's a good question," he said as he held out his hand and pulled me towards him. He pulled a little too hard and we fell sideways, landing in the dirt next to each other, nearly rolling down the hill. I lay there, waiting for an answer.

"Let's just say, if Joseph wasn't madly in love with you, I would very happily take your place in his affections." I think my eyes were nearly popping out of my head. I had never heard of such a thing. Shock didn't even cover it.

"Does…Joseph…know?" I managed to stammer. I was reeling at this information.

"Yes, but don't worry," he said sadly. "He has always made it clear that he considers me a friend, nothing more. He never asked me to come; I made that decision for myself."

I felt quite sad for him. Even if it weren't Joseph he loved, in the Woodlands his would always be a life of constant lying and unhappiness. In Pau, and I assume everywhere, one was expected to marry and produce a child. Life was hard enough without the added burden of living a lie. I understood why he left. Anything had to be better than that.

"I'm not worried," I said, "but I'm glad to understand you better." I knew what it was like to love someone from a distance. I guess sometimes that's all you get.

"Maybe you'll let me understand you better then?" he said as we pushed ourselves up to standing.

"Maybe."

We pushed on. It was getting steeper and the vegetation was clearing. Now it was mostly crumbling dirt and orange gravel. It was very slippery and hard to negotiate. As we neared the top, we were both crawling on our hands and knees. I got to the top first and hauled Deshi's slight body over the edge. We both stood up, dusting orange dirt off our knees and palms.

We both looked down at our feet; we were standing on large slabs of wood evenly spaced apart with two metal rails lying across them. It snaked off into the distance as far as we could see. This had to be it.

It was joyful and frightening at the same time. The tracks followed a line of trees, pines and spruces, green and towering. They leaned into the track, casting spiky shadows over it but never covering it. The track itself was in remarkable condition. It was rusty and the wood was grey and rotting, but it was not engulfed in vegetation as Alexei had expected. From our vantage point, we could see the whole world. It was foreign, ancient, and beautiful.

Deshi handed me his canteen and I took a large gulp of water. Almost immediately, I needed to go to the toilet. As I went on, I was finding more and more that this child inside me was encroaching on my physical well-being, changing things I didn't want changed and always making life harder.

"I need to go to the toilet," I said, embarrassed.

Deshi rolled his eyes but he was used to this after travelling with two pregnant girls for days.

"Ok, well, why don't you stay here and do what you need to do and I'll go back and get the others," he chirped. He couldn't get out of there fast enough. He was scrambling down the incline before I could even reply.

It was getting dark. I hoped Deshi wouldn't take too long. Even though there was no one around, I felt conscious of being exposed so I decided I would climb down the other side, which was less steep, and offered some privacy. I skidded lightly down the other side and found a bush to crouch behind.

Just as I finished, I noticed a form moving towards me. At first I thought it must have been someone from the group but no, it was coming from the other direction and it was moving lower and faster than a person. I was fascinated, watching this fuzzy form move from tree to plant to rock, bowing its head and then moving on, getting closer and closer to where I stood. There was no noise as it approached. Its padded feet walked soundlessly across twigs and gravel. I hadn't moved since I spotted it and tried to shift my weight, as I was standing with one leg on the incline and one on the flat ground. That small movement made it stop, still. It turned its head to the side and lowered its body, gliding softly towards me, ears back, eyes wide. Even in this cold air, I was sweating. It put its nose to the sky and sniffed, snorting the air from its nose like the smell was unpleasant. It was only a couple of meters away from me now and I could see clearly what it was.

It was a magnificent creature, standing as high as my shoulders. It was covered in a thick coat of brown-grey fur, yellowing as it reached down its long, lean legs. This was a dog. No, it was far too big. A wolf.

It was upon me now; it lowered its head to my feet and tracked its nose up to my stomach. I was as still as stone, feeling an odd sense of protectiveness about its nose nearly touching my belly. Wanting to turn to the side, so the baby was out of the way. It was so close that I could feel its hot breath on my skin. I was mesmerized by its beauty, its presence. It was majestic and powerful. It could kill me in a second, but it was all I could do to resist the ridiculous urge to run my hands through its thick fur.

Like a trap snapping shut, it whipped its head around. It sniffed the air again and cantered gracefully away from me, making its way to the crest of the incline. Standing on the tracks, our path. It howled one long note and other howls not far away joined the chorus.

Run, a voice in my head uttered urgently. *Run now.*

I scrambled up the graveled hill, just in time to see the creature bounding down the tracks in the opposite direction to me. I knew I had to be quick. It was a scout, soon it would reach its pack and they would be after me.

I slid down the other side on my backside, all the while screaming for Deshi. He couldn't have been that far ahead of me, surely. Tramping through the thicket, I cut through to clearer ground, my arms and legs scratched and bleeding. I broke into the quickest run I could manage, which wasn't very fast. All the while thinking, *what if they get to them first or what if they get to me first?* I was struggling to suck in breath, struggling to keep moving, but I did. I started screaming all of their names, hoping for any reply.

"Joseph, Deshi, Clara, Apella, Alexei, *anyone?*"

Finally someone answered. It was Joseph, sprinting in my direction. His large body barreling towards me so fast, he had to dig into the dirt to stop from knocking me over.

"What? What's wrong? Is it the baby?" He sounded panicked. He grabbed my arms, casting an eye over the blood and scratches. They all had their packs on their backs. Deshi must have made it back and they were preparing to come meet me at the tracks.

"No!" I said, pulling away from his grasp violently with irritation. "There's a pack of wolves nearby and I think they are hunting us or will be soon."

"Oh," he sighed in relief. I was confused by his reaction. We were no match for a pack of wild animals. I didn't think we even had any weapons.

"Alexei, what do we do about wolves?" he said, with an edge to his voice I didn't recognize—commanding and directive.

Alexei took out his reader and scanned it for some information, flicking his finger occasionally to enlarge something he was reading. "Wolves," he said in his intellectual voice, "hunt in packs. To avoid being attacked, climb a tree. The pack will eventually lose interest and move on."

"Right, let's put our packs up in a tree and then up we go," Joseph said with authority. But it was too late. As we were organizing ourselves, I could see glowing eyes hovering in what was left of the day's light. There looked to be at least five pairs. I imagined them licking their lips and baring their teeth but all I could see was eyes. There was no sound. Everyone was still fussing around with their packs. I grabbed Alexei's shoulder roughly and pointed towards the eyes. They would have been about four-hundred meters away. They were moving slowly and deliberately in our direction, stalking us.

Alexei grabbed Apella and hoisted her into the branches, whispering through his teeth, "Climb." She still had a tiny pack on her back. Come to think of it, I'd never seen her take it off. Luckily, the radiata pines that surrounded our chosen meeting place were tall, strong, sturdy trees with plenty of straight, easy-to-climb branches. The only problem being, the first branches started a couple of meters off the ground. Joseph went to pick me up and push me up into the branches with Apella.

"No, help Clara," I said. He looked at me as if he were going to argue but then went to Clara and gently raised her to the first branch. His arms flexed under her weight, but his face showed no exertion. Apella held out her hand and pulled the tiny ball of a girl into the tree. She looked ridiculous, a tiny ninth months' pregnant girl balancing on a branch like a swollen songbird. She looked scared, but I was confident she would be safe.

Apella was looking anxiously to Alexei, beckoning with her hands for him to follow. Her selfishness never stopped surprising me. I wanted to take a rock, aim it at her porcelain face, and knock her out of the tree. Let her be devoured by these hunters. Not that they would get much of a feed from her bony body. I turned to see the eyes were closer now. I could see their padded feet silently creeping towards us, their heads low.

Alexei and Deshi both clambered up the tree, helping each other. Clara and Apella were quite far up now, and the tree was swaying under the weight of four people.

We could hear them now. They had separated and were circling our little campsite, sniffing and panting. Without asking, Joseph swept me into his arms and unceremoniously catapulted me into the tree. I couldn't get a grip on the branch and I slipped, just hanging from the rough bark by my hands, my feet a foot off the ground.

Alexei's voice carried down. "No. The tree won't hold all of us." He was aiming his whispers at Joseph. "Take her to the one over there." He pointed across the circle to the other big pine. Joseph growled as he held his arms out for me to fall into. I let go and he caught me but I quickly wiggled out of his grasp and to my feet.

We ran to the opposite tree. Joseph was about to lift me when I stopped him. "You first," I didn't want to be thrown again.

"Are you joking? No!" he whispered tersely. He was angry but I knew it was the smart thing to do. The wolves were moving in, watching our little performance with hungry eyes. A black wolf had taken the lead. It was so close to the ground, it looked as though it was slithering, only a couple meters away from us. Its yellow eyes were menacing in the almost dark. A soft growl emitted from its bared teeth. We didn't have time to argue.

"I need you to pull me up!" I shoved him. I think it took all his strength to obey me, but he did. Once in the branch, he grabbed my arm and pulled. But something was wrong. I was stuck. No, not stuck, something was pulling me backwards. Did it bite me? I felt no pain. I turned around to see the black wolf had a hold of my pant leg. It was tugging me to the ground, my toes desperately trying to find something to push off but finding only scrapings of dirt and air. Joseph eyes looked crazed with worry as he grabbed me with both arms and pulled as hard as he could, my arms straining at their sockets. Then I felt teeth sink into flesh and I screamed. For a split second, the animal paused, which was long enough for me to kick it as hard as I could with my good leg. It yelped and then it lunged. I closed my eyes. This was it. Air rushed across my face and I was flying.

When I opened them again, I was in Joseph's arms and the wolves were surrounding the tree, moving in unison as if in a dance, taking turns jumping and scratching at the trunk and trying to snap at our toes.

Joseph was breathing hard. So was I. He was holding me so tight that I was starting to feel suffocated.

"Joseph," I whispered, "I'm ok, you can let me go." He looked at me and it registered. He loosened his hold on me, but he didn't let go. After a few seconds, he put his large hands on either side of my waist and helped me to stand on the branch. A flicker in my chest made me pause. We needed to climb higher, just to be safely out of reach of the frenzied clawing that was taking place beneath us. I pushed up onto my toes, feeling the squelch of the sock in my left boot, which was filling with blood.

As we climbed higher, we heard them shouting from the other tree. It was Clara I could hear the clearest. "Are you all right, Rosa?" Her voice sounded high and strained. It must have been very uncomfortable for her, sitting in a tree. I hoped Deshi was looking after her.

"She's safe," Joseph answered for me. "What about you?"

"All good over here," she said, adding, "Beautiful moon, don't you think?" My eyes were starting to get sore from all the rolling I had done since I met her. She always managed to find a positive even in the worst situation possible.

Joseph chuckled. I looked up at the sky, and sure enough, there was a beautiful moon rising, casting pointed, ghostly shadows on the forest floor.

"Joseph, I'm not ok. It bit me," I whispered.

He nodded tightly. "I know. I just didn't want to worry her," he confessed quietly. I was grateful that, for once, we were on the same page.

2.3
Rosa and Joseph
Sitting in a Tree

We sat together on the strongest branch we could find, that was high enough to keep us safe from the snapping jaws of the wolves below. I had said I could sit on a branch on my own, but Joseph absolutely refused to let me go and we were balancing so precariously, I couldn't really start a fight. If I had tried to pry myself out of his arms, I was liable to fall. So I allowed him to hold me, reminding him every so often that he was squeezing a little too tight.

It was a strange set of senses I was experiencing. The smell of the pine needles was refreshing and stirred up pleasant memories of a life past. I know I should have been fearful but I wasn't. From here, the wolves looked less menacing and more entertaining. And with Joseph's arms around me, I felt calm. I thought about how many times I had wished to be in his arms before. Before everything had changed. I felt safe, certainly, but I was sure it couldn't last. Nothing ever did.

On the ground, the wolves were scratching the tree trunks, jumping up, and sometimes fighting with each other. Their sharp claws made shredding noises as they tore large chunks of bark from the poor bleeding tree. Yelping and howling. Every time I thought they had given up, they would start again. They were ravenous.

Despite this, I still found them stunning. Their long fur was standing on end and they were mad with hunger, but there was something so fierce and powerful about them. We were in their world now and I was fascinated by their behavior. The black wolf was clearly the leader and two other, bigger, stronger wolves flanked him. One of them was the scout I had encountered earlier. They behaved how I imagine a family would... Helping each other most of the time, occasionally fighting, but all working towards the same goal—to kill and eat us.

"Look at them," I whispered. "Aren't they beautiful?"

Joseph scoffed. "Yeah, they're gorgeous; I particularly like the look of the one that sank its teeth into you." I didn't really think he would see them the way I did.

He was shivering and I noticed that he was only wearing a thin shirt. He must have dropped his jacket on the ground when we ran. I was sitting across his lap, with my back against the trunk of the tree. I leaned into him, trying to warm him with my own body. Slowly, his breathing steadied and he stopped shaking. I could just make out his face in the moonlight. He smelled like the woods, like damp dirt and wood fire. I liked it. After being in an artificial environment for so long, these natural smells were intoxicating to me.

He slid his hand down my leg slowly and gently tried to lift my boot off. I was shivering but I wasn't cold. I was not used to this closeness and every touch felt charged. I winced as he carefully pulled it. The blood was drying and the boot and sock were stuck to each other and my foot. He dropped it down and I watched as it bounced off branches and landed amongst the wolves. They jumped back then leaned in to sniff it, shaking their heads in frustration when they realized it wasn't attached to one of us. Then Joseph started working his fingers into my sock. I shuddered.

"Please leave it! It has stopped bleeding," I said a little too grumpily. He let my foot fall and I let out a small squeak in pain.

"Are you all right?" His hand was searching for my face. I held still. He traced my lips with his finger. "I can't see you; you have to tell me if this is ok." I wasn't sure what he meant. Was he asking me if my foot was ok, or was he asking if his hand on my face, his other hand gripped tightly around my waist, was ok? I didn't know, so I didn't answer. I didn't want to feel this way but a very big part of me was more content than I had ever been—which was ridiculous given our situation. We had each other captive; there was no running from him now.

"I can see you," I said. He was smoothing my hair back from my face, running his hand down my neck. Warmth was all I could feel, like liquid gold running through my veins.

"You must be part wolf," he joked. I could feel his breath, warm, drawing me in. His face lit up by the moon, eyes earnest, painful in their restraint. I knew I should stop him. I knew what he wanted, and that he wasn't going to get it from me. His lips were brushing my neck. I reacted, giggling. It tickled.

Suddenly, the sound of tearing fabric interrupted us. Initially panicked, thinking someone had fallen from their tree, I saw the wolves had moved on to our packs. I could hear plastic wrappers being torn open and wolves growling and fighting over our dried meat and bread.

"There go our supplies," yelled Deshi from the other tree. I was staring down at the ground, straining to see what the wild animals had done. They didn't seem so scary this far up. They were just puffs of fur moving around each other in a destructive dance. Joseph's hand was pulling my face towards his own. He was clumsy because he couldn't see, but his intent was clear. I went rigid. He sensed my hesitation and spoke.

"Please, I need to do this. I need to finish it." He sounded so determined.

"Finish what?" I asked, confused.

"I owe you this kiss; I need to kiss you back. The way I should have back in Pau," he said sincerely, nervously. Like he had practiced this speech before. It wasn't like him to be nervous. I couldn't help myself.

"Geez, could you be any sappier?" I laughed. I could see him smiling, his strong jaw and cheeks looking more angular in the moonlight. And then his lips were on mine and I forgot everything. Every logical argument for why this shouldn't happen flew out my head. We were both overcome. It was more than I had expected, more intense, almost to the point of being painful. I couldn't pull away. He was never going to pull away. He was right. This was what it should have been like the first time.

I don't know how long it lasted. It could have been a minute—it could have been hours. Slowly though, we disconnected from one another. I forgot where I was and over balanced, teetering backwards just slightly, he had me though. I felt like, perhaps, he would always have me. He held me tightly, running his fingers gently up and down my arm and kissing me lightly on the neck. I buried my head in his chest, listening to his heart, feeling the rise and fall as he breathed. I wondered if we needed to speak. Should I say something? Was he going to say something? The biggest question would spoil everything, so I left it. I wanted to stay here, with him, as long as I could. The gold spread through my body. Like a drug, it found its way through every part of me, threatening to dislodge that stone in my heart.

Somehow, I must have drifted off, because when I opened my eyes, it was dawn. I felt stiff and achy. My ankle was throbbing and crusty with blood. Joseph was awake. He was looking down at me, eyes protective, but with a slight smile on his face.

"How are you feeling?" he said. He was still holding me tight. I was still curled up in his lap, very reluctant to move at all. This was the safest place in the world to me; I didn't want to give it up.

"I'm fine," I said croakily. I took his hand in mine and kissed it. He held out my arm to inspect it and traced the numerous scrapes and scratches lightly with his fingers, sending more shivers through me.

"Are you cold?" he asked. I shook my head, attempting to make myself smaller, so he could wrap himself even more tightly around me.

I looked down through the branches. The wolves were gone but they had left a huge mess. Everything was destroyed. The others were already out of the tree. Clara was standing with her hands on her hips, arching her back and beaming at us. She looked very tired.

"Good morning, you two," she said. I didn't like her tone. Joseph eased me off his lap and helped me climb down from the tree. The stench burned my nostrils as soon as my good foot hit the ground. The wolves had certainly 'marked' their territory.

I surveyed the torn bags and crumbs of food, shaking my head. There was very little we could salvage. Clara sidled up to me, slipped her arm in mine and whispered in my ear, "Joseph and Rosa sitting in a tree k…i… s…s." I cringed. I gave her a look, which she understood to mean: I don't care if you're pregnant; if you finish that sentence, I'm going to finish you. She stopped and grinned at me. Threats never worked with her. Joseph jumped to the ground with ease, barely able to control his glee. Then Clara saw my foot.

I've never had someone fuss over me so much. She sat me down and cleaned the wound, chastising me constantly for lying to her. I pointed out that it was Joseph that lied to her. She whacked the back of his legs as he passed. "Ouch!" he said in mock pain. Their mood was easy to read, like co-conspirators, they just had to give each other a knowing look to work out what the other was thinking. She may as well have congratulated him. But now that I was back on the ground, reality was creeping back in. I was a bit embarrassed. Conscious that maybe the others knew as well. Although, they didn't seem to show it. They were too concerned with sifting through the chaos our four-legged pursuers had left for us.

Looking at the bite marks, it seemed I was pretty lucky. I had two neat gashes where the wolf's teeth had connected with my flesh and dragged across it as Joseph pulled me up. They weren't too deep. I shut my eyes, remembering the pain as the beast had sunk its fangs into my ankle. The bleeding had stopped. It was going to be hard to walk on though. While Clara was bandaging it up with some torn-up scraps of fabric she had found, care of the wolves, Alexei was busy scanning his reader. He said we needed to get moving. We needed to evacuate the wolves' territory before they returned. It would mean walking all day, with very little breaks.

Joseph scooped me up in his arms; he touched his forehead to mine affectionately. Our eyes connected—it was easy to get lost in those green eyes. But I was aware that everyone was looking at us. I asked him to put me down. I would walk, at least, for a while. He looked like he hadn't slept all night and we all needed to save our energy. He scrounged around and presented me with a long piece of wood with my missing boot on the end of it. I tried to shove the boot on my foot but it was hard with all the bandages. Joseph walked towards me. "Sit down," he ordered. I obeyed. Gently he lifted my leg, sliding both hands down from my knee to my foot, slowly. I trembled. He balanced my foot on his bended knee and loosened the laces on my shoe. As he positioned my shoe, he winked. As infuriating as ever. "You're blushing," he whispered, as he helped me to my feet and handed me the walking stick. I tried to hit him with the stick but he was too fast for me. He ducked and ran to the front of our group, consulting Alexei about what we needed to do next. Although, he may as well have skipped off for how pleased he was with himself.

We put everything we owned into a couple of packs, which Alexei and Deshi took turns carrying. There wasn't much. We had lost all our water and dried food. What we had saved or really, what the wolves had decided they didn't want, were empty water containers, our blankets, and the grey box that had dispensed my breakfast. Apella still had her little pack, which I reminded myself I needed to ask her about.

Deshi led us with the help of my instructions to where we had found the railway line.

24

Food and Water

When we arrived at the railway line, Clara was already completely exhausted, and we'd only been walking for about twenty minutes. It had taken a lot out of her scrambling up the hill, and Joseph was unable to help her because he was carrying me. With my injured foot, I was struggling to do very much. I hated being dependent on anyone, let alone Joseph. I hoped once we were on the track, I would be able to walk on my own. After months underground, Clara and I were both quite unfit, despite the 'exercise'. Joseph let me stand when we got to the top, and we watched as Alexei and Apella celebrated the finding of the line.

She took his pale face in her hands and kissed him. "We found it."

He pulled her into his chest, his thin fingers pressing into her back. "I knew we would sweetheart." Yuck! "We might just make it."

She gazed up at him, her blue eyes hopeful.

She was pathetic. I honestly couldn't understand what he saw in her. Alexei had proved useful so far. He had knowledge and survival skills. He was also strong, despite his slight appearance. But he loved her. The way he held her and looked into her eyes, that much was obvious.

"So which way do we go?" I asked. My sense of direction was never very good and I was so turned around, I really had no idea where we were.

"We head east." Alexei pointed towards the track that snaked off into the distance, looking like it climbed, looking like it was carved into the side of the mountain.

"Fabulous!" I said, sarcastically. I looked at my group of travelers. Deshi looked as doubtful as I was. Joseph and Clara were smiling, although Clara looked a bit drained, her skin looking sweaty and green. At least the weather was warm and we had a track to follow. Thinking of the sun and the warmth, my mouth felt suddenly dry. Deshi vocalized what I was thinking before I could.

"Has everyone forgotten that we have no water?" he said, irritated. I wondered what he knew of last night. I felt bad that it may have hurt him.

Alexei took out his map from his back pocket. He was wearing sturdier clothes than the rest of us, who were in Class uniforms. He had thick, cotton pants on, dark green in color. He was studying it intensely. I hoped there was a line of blue somewhere on this map that would lead us to water. I didn't notice that Joseph had come up behind me, until I could feel his breath on my neck. I wasn't ready for this. I didn't want to have this conversation, especially not in front of everybody else.

"I just want to tell you…" he hesitated, stepped back from me, and wiped his nose with his hand. His face was scrunched up—was he in pain? "Oh Rosa, you stink!" he laughed. I smelled the air. Something certainly smelled revolting. It was the same smell as back at the campsite and it was coming from me. My boot. Once we were standing still, it emanated the pungent stink of wolf urine. Joseph was doubled over laughing. Deshi slapped him on the back and was smiling too. Even the corners of Apella and Alexei's mouths were turned up.

The only person who wasn't amused was Clara. She came to my defense, smacking them both lightly on the head. "What's the matter with you two? Hasn't she been through enough?" The boys sucked in their laughter and looked at their feet like they were about to get detention. "We need to move. Now. Stop playing around and start walking," she said sternly, but with a twinkle in her eye. I smiled. Sometimes, when she wasn't talking about moons and rainbows, she took on this tone that sounded so much older than her years. Motherly almost. Deshi pulled Joseph to his feet and they strode off, laughing and talking. I stayed downwind, at the back of the group with Clara. We were the slowest anyway, with her waddling and my limping.

After a few minutes, Joseph and Deshi calmed themselves and took on the task of scouting for water. They would divert from the tracks every few kilometers and head into the forest. They always came back with their hands in the air. Nothing. They were way ahead of us. Apella and Alexei walked hand in hand in front. Joseph kept looking back at me, but thankfully, he was giving me the space I needed. He knew me well enough to know I didn't want to talk to him just yet. Or maybe he was afraid of what I would say.

Clara took my hand. It felt tiny in my own. She swung our arms together like we were schoolgirls. She was like a tiny ray of light—always smiling, always a comfort. She looked to me and smiled, shiny white teeth gleaming, her springy, black hair bouncing up and down as she walked.

"I'm glad to have you to myself for once." She gave my hand a squeeze.

"Me too," I said. Distance from Joseph was a good thing at that moment.

"It is so beautiful here. In Palma we wrote about the Wilderness but only from our imagination. It's so much more than I had expected," she said, her face full of wonderment.

She was right. From where we stood, we could see a carpet of alternate greens. The sky was clear blue. The spring weather brought with it warmth but not heat. The grey, rocky mountains contrasted with the pines. There was life everywhere. She patted her belly.

"Yes, we could be at home here." She was talking to her child, so dreamy. Sometimes I did wonder if she was 'all there'. She was full of hope, which was not a bad thing, but I couldn't understand from what source it originated. After everything she had been through, she seemed unaffected. It had to be the baby that kept her so buoyant, something I neither comprehended nor wanted.

Something occurred to me that hadn't before. Spring weather.

"What month is it?" I yelled to Alexei.

"It's just turned to April today," he replied. "Why?"

"Just wondering," I said unconvincingly.

Alexei shrugged his shoulders and returned to his conversation with Apella.

Clara was looking at me curiously. Her eyes asked me, what that was about?

"I turned seventeen two days ago," I said with a sigh.

"Happy birthday!" Clara said, clasping her hands around my shoulders and pulling me to her. I had never heard that phrase before. A change of age was not marked by anything in Pau, except access to a new ring. She was giving me a big squeeze when she jumped suddenly, like someone had kicked her.

"Ouch!" she exclaimed. Then in the sickly sweet voice she reserved for her baby, she said, "Naughty child, you shouldn't hurt your mother so," with her finger raised in mock disdain.

"Are you ok?" I asked. She looked weary. We needed to rest. I flagged the others and we let her sit for a while.

"I'm all right, really. I'm just hungry, and thirsty, but so is everyone else," she said, waving her hand, shooing us away like bothersome flies. We had to find something soon. We were all getting hungry and weak after our night in the trees. I scanned the area. I felt like there was a memory pinching me, something to do with Rash. He was making fun of me in the Arboretum. I was saying something was surprising, interesting. I remembered him telling me I was confusing boring with interesting.

"Rash," I whispered, smiling to myself. Forgetting where I was for a moment. Joseph looked at me. Eyes searching but I was replaying a memory in my head, looking right through him. I was reading about the pines. Rash was teasing me about having no life. I punched him in the arm. What I was reading was interesting because the plaque described the spring needles as being edible and that the male pollen cones were sweet. We needed sugar. I limped down the side of the hill, and picked a few of the small, yellow cones. I put one in my mouth. It was sweet, chewy. I filled my pockets and dragged myself back up the hill. I handed them out.

"Try it," I urged. Joseph chucked one straight in his mouth, always the trusting one. Clara did the same. The others waited until they were sure I wasn't planning a murder-suicide, but eventually they tried them. It wasn't going to satisfy for long, but it was something until we found water. When we got up and started walking again, I tried to remember anything else about the plants I had read about, opening my eyes and really observing our environment. I was hoping it would come back to me. We split up again, the boys still searching for water. Clara and I, arm in arm, headed up the back.

"What's rash?" she asked innocently.

I laughed, but it came out stiffly. "Rash was the name of my friend at the Classes. I mean is—Rasheed is his name." These memories were painful, dredging up feelings my conscious had not had time to deal with. Although it had been months since I had seen them, for me it felt like only a couple of weeks. I had had no time to grieve, or even decide whether I should grieve.

"You hurt him," she said plainly. I wasn't sure what that meant.

"I guess so, I mean, no not really." I was confused. I didn't hurt Rash, well, not directly anyway.

"Joseph doesn't understand your feelings for this Rash; you need to explain it to him." She said it like it was the most obvious thing in the world. She thought I had hurt Joseph.

"I can't talk to him. I don't know what to say," I explained, upset. She could cut right through me. She saw things I couldn't see, or didn't want to.

"Do you love him?" she asked, stopping us mid-stride, turning to face me. Her face was imploring, kind but urgent in its need for an answer.

Without question, I knew the answer, "Yes."

She looked baffled, "Then why? Why don't you go to him, tell him?" For her it was simple.

"I don't love this thing inside me, and I think he does or he will." I knew he did.

"Oh, is that all?" She waved her hand in dismissal. I stared at her in disbelief. "Rosa, it's obvious to everyone here, except you, that he will choose you, every time, he will choose you." I didn't need to hear that.

"He shouldn't have to make that choice," I uttered, mostly to myself.

I didn't believe her anyway. I knew she thought I would change my mind, that when it was born, somehow something would kick in and I would be a mother. Then we could be a family. But the idea made me feel ill. It wouldn't be real. None of this felt real. It was all backwards.

I was staring out at the trees, scanning the foliage, looking for a point of difference, when I saw it. In from the tree line and standing out like a splash of paint was a patch of purple.

"Siberian Irises love water!" I cried.

"What?" she called after me, but I was already stumbling, halfway down the gravelly hill.

Joseph caught up to me as I was entering the thicker part of the wood, the group disappearing from sight. He put his hand on my shoulder.

"Wait, where are you going?" he sounded out of breath and worried.

"I'm not running away. I think I can find water." I panted, feeling light-headed from the lack of water and the sprint down the hill.

Surprising me, he held out his hand, indicating for me to pass him and said, "Lead the way."

It was cooler down here, with only small snatches of light shining through the gaps in the trees. I kept a straight line, hoping that I hadn't led us off course. We walked for about half an hour, the dense foliage closing in around us as we moved deeper into the forest. It was mossy and damp with spatters of small, white flowers tucked in the tree roots. I was sure we should have hit it by now and I was beginning to doubt that I had seen it at all, when I heard something. Joseph must have heard it too because he stopped dead in his tracks and pulled me backwards into his arms. Quietly, we crouched down, watching a large form shuffling through the undergrowth. All I could see was small patches of brown fur catching the light every now and then. The plants were higher than my eye line. I wanted to get closer but Joseph had his hands clamped around my arms. I put my hands over his and gently pulled his fingers off me one by one. I stood. Joseph stood behind me, so close I could feel the heat from his body. Having him close was distracting and I needed to think clearly.

It must have been at least four times the size of a man. It turned in our direction and sniffed. A fuzzy face presented itself, with a squashed muzzle and a big, black nose. I became as still as a statue, not daring to breathe. Slowly but deliberately, Joseph moved his body between me and the great beast. Still unmoving, I hissed at him, "You're not wrestling a bear for me, you idiot!" He let out a stifled laugh, swallowing the noise as it escaped his lips. We both backed away slowly. It wasn't interested in us. It turned its attention to something else and lumbered through the brush.

Leaving a good distance between himself and the bear, Joseph followed. He told me to stay, so of course, I followed them both.

We followed for about fifty meters and were rewarded for our bravery, or stupidity. The bear had stopped and was taking a drink from a wide stream. Dotted along both banks were the purple flowers of the Siberian Iris. Their long green stems extending from the bank, looking like beckoning arms. The soft purple and yellow petals reminded me of a woman's mouth parted and ready to speak.

We sat and waited, giving the huge creature a wide berth. Joseph was distracted, tracing patterns in the dirt with his finger. I kept my eye on the bear. It finished drinking and padded off in a different direction to where we had come from.

"You know, if I'm part wolf, I think you might be part bear," I said cheekily.

"Why's that? Are you saying I'm big and hairy?" Joseph said, looking up from his dirt tracing, his eyes sparkling. An old feeling resurfaced.

I roughed up his hair. "Ha! Maybe. Well, big anyway." I swayed from side to side, grumbling. "It's the way you move; you're not the quietest person in the world."

He grinned at me. I found that broken tooth. Chipped and grey. My little beacon of imperfection.

After a while, we decided to venture towards the stream. Thirst ran hot sandpaper across our tongues. I ran to the water and plunged my head in. I took off my stinky boot and threw it into the water downstream. Joseph drank and then scooped the water up in his hands, washing his face and running them along the back of his neck, smoothing his blonde curls from his face, water dripping down his neck and onto his chest. I didn't want to look but he was hard to ignore. What had Rash said? He was an impossibly beautiful man. Unaware of it too. I blushed, realizing my own hair was crusty and unkempt. I undid my plait and dipped my head in the water again, trying to wash out some of the dirt it had accumulated out here in the Wilderness. It had grown quite long over the time I was underground and now lay midway down my back. When I flipped my hair back, he was giving me that look again. I guess I was the only girl in the world, right at that minute. Apart from me, there were only the birds and bugs.

Before he could speak, I said, "We'd better fetch the others." He shook his head and got up. I suspect he found my behavior frustrating. I did too.

We didn't need to get up. We could hear them crashing through the trees, not even trying to be quiet. Deshi burst through first, looking at us like he had caught us doing something inappropriate. I gave him a scowl for his insinuation.

"What's going on?" I asked.

They all looked panicked and breathless. Clara stumbled up behind them, lagging. I was annoyed by the fact that they let her fall behind. Once they all stopped talking at once, I could hear what had sent them barreling through the forest. The familiar sound of chopper blades cutting through the air sounded unnatural under the canopy of the trees. It started quite far away but slowly the noise increased, until all we could hear was the brrrrr of the aircraft. The trees were swaying. The birds had stopped singing. We all dove down and hid under bushes, rocks, or whatever we could find. I grabbed Clara and shoved her under a sage bush. Searching for a place to hide, I could see Joseph calling me over to him. He was squashed under a rock ledge near the water's edge. I saw a fallen branch, between them both, and pulled it on top of myself. Being small, it covered my whole body quite well, my grey uniform blending into the rocks around us. I curled up. From the air, I would have looked like a rock that a branch had fallen on. Out of the corner of my vision, I could see Joseph rolling his eyes at me. It was catching.

The Woodlands

The craft hovered temporarily, sitting in the air like a giant dragonfly, but after a few minutes, it veered northeast. I breathed a sigh of relief—we all did. At least it was heading away from where we were going.

That was the first day we saw the choppers. From then on, they were our constant companions.

25

Sisters

The choppers were unrelenting. Always drawn to our position, like flies to rotting carrion. There was no pattern to follow. Sometimes one would come in the morning and that would be it. Other times, three or four would come at different intervals throughout the day. We decided we would walk alongside the tracks, rather than on them, so that we had time to hide when we heard them coming. What I was unsure of was whether they were looking for us. They never hovered over one place for very long. They always veered off to the northeast eventually. As far as Alexei knew, there was no settlement out that way.

We all developed our own methods for hiding. Clara dropped and rolled under a bush. I always pulled something over me. Alexei and Apella always wasted time looking for a place big enough to hide them both. Joseph and Deshi went for whatever was closest. We started to get into a rhythm, warning each other when one of us heard them coming. It slowed us down a lot though.

Water was no longer a problem either. We knew what to look for, and once we did, we found there were bountiful streams meandering through the woods. They cut through the land, like shards of a shattered mirror, beautiful and strange water plants poking out around the banks. Alexei even managed to catch us some fish. He squatted over the water, watchful, eyes darting impossibly fast. The fish zipped in, out, and under rocks, like they knew. Poised, he waited for his moment and snapped, quick as a whip, pulling a fish out with his bare, shaking hands. Joseph and Deshi had a try. It was hilarious to watch them. Most of the time they both ended up in the water, laughing and pushing each other over. I tried too but my balance was so off I couldn't squat over the water for very long. It just irritated me, so I gave up.

It was also nice to be able to wash. I don't know why it made such a difference, but I felt so much better after I had bathed. Clara and I would walk down to a stream before dinner. Wash ourselves and clean our hair. We rinsed out our clothing and letting it dry in the sun. Clara would braid my hair in all sorts of odd configurations. I let her, but wished I had a mirror so I could check that she hadn't made me look too ridiculous.

She pestered me about Joseph constantly. Pulling my hair back with her thin fingers, she asked, "So what are you going to do about him?"

"About who?"

"Really, Rosa?" I could sense her eyes rolling at me behind my back. She pulled my hair back sharply. "Ouch! Not so hard"

"You're not being very fair to him. Have you even thanked him for rescuing us?" she said in that motherly tone.

"Save your mothering for that little monster you're carrying," I snapped.

"Hold still."

"Ouch!" Clara's fingernails were digging into my scalp.

"Oops, sorry," she giggled, returning to her girlish self.

That night I returned to the campfire and Joseph and Deshi fell backwards off their seats with laughter. Apparently, I looked remarkably similar to an octopus. I touched my head, eight chunky plaits protruding from it at different angles.

"Thanks Clara," I said, frowning.

"Oh, come now," Clara said between fits of hysterical giggling. "I think you make quite a beautiful octopus."

I smiled, shaking my head around, my tentacles bashing into each other. I felt like she was peeling layers off me, stripping back the roughness. Shining her faith into me, and airing out the darkest corners.

Once, Clara pulled just the front part back into two thin plaits, letting the rest of my hair fall down around my shoulders, placing tiny, white, star-shaped flowers around my crown like a wreath. When we returned, Joseph stood. He looked stunned. I worried she had made me look stupid again. I went to pull it out. Joseph put his hand up, "No, leave it. It looks… it looks good." Now he was blushing.

The group mostly ate from the box but I preferred to eat what I could find in the forest. I discovered I had absorbed quite a lot of information from my time at the Classes, and I enjoyed foraging for food.

At night, the non-pregnant members of the group took turns taking watch. We always camped under trees that would be easy to climb, in case the wolves returned, but we never heard from them again. I wondered whether the choppers had scared them off. Then again, we had walked quite far. We may have managed to get out of their territory.

Clara was so slow. She said she felt good. But to me, she looked ill. That thing seemed to be dragging her lower to the ground. I was very worried about her. My foot was healing well and I didn't need help to walk anymore, so I insisted that Joseph help her and carry her when he could. When I did stumble, Deshi was kind enough to offer a shoulder to lean on.

Deshi was a good friend to Joseph, and even though there would always be a slight unease between us, he helped me when he could. We were starting to be friends. If anything, we had a mutual interest. I don't think he resented me; maybe he was just a little sad.

Clara seemed like she must only be days away, judging by how long we had been out here and my vague memories of them saying she was thirty-six weeks when she had her 'scare'. I resolved to speak to Apella about Clara's condition and what we needed to look out for. I had only a vague idea what labor would be like. It was not something my mother ever talked about, but I was sure it would be painful. And without the normal facilities, it was going to be very challenging and probably dangerous.

As we were walking, I decided to catch up with the spindly couple and talk to Apella. I had barely said two words to her since my rescue, so the surprised look on her face was expected.

"I need to talk to you about Clara," I said directly. She nodded.

"How long do you think she's got to go?" I asked.

"It could be today or a week from now, any day really," she said calmly.

"Ok, so what do I need to look out for?" I wanted to know if there were any signs. I needed to prepare myself, as well as Clara.

"When her labor starts, she will have contractions. They will be painful and will last for a minute or two. They will come at even intervals. Don't worry, Rosa. Clara and I have discussed it all. She is as prepared as she is going to be." Apella's pale blue eyes were avoiding my gaze, her fair eyelashes lapsing over them longer than necessary. It didn't surprise me that Clara had spoken to Apella. She didn't subscribe to my dislike of the woman. Clara didn't dislike anyone.

I went to say thank you, but I couldn't get the words out. It was like trying to rearrange my bones. It wouldn't sit right. I stopped walking until Clara had caught up to me. She linked her arm in mine.

"Find out anything interesting?" she said with a wink. I shook my head. Apella was useless. I felt like we were alone in this. We had a doctor, but she seemed to distance herself from the very real scenario we were about to face. I don't think she had ever asked me how I was feeling or checked on the leech. I knew if things went wrong, I would do anything to help Clara. Even if that meant holding Apella at knifepoint while she assisted.

I kept these violent thoughts to myself and walked. Monotonous trudging. Boots crunching gravel, sounding like scraping frost from the freezer. Walking, always walking.

"So you know you're going to be an aunt soon," Clara announced, beaming. If Joseph was liquid gold in my veins, Clara was light. Pure white light, shining through me and surrounding me. She lifted me because she was better than me. I was never going to be as fundamentally good as she was.

This word aunt meant very little to me. The way she spoke, sometimes, it was like she was from another world or another time, a place where families existed: aunts, uncles, and grandparents.

"How's that?" I asked.

"We are sisters," she said, like it was the most normal thing in the world. "So when my baby is born, you will be an aunt."

I was too touched by what she had said to make my normal sarcastic comments. Sisters. The word warmed me. Like I could hold my hands up to it and thaw my fingertips. I liked the sound of it. We were sisters and as soon as I had accepted it in my head, it was so. It was probably always the case, just without the label.

All I said was, "I suppose I will be."

I had a sister. I smiled to myself, letting a little light in, cracks starting to show in the stone.

26

Lights Out

Blood surrounds me, life-giving and life-taking. I am swimming in it and drowning in it. No matter what I do, I can never escape it.

Unfortunately for me, Apella walked with us for the next couple of days. Clara had asked her to and I couldn't object. She was the only one who knew anything about what was going to happen to her.

The railway had started to lead us upwards. Grey rock dominated the landscape more and more. Joseph carried Clara most of the time. So our duo became a group. They talked amongst each other a lot, for which I was grateful. I didn't need or want to talk to either Joseph or Apella. I wanted to be close to him but I still didn't know what to say. Apella, I could have easily thrown out in the open. Let the choppers see her. As I got bigger, surprisingly, I felt stronger. Apella was a waif, her thin frame inviting me to snap her like a twig. I daydreamed that I threw her in the path of a passing helicopter, her perfect blonde hair whipping around her face, as a long claw reached down and pulled her from our group. But Clara wanted Apella close, so I kept my hands fisted at my sides and gritted my teeth through the polite conversations.

The choppers were fewer now. The last one we saw was a day behind us and I knew it wasn't looking for us; it was carrying a giant curve of concrete wall. It twisted and swung in the wind, a somber arc. I wondered whether it was part of something they had torn down or something they were building. My mind went to all those girls we had left behind. Had some escaped? What about all the babies? The haunting question was—*what were they going to do with all those children?*

Around noon, we sat down for lunch. I ventured into the forest, searching for some berries I had tested out a few days ago. They were so sour, I felt my mouth salivating at the thought of them, but they weren't poisonous and that was good enough for me. Joseph had started following me into the woods, asking questions about the plants. This was easier. I didn't mind sharing this information and it gave us a way to communicate without touching on the subjects I couldn't handle. Every now and then though, he looked at me like he wanted to say something more. I was good at reading those times and quickly changed the subject, bending down and picking up a leaf or a pinecone, shoving it in his consternated face and telling him to look at it. I knew he was frustrated with me. I knew it was only a matter of time before he confronted me, but not yet. I wasn't ready, the leech made sure of that.

When I came back, they were all staring at the box like they were waiting for it to burst into song. There wasn't much sun and it was taking a while to charge. Slowly, the light came on and they started preparing their lunch. I declined. I had some pine nuts, some dandelions, and the purple berries. I did take some water.

Clara inhaled her lunch. She then complained of a stomachache. So we sat with her for a while until she said it had passed. Just indigestion, she said. Just to be safe, I stayed right by her, exchanging worried glances with Apella.

It became increasingly difficult to walk off the railway line. On one side it fell away steeply. On the other side, we were looking up at the mountainside, straggly pines clinging to the loose, grey dirt. Pebbles constantly dripped down, pinging off the ground. The line was cut into the rock now. Alexei announced that we were not going to be able to hide anymore. We would have to take our chances in the open. We would be hard to spot anyway, all in grey except Alexei. We could hide against the cliff side if we heard the helicopters coming and be quite well camouflaged.

As we rounded a bend, the line seemed to just stop. In front of us was a steep mountainside covered in grass with a heavily wooded peak that went on forever. Juvenile pines, only my height, stretched as far as the eye could see. I could no longer see the railway snaking its way up the mountain. It was a dead end. Without thinking, I grabbed Joseph's arm.

"What do we do?" I asked, pointing straight ahead and then letting my finger rise to the sky. This was our only plan. What would we do if there were no line to follow?

"It's all right, look a bit closer," he said, chuckling. Sure enough, on closer inspection, I could see two black holes punched into the hill. Tunnels. The thought of being underground again filled me with dread. So much so that I didn't know I was digging my fingernails into Joseph's arm, clinging to him like a half-drowned animal. He gently put Clara down and grabbed both my shoulders. I was gasping for air.

"Rosa, breathe slowly." Joseph's green eyes were locked with mine. I searched them, picking out flecks of gold, watching his eyelashes flutter and close. I concentrated on that, as I tried to slow down.

"I can't go in there," I stammered, shaking. I was picturing all the earth piled on top of us. No air, no light.

"Ahhhhh," Clara emitted a slow, painful sound. She was crouched on the ground, holding her stomach, rocking back and forth. Like that, I snapped out of it. This was no stomachache. Apella knelt down beside her and touched Clara's enormous belly. She nodded to me.

"We need to find some shelter," Apella said. I knew there was only one place we could go. Joseph scooped Clara up in his arms and walked briskly towards the black holes. Deshi and Alexei were running ahead. They arrived at the tunnel and entered, disappearing into the blackness like it was a solid curtain. I shuddered.

When I got to mouth of the tunnels, I peered in suspiciously. I couldn't see a thing. Deshi clicked on his torch and scanned the area. A stone archway curved around and disappeared. There was no light, no end to it, only stark darkness. On both sides of the railway tracks, there was a narrow ledge built up with more carved stone blocks. It was dirty and black, hundreds of years of grime and smoke layering the surface.

Apella spread out one of our blankets and rolled another one up for Clara to rest her head on. It was cold, damp, and completely uninviting.

I had only one boot inside the tunnel and that was enough. I volunteered to collect some wood for a fire. They didn't seem to hear me, too busy arranging Clara comfortably. I sighed in relief as I turned around, heading away from the darkness. Deshi was close behind me.

We collected the wood in silence. Large, dry branches had fallen from the straggly pines above and there was more than enough. Every now and then, we could hear Clara moaning in pain. The sound bellowing out of the entrance, like the tunnel itself was a dark mouth calling out to us. I told myself I had to go back, that I was being a coward. She was going to need me, but my feet were cemented to the ground.

Deshi put his hand on my shoulder. "We better go back," he said, his eyes full of concern for Clara. We had all grown to love her. You couldn't help it. He actually had to pull me there quite forcefully, but we made our way back.

What I saw when we got there was not what I had expected at all. Joseph was sitting next to Clara, holding her hand. "You're doing great," he said kindly, running his other hand through his hair adorably. It was an action that only I would recognize. Because even if he felt out of his depth, he wouldn't show her. She didn't know the little things he did that conveyed his nervousness, not like I did.

Clara beamed at him. "You're lucky to be a man," she said.

He chuckled. "Yeah, I think in this case that's probably true."

Clara turned to Apella, her face more serious, "How long now?" She patted her belly and leaned against the wall.

Apella whispered something quietly to her. Clara frowned for a second and then cooed at her stomach, "Not ready to come out yet, are you? I know it's safe and warm in there but Mama wants to meet you."

I tried not to roll my eyes at her and bent down to build a fire, watching its light transform the darkness, bringing warmth. Sometimes, Clara would close her eyes and make a noise. She was clearly in pain, but it never lasted very long. She was amazing. She made it look manageable.

I moved to her other side and held her hand. She was sweating and pale but beautiful in the firelight. Showing a woman's strength in a delicate vessel, holding strong like a warrior. I have never admired someone more.

But after a few hours of this, she was starting to get very tired. She slept between contractions, waking with a start and then falling unconscious when they ended. I fed her small sips of water and rubbed her back.

Joseph was impressive; he helped her through every painful moment. Unlike Deshi, who was standing back from us like labor was catching.

Gritting her teeth, she screamed into the blanket. "C'mon," Joseph said as he wiped the sweat from her forehead with his sleeve. "That was nothing. What's all the noise about? You're scaring the baby back in." He winked at her. She let out a breathless laugh and tried to swat his arm. Even I had to laugh at that. They were so alike, never letting anything get to them, rising to the challenge like it was something they did every day. I touched my own stomach, wondering what lay ahead for me. I doubted I would handle things as well as Clara. Would I become an out-of-control, screaming mess? Would Joseph be able to cope with me being in that much pain? Would I even want him there?

Then it changed. The pain no longer seemed manageable. She was screaming and tearing at her clothes. One minute she wanted to stand, the next she was lying straight out on the cold, hard stone, her ear pressed to it like she was listening for something. I tried to talk to her, but it was like she had disappeared, retreated. She was in another zone—one filled with agony and waiting.

Apella asked us to get her to sit down. She needed to examine her. Clara was pacing back and forth. We gently coaxed her down to sitting.

"Is she ok? She's acting crazy. Is this normal?" I asked, touching Apella's rounded shoulder.

Apella didn't look up. She was focused and talked as she worked, lying Clara down and covering her with a blanket. "She's fine, she was like this in her last labor," she said as she removed Clara's boots and pants.

It hit me like a sledgehammer. I actually felt myself blown backwards against the stone wall, digging my nails into it, trying to find something to hold onto, to stop me. Stop.

Apella, unaware of the information she had let slip, peered between Clara's legs, completely unaware of my growing anger.

"What do mean, her *last* labor?" I stammered, my lips barely able to commit to speaking. I was trembling with rage, with fear. This wasn't Clara's first pregnancy. I moved towards Apella, my body sliding off the edge, slow. I was so close to her face that I barely had to speak for her to hear me.

"How many babies has she had?" I hissed through clenched teeth. She looked away, biting her lip. I grabbed her, squeezing her thin arms, hard. I pulled her away from Clara for a moment. "Look at me. How many?"

"Four," she said in a barely audible whisper. She sighed it. Four. Like it could be exhaled and expelled from her conscience.

Before anyone could stop me, I slapped her as hard as I could. "You're a monster," I screamed, my voice echoing down the tunnel. "You deserved that and so much more."

She touched her hand to the already bright red handprint on her pale cheek. "I know," she said quietly as she returned to tending to Clara. Joseph had a hold of me now, but even he was struggling to hold me back. If he hadn't, I would have strangled her.

Clara was sitting up now, looking at the three of us. Scared. I don't think she heard us but she was startled out of her dream state by my screaming. I felt sick at the thought that she didn't know. She didn't know she'd had four babies taken away from her. It would kill her. I ran my fingers through my hair and tried to breathe when all I wanted to do was scream. Clara needed our help now. Whatever problems Apella and I had would have to wait.

I returned to Clara, wiping the sweat from her face. Her once springy curls were plastered to her forehead. I felt so protective of her. I wanted to wrap her up in a blanket and run away from here. Like if we ran fast enough, arms linked together, somehow we could escape the pain. Apella finished her examination. She said she didn't have long to go. I was hoping she would say it was time to push, but no.

Clara said she wanted to stand so we tried to help her to her feet. The contractions were so close together she didn't even get halfway up before she was screaming again. When she stood, I could see she was sitting in a pool of blood. I hadn't noticed before that Apella and I were both bloodied as well. It was dripping over the ledge and onto the railway line, spreading like a ghastly, growing shadow.

Deshi and Alexei were standing back, keeping the fire going. They looked worried. We were all worried.

Clara started to speak, in breathless whispers between the contractions. She was in so much pain; it was agonizing to see her this way. "I can't, I can't. It's too hard, please," she whispered.

Joseph took her burning face in his hands, forcing her to focus on him. "Listen to me, you can do this, it's nearly over. Then you will see your baby." She blinked once, listening to him. She took a deep breath and focused all her energy on this last task. The pains were on top of each other, leaving barely a second to breathe. But she stopped screaming. She bore down and took control. I could almost see light shining from within her. White hot in its intensity.

It took two hours to get to the point where Apella said she could push. Clara was beyond exhausted, but the reminder that she would soon see her child sustained her right to the end. We lifted her tiny body to a squatting position, Joseph and I holding her up by her arms. It felt like holding nothing. She was air and light. Apella told her that on the next contraction she had to push. I don't know where she found the strength, but she took a breath and let out an almighty scream. Joseph cried out that he could see the head. I closed my eyes. I couldn't look.

Clara held herself in that position, waiting for the next assault of pain to tell her to push the baby's body out. She did this quietly—eyes squeezed tightly shut, body and face tense. Her usually dark skin looked pale, ghostly in the firelight. And then there was a baby in Apella's arms. A screaming creature, covered in blood and muck. Clara held out her hands eagerly and Apella placed the child across her chest. A boy.

Joseph was grinning at me. "You're an aunt!" he said. I felt my own mouth creeping up at the corners, smiling too. It was over. Thank God it was over. I looked at him. I wondered if he found that as terrifying as I did, or whether he was looking forward to the birth of his own child. I leaned into Clara's face and whispered, "I'm glad it's a boy." I was thankful there was not going to be a Rosa the Second running around.

She didn't respond, too engrossed in the baby boy clinging to her chest.

Apella was busy cutting the cord with instruments she pulled from her mysterious pack. So that's what was in there, medical supplies. Joseph had walked over to Deshi and Alexei, all smiles, relieved. The baby screamed again. Clara was still. The poor girl must have been so tired. Her eyes were closed lightly, her arms haphazardly flopped across her body. I motioned to Alexei; he came staggering over like he'd just been in labor. "Can you take the baby? We should let her get some rest," I said. He took the child, wrapping him up tightly, just his springy, black hair poking out the top of the blanket. Clara didn't move. I swept the hair back from her face, her cold face. It left a smear of blood like a brand across her forehead.

No.

I looked to Apella. She took Clara's limp hand in her own, her fingers on her wrist, searching for a pulse. She shook her head minutely. She checked again, putting her head to Clara's chest, tears forming and spilling down her cheeks. I stood. Joseph took broad steps towards me and I slipped, feeling cold liquid soaking into my clothes.

No, no, no.

The panic was rising. My mouth felt dry, bile rising in my throat. I slid off the ledge and pushed Apella out of the way. I grabbed both of Clara's arms and pulled her towards me. "Wake up!" I yelled. Knowing she wouldn't, knowing she couldn't open her beautiful brown eyes and smile at me. The light was out. She slumped forward and fell to the side, limp like a ragdoll. Blood. There was so much blood.

Somewhere inside of me, something snapped. It shattered and splintered, sending slithers of debris coursing through my veins, grating and fraying the sides. I held onto the metal bar of the railway line, like it was the only thing stopping me from sinking into the ground. The sun was rising, light penetrating the darkness, showing the devastation the night had hidden from our eyes.

It was over.

She was gone.

My beautiful sister.

I crumpled like a piece of paper in a flame, disintegrating to dust.

2.7

Wash Away

I don't know how long I stayed there. I heard muffled voices—people moving around me, sharp rocks clunking dully together.

Strong arms tried to pull me up from where I squatted, head between my knees, clinging to the rail. A baby cried. Someone punched the wall. I stayed there still.

The light was touching my hands, bare-knuckle white. My body tensed. Someone was talking to me, but it was like I was underwater. His voice warbled and I couldn't make sense of it.

I was teetering on the edge of a precipice, wind in my hair, staring down into blackness. With all my courage, all my energy, I made the choice. I let go and I let myself fall, endlessly falling, cold air pulling my hair up over my head.

One finger at a time, detached. *Tick, tick, tick.* Heavy cloth shrouded me.

He picked me up in a blanket and walked outside. Silent. It was bright. I closed my eyes and focused on his footfalls on the solid earth. Thump, thump, thump. I felt us descending. I opened my eyes and it was cooler, darker.

He lay me down gently, kissing me on the forehead. I felt numb with no senses, like there was a barrier between me and the outside world. He rolled my shirt up and pulled it over my head. The cotton stuck to my skin. Carefully, he used his hands to peel it away from my stomach and chest, push, pry, rip. A faint copper scent stung my nose. He stood me up, removed my boots and trousers, dunking everything in the shallow pond he had brought us to. I sat there. Blank. Cold. Watching the water change from clear to pink and then clear again as it washed away. Washed her away.

He soaked a cloth in water, and begun carefully wiping the rust-colored blood from my body. I didn't care anymore. I let him touch me, lifting my arms, turning my head, pulling my hair back and cleaning my neck. He did it all slowly and deliberately. There was no charge in his touch. This was a kindness to one who was broken.

When he was done, he wrapped me in the blanket and propped me up against a tree trunk like a wooden puppet. I watched, disconnected, as he soaked my clothes and rinsed them until the water ran clear.

He gathered me up, in only my underclothes and a blanket, and slung my wet uniform over his shoulder, taking me back into the sunlight.

28

Wake Up

The world was grey. The color washed away, dripping down the sides of the trees like it was soaking back into the earth. I moved through the world but not in it.

We kept walking, leaving it all behind.

We walked through the darkness for miles. When the light started to show at the end, I took up my initial position, clinging to the rails. I didn't want the light on me. It burned my eyes. *Coward, coward, coward*, the light screamed, balancing a slant over my face. *You couldn't save her.*

From then on, he carried me as much as his strength would allow and, after his arms trembled under my weight, he held my hand and led me like a child. I followed him. I let him carry me. The fight in me was gone.

He talked as he walked but I didn't listen. I couldn't hear him from behind the wall. Occasionally a baby's cries would punch through, but only for a second before it closed over, enveloping me in buffered sounds.

I wanted to speak but the words were buried. With her. If I could have cried or talked about it, maybe I would have healed faster. But nothing came.

I kept expecting her arm to link in mine, to hear her voice telling me to snap out of it. She believed things would work out. She was wrong.

I walked, ate, and slept, but that was all. My eyes focused on something far away. Just over the hill, just behind a tree, never on what was in front of me, or who was walking beside me.

The Woodlands

At night I slept by the fire, my body warm but shaking uncontrollably. Closing my eyes brought on nightmares soaked in blood. He lay with me, holding my arms down to stop me from hurting myself. He spoke but all I could hear was calming whispers. No words.

I tried to recede to the point where nothing could reach me, but something was always tugging, pulling at my shirt, trying to drag me back into the light. But without her, the light was dull, insipid, lying over the forest like a silty blanket.

For weeks, I stayed inside myself. Joseph tried to coax me out, but even he stopped trying after a while. On the twenty-third day, I heard words. My head rose above the waves of my grief and I heard them talking.

Apella was cooing to the child.

"You'll make a wonderful mother to little Gabriel," a stuttering voice said lovingly. Gabriel?

I kicked my feet, trying to keep my head above water a little longer.

"Thank you, darling, you will make a wonderful father too." Apella's sweet voice was like a booming bell, reverberating and hurting my ears.

"His name is Hessa," I said, my voice a tiny crackle.

Everyone stared. Apella sheltered the child in her arms, like she thought I was going to hurt him. I wasn't going to hurt him. The couple was sitting, cradling the child under a tree. It was a spring sapling that was bending and swaying in the breeze, making shushing noises as the leaves grazed each other. Apella was holding a bottle full of grey liquid, which the baby was sucking. My head fractured as I thought of our grey milkshakes.

The trees were no longer grey, the color returning slowly. Green leaves touched by sunlight. I moved towards the couple on my hands and knees, aware that Joseph was behind me, shadowing my movements. I sat back on my heels and gently folded the grey blanket they had wrapped him in away from his face. He had springy, black hair, caramel-colored skin, and big blue eyes. He looked just like her and nothing like her at the same time. He was definitely All Kind. But it was there, that light had passed to the child. It shone in and around him, protecting him, announcing him as Clara's son. I held out my arms. Apella shook her head. But Joseph was right there. So was Deshi.

"Let her hold him," he said quietly but with force. Deshi was standing next to Joseph, looming over Apella with a stern look on his face. They both knew I would never hurt the child. I think Apella knew it too—that wasn't the reason she didn't want me to hold him.

Apella gently handed the bundle to me, uttering "careful," as she let go of the child painfully slow. I peered at his face, pulling one of his arms out of the blanket and letting him wrap his fingers around my own. That touch wrapped around me like a bright white chain, binding me light as a feather but strong. I knew this child was mine. I was his family now.

"Hessa," I whispered as I traced his tiny lips with my finger. I turned to Apella and Alexei's pleading faces. I did not relish the disappointment I was about to bestow upon them. "You know you can't keep him," I said plainly, not meaning to repeat the words I had spoken to Clara back when we were underground. After everything she had done, what she had kept from us, this was not Apella's redemption. She was not his family and had no place in his life. I knew now why Clara had named me her sister.

Apella didn't speak. For the first time, that perfect facade contorted as she burst into tears. It lasted all of thirty seconds, then she patted her tears, straightened her clothes, and walked away. Alexei followed.

I held the child, not overcome by the decision I had made. It was simple. It was fact. It was the easiest thing I had ever done. I felt two distinct hands on my shoulders.

"Welcome back, zombie," Deshi said with a grin. He looked tired and thin.

"I'm sorry," I said, without looking away from Hessa. "I'm sorry it took me so long."

"Don't be sorry. We're just glad you're back," Joseph said, smiling. "So you're a mother now." There was a hopeful glint at the end of his sentence and I knew what he was thinking, but I wasn't sure this changed anything.

"No. Not a mother, an aunt," I said, already feeling something absolute solidifying inside me, *love*. Joseph shrugged, seeming to accept that was all I could manage for now. He ran his hands through my hair and tied it back with a piece of twine, my skin buzzing from that barest touch.

"Thank you," I said, feeling a bubble of that liquid gold pushing through my veins. I looked at his earnest eyes, green with flecks of gold, and wondered if he would always be this patient with me. If I pushed him away now—would he come back? I held out my free hand for him to hold, which he took eagerly but gently. It was an uphill battle and the gold rose and receded, not quite able to push past the pain.

"Are you all right?" Joseph asked. I looked down at Hessa. The baby blinked uncomfortably as drops of water hit his perfect little face. I thought it was rain at first, quickly realizing they were tears. For the first time since I had watched my sister slip away, I cried. I rocked the child and let it all out. I saw her face as she left me; I saw her face in her son. But it was not painful to see him. It was comforting. She would always be here with us, in him. The boys sat back and let me go until I could cry no more, my face red and salty.

Hessa was sleeping. Peaceful. He was unaware of our journey. For him, home was under the trees. He had never seen the grey walls of Pau or the Classes, never seen the towering, concrete prison of the rings. He could have a free childhood. It was an exciting prospect and it motivated me even more than before.

Joseph filled me in on what I had missed. We had covered a lot of ground but there was still a lot ahead of us. Looking around, it seemed the scenery had opened up a lot. We were sitting at the edge of a field, tall grass and saplings dominating the landscape. It was much flatter than before and it made me feel exposed.

"Have there been any more choppers?" I asked. I felt foolish for not knowing, for being so unaware of my surroundings.

"No," Deshi replied. He was preparing a bottle, spooning the grey sludge from the box in and watering it down, giving it a sharp shake.

Hessa awoke with a start, screaming. I panicked—had I done something? Deshi saw the fright in my eyes and answered my question.

"He's hungry," Deshi said as he opened his arms. I gently handed the child over and watched as Deshi adeptly fed and changed the child. He played with him for a while and then rocked him to sleep, placing him, tightly wrapped, in an emptied-out backpack. He looked at the child with a love that was unmistakable.

Joseph laughed at me, which I didn't appreciate. "It's just a baby, Rosa. You don't need to be afraid of it. It cries, eats, and needs to be changed." I had a bit of catching up to do. "Don't worry, we'll all help you."

Hessa now had three parents.

Apella returned, her face composed but shaky, her lip quivering unappealingly as she spoke. "I know I can't keep him. I know I don't deserve him but I want to help. Will you let me help you?" She was humbled to the point of begging. I wanted to say no. But something softened in me. I would need all the help I could get. I wasn't going to be her friend. I was never going to like her—but I could use her.

"Sure," I said, deliberately trying to sound like I didn't care. But I would be watching them both. We all would.

Watching Hessa sleeping on top of the backpack gave me an idea. It wouldn't do for him to sleep like that, and we needed the backpack to carry other supplies.

"Can I have a knife?" I asked, surprised faces all around. I guess it was hard going from zombie to fully functioning human without people wondering whether you were insane.

Deshi searched around the site and found one. I set to work cutting down some of the bendy green saplings. As soon as I cut into the trunk, the right feeling was overwhelming. I ran my hand over the trunk, enjoying every little bump. I had missed this. I sliced through the sapling, sticky sap oozing from its wounds. I cut down about eight small trees and went to work skinning them and bending them. I know everyone probably wanted to get moving but they let me work. I must have looked possessed. I didn't speak. I just worked. I bent the wood into the shape I desired and tied it with the tough grass we were surrounded by. I felt like I was made for this. I saw things differently to the others. I could see there was a life to be made out here. The forest was abundant and provided everything we needed.

When I was finished, I cut up one of our blankets, trying hard not to picture its last use. With a pointed stick and more grass, I sewed it into my cradle to make a lining. I had made a crude capsule. I sewed strips onto the underside so that it could be carried on my back. It wasn't pretty but it would work. We slipped Hessa inside it still wrapped. He was cozy and protected.

Apella put her hand up timidly. "Are you sure that is safe for a baby? He is so tiny. What if he slips out the bottom?" Both Joseph and I glared at her and she sealed her lips.

"It's amazing!" Joseph said, congratulating me. "I had no idea you could make something like that."

"Well, this is what I was going to do. Before…" I said. He looked at me sadly. I wished he would stop punishing himself. This was not his fault. None of it was. I didn't blame him, but I couldn't look at our situation the way he did, the way Clara did. It was not a blessing.

I grabbed his shoulders, heat pulsing through my fingertips, having to stand on my tiptoes to look him in the eye, my stomach touching his.

"This isn't your fault," I said. "Don't look at me like you need to make up for something—you don't." I sounded angry, which is not what I meant. I just wanted to release him from this obligation he felt, this guilt.

He smirked. "There she is," he said. He always confused me with his reaction to my anger. Like he enjoyed it or at the very least, expected it. I let him go and laughed. He was so annoying, so charming.

Deshi volunteered to carry Hessa first and I didn't object. I was tired from all that work and could not ignore my heaviness and awkwardness. Over the last three weeks, I felt like I had doubled in size. It got in the way of everything and it moved more and more, less like a kick and more like a stretching of my skin, squashing my organs and bruising my insides.

I was even more frightened of it than I was before. Especially after seeing what Clara had gone through and how it had ended. I had to hope that I would not suffer the complications that killed her, but even the idea of all that pain was too much to consider. I tried really hard to put it out of my head. I had some time and there was no point in worrying about something that was out of my control.

There were miles of track in front of us. It stretched as far as the eye could see. I felt Clara's arm link in mine. I imagined her dragging me forward. I looked at Hessa's beautiful little face poking out of his capsule. He was content, shadows of leaves playing games with his eyes. I felt a surge of energy with the revelation that his happiness and that look on his face had to be maintained. No matter what, we had to protect this child.

2.9

The Choice

Clara, I miss you so much. I wake up and I'm trying to find you. Where are you now? I need to make sense of what happened to you but there are no answers. I hope I am doing what you wanted. I know I can never replace you. I won't even try. But I promise, I will treasure Hessa, we all will. Please don't leave me.

The days took on a peaceful current. Being so focused on caring for Hessa left no room for arguments. We took turns carrying him and feeding him. I let Deshi change him, finding the stench created by drinking that grey stuff too powerful for my sensitive nose. Joseph stoically offered to wash out the soiled cloths but made a loud fuss as he ran, holding them in front of him, pinching his nose.

The nights were harder. I insisted on sleeping with Hessa. I needed to hold him; scared he would disappear if I let him go in the darkness. Even though Apella promised she wouldn't run away with him, I didn't trust her. I held the child close, tucking him into my sleeping bag every night.

I woke up to yelling. Hands frantically waving, Apella said, "Rosa, put Hessa down."

"Yes, gently," Alexei stammered.

"Easy now, don't panic," Joseph said, although his eyes said differently.

"For goodness sake!" Deshi cried out.

Four pairs of panicked eyes were all stalking me slowly. Deshi had his arms out, eyes wide with terror. He was edging closer, taking tiny, timid steps that didn't disturb the dirt around his feet. Approaching me, as I imagine, one would approach a wild animal that was about to charge. Joseph was standing across the fire. "Rosa, stop." My head was muddled—stop what? I looked directly in front of me. I had Hessa in my hands. I was holding the plump little baby out in front of me over the fire. The heat was starting to hurt my hands.

"Oh no!" I exclaimed as I pulled the baby towards me and held him close, his too warm face pressed into my neck. I recalled my dream, feeding the fire that I had made in the tunnel. In my arms was a piece of wood; I had nearly flung Hessa onto the flames. I couldn't believe what I had almost done. Deshi stormed over to me and took the baby out of my arms. I let Hessa go without a fight. Deshi was distraught. I felt the sting of disconnection. Without the light, I felt myself crumbling again.

"That's it! I'm sorry, Rosa, but it's too dangerous. I could put up with the screaming and the nightmares but you could hurt him. You can't sleep with him anymore," Deshi said, telling me off like a child.

"I'm sorry, it's the dreams. I can't control it. He needs me," I pleaded, lying selfishly. I knew the truth was—I needed him. It was no use anyway. Deshi put Hessa before everything else. As he should. As I should. I knew I couldn't put the child in danger. Deshi tucked the beautiful baby in with him, muttering to himself about me being easier to handle when I was a zombie. Hessa cried for a second but Deshi patted his head and soon they were both asleep. Apella and Alexei waited until they knew Hessa was safe then went back to sleep, exhausted from all the walking.

Joseph had returned to his sleeping bag; he lay with his arms folded behind his head. His eyelids fluttered as sleep found him. His strong arms looked so appealing to me. I wanted to curl up next to him and lay my head on his muscled chest but I stopped myself. It was only inviting more pain, confusing an already extremely confusing situation.

I climbed back in my bag, knowing sleep would not come easy to me that night. Missing that warm, precious baby lying with me, I felt lost. I watched the fire, the way the orange light curled and consumed. Without fail, it found a way to devour its fuel. I closed my eyes and the flames licked up the wall of the blackened tunnel, hunting me down, singeing my flesh. Heart thumping in my chest, I opened them again.

I picked up a stick and traced shapes in the ground. Concentric circles, things we left behind. How long would I feel this way? If I let go of the pain, was I forgetting her? When I looked at Hessa's face, when he grabbed my hand, I felt a joy I had never felt before. Then immediately, guilt would follow, knowing that I could see these moments in his life and Clara could not.

I thought about when I first met her. Those beautiful dolls painted on the wall. Her giggly exterior hiding such wisdom. I pulled a knife out of the pack. My eyes fell upon Joseph's resting face again. They wandered over his body, taking in the things I could not when he was awake. His fair skin was looking darker from the sun, tiny freckles forming over the bridge of his nose. And of course, he was smiling, even in his sleep.

"You know, if you're going to kill me, you should just get it over with," he said, propping himself up on his elbows, his voice low, trying not to wake the others. I jumped, startled, and dropped the knife.

"I wasn't, I mean, oh you know I wasn't." I was so embarrassed that he'd seen me staring at him.

"You so beautiful when you blush," he said, staring into the fire. Watching him now, it was clear. He was no longer the boy I met in Pau. He was sure of himself, strong. I wished I had that confidence.

"I wish you wouldn't say things like that," I said, throwing the stick in the fire, watching it wrap its orange and yellow flames around the thin arm of wood and draw it into the heat.

Joseph sat up and pulled himself out of the bag. He made his way over and sat down with a thud. He gently nudged me with his shoulder. "Why?" I found it surprising that he didn't know the answer to that question.

I picked up a stumpy piece of wood and retrieved the knife from the edge of the fire. Brushing the dirt off the blade, I began working my way into the bark. Carefully stripping away the outer layers, the dark grey skin peeled away easily.

"It just makes it harder to..." I wasn't sure what to say next so I let the words fall away to silence.

"To resist me," he said jokingly, raising his eyebrows.

I carefully dug the knife in at an angle, slicing away at the bone-colored flesh, removing small pieces and flicking them into the fire. "Well, yes, I suppose." My nervousness at this conversation was showing, my legs rattling uncontrollably. I wanted to be calm. Cooler.

"Oh," he said, half-laughing, half-sighing. "Why do you have to?" he asked genuinely.

I whittled the wood further, using the thin edge of the knife to smooth out the shape. Adding sharper angles, refining and defining the shape I was trying to bring forth from the timber.

"Because I know what you want and I'm not sure I can give it to you. Whatever I feel, it doesn't matter. I'm carrying your child and you want that child. I just don't know if I want it. If I could even tolerate it," I blurted out in one breath. I had hoped I could say it better, but it was too late to take it back.

"Rosa, you are so frustrating." He was angry—I knew he would be. "I know you have been through hell and I know you don't know whether you can love this baby." I wasn't expecting that. He took my hand in his. "We have months before we have to face that problem. I'm not going to force you to make a choice. Just tell me..." He stuttered over the last part, trying to choose his words carefully. "How do you, I mean, um, do you love me?" He removed his hand from mine and clasped his own two hands together tightly, awaiting my reply.

There it was. I could have lied. Perhaps I should have, but he was looking at me so intensely, his beautiful eyes searching mine. Begging me for an answer. "You know I do," I whispered, feeling the blood run to my face. Feeling the gravity of my words anchoring me.

His laugh boomed out across the forest. Our traveling companions stirred in their sleep, but thankfully they did not wake. I was shocked— what was so funny about that?

"Why are you laughing at me?" I said, glaring at him, unconsciously waving the knife in his face.

"I'm sorry, but I can't believe you would think that, somehow, I would know that you loved me. You are always pushing me away." I suppose that was true, but I had always thought he knew why I was doing that, that my feelings were obvious. I was trying to protect him. Then I remembered that day, when Clara told me that I'd hurt him. That he thought I was in love with Rash, which was ridiculous. Perhaps it was obvious, only to her, how much I cared for him. I held my heart, feeling pain creeping in.

Joseph's face flickered with concern. "You ok?" he asked.

I nodded. "It's just...Clara," I whispered. He nodded in agreement. Sometimes the pain was physically crippling. I wondered if he was scared I would regress to that shadow state again. I wouldn't. I couldn't

"So what do we do?" he said as he pressed his cheek to mine. I leaned into it, feeling liquid gold rising. Like the sun, I had no power to stop it. What could we do?

I used the point of the knife to create swirls, working the curves into the wood, linking each curl together in a flowing pattern. "I'm open to suggestions." I shrugged in a failed attempt to look unaffected. It wasn't working. Nothing would work now. I had said the words. My heart was beating so fast at the realization that I couldn't stand the idea of him walking away from me now. If he said we had to stop, I would fall to pieces. But if I chose him now, what would happen in two months?

"Well, if we love each other then we should be together."

"You say it like it's so simple."

"It is."

I wasn't sure what to say. There was the future to consider, but I had resolved not to think about it. We didn't know what would happen next. If I died tomorrow, I knew I would regret not saying yes to him tonight. Was it simple? I carved the dent of a chin into my piece of wood, scraping the neck down. It needed to be thinner. I closed my eyes. Threatening myself. Just speak. It would be better to lose this, than to not have had it at all.

"Ok," I managed to utter softly.

He raised his eyebrows. He was surprised. I guess he didn't always know what I was going to do. I smiled at him. He pulled me towards him in a tight embrace, my stomach, as always, getting in the way.

"Rosa, thank you," was all he said. It was relief and fear mixed together. I knew that now I had made this choice, there was no going back. Everything that I had held back came spilling over. I allowed the liquid gold to spread throughout my body, finding its way in the dark. Opening me up, making me brave and vulnerable. It felt good.

"Will you lie with me?" I asked.

"Of course," he said, still surprised. I watched him nervously and clumsily zip the bags together. Stumbling over the logs we had stacked for the fire. He was the sweetest man I could have found. I let it in. I let him in. I would let it heal me.

I gently placed the piece of wood and knife on the ground by the fire. I would finish her tomorrow.

Joseph lay down and I curled up in his arms. He swept my hair back from my ear, tiny tendrils of electricity making me shiver. He whispered, "I love you." There was no urgency, no pain to his voice. It was simple. I knew this was where I should be, probably where I was always supposed to be. I didn't reply, but placed his hand to my heart, hoping nightmares would not find me that night.

30

Revelations

To say I was happy wouldn't be the right word. It was more like, once I had made that choice, I felt *released*. Released from the angst of denying myself something I had wanted so very much. A pressure in my heart let out. I felt normal.

Joseph still irritated me, with his permanently cheery outlook and terrible sense of humor. That would probably never change. But I never understood why anyone would want to be with someone who was the same as them anyway. I think that would be the worst of all. Always agreeing, never having someone challenge you. I would die of boredom. But when he held my hand, or sidled up behind me and whispered in my ear, I disappeared into a bath of gold. I still thought of Clara constantly, but I was sure this was the path she had been trying to put me on ever since we were found in the forest.

When we awoke, our confessions, our decisions, were laid out for everyone to see. But there was no interest in our sleeping arrangements whatsoever. I don't know what I was expecting, perhaps a raised eyebrow or a sarcastic comment from Deshi, but none was forthcoming. It didn't bother Joseph. Maybe they expected it would happen eventually. I don't why it should have mattered, but I didn't like the idea that people thought they knew what I was going to do.

After nearly throwing Hessa in the fire, I resolved to spend as much time with him as I could during the day. Not being able to sleep with him was hard and I was determined to make up for what I'd nearly done. I had almost finished my gift last night when I was interrupted. So I picked up the knife and carved the last details into her face and clothing while the others were eating breakfast.

There. I was done. Joseph put his hand over mine. I withdrew sharply, not used to allowing his touch. His eyes widened, worried that I had changed my mind.

"Sorry, old habits," I said, turning to him and holding out my hand for him to take.

"It's ok," he said, slapping my hand away, "but that wasn't what I was after." He held out his hand, palm upwards. I placed her on top. "Wow!" he exclaimed as he turned it around in his fingers, tracing her hair and face, smiling to himself. "It looks just like her. Rosa, it's beautiful."

"Thanks," I said shyly. I walked over to Deshi, who was arranging Hessa in the cradle. "Here, it's for Hessa." I handed the carved doll to Deshi. He eyed it suspiciously. "It's ok; I used a really hard wood so even if he chews on it, it won't harm him."

Deshi took the doll, examining it carefully, and then smiled. "It does look very much like his mother," he said as he held it in front of Hessa, who grasped at it and then proceeded to slobber all over her head. "You're sure it's safe?" he asked.

"Absolutely," I assured him.

I left them to pack up, announcing that I wanted to collect a few things for the walk, some nuts and fruit I had seen growing a few hundred meters away. Joseph offered to go with me, but I said I would be fine. He could keep packing and I wouldn't be very long. I walked towards the blossoms I had seen in the distance, hoping they would be wild apple. As I approached them, I could hear the soft padding of feet behind me. I felt the hairs on the back of rise, thinking it was an animal. I turned around slowly and was face to face with Alexei.

"You scared me," I sighed as I moved to the tree to collect the fruit.

"Sorry, just thought you could use some help," he said, unconvincingly.

"Um, all right, well just put the apples in your pack and I'll collect those nuts over there." I left him, but he followed me. I spun around and faced him, "What's going on, Alexei, you're not being very helpful. What do you actually want?" He obviously wanted to talk to me about something and I was never one to wait. I wanted him to get on with it. He fumbled around with his reader. "Spit it out!" I said, probably a bit too impatiently.

"It's about Apella," he said quietly. Of course it was. "I was wondering if you would let her spend more time with Gab...I mean, Hessa?" *What a question,* I thought.

"No. I don't think so. Sorry." I shook my head. I didn't trust either of them.

"I know you think she's a bad person but she's not. If you understood more about her, maybe you would see things differently—maybe you would see her as I do." He was pleading with me now, hands shaking. I didn't want to know anything about her. I couldn't feel sorry for her, but I suspected he wasn't going to give me a choice. He sat down under the blossoms. An odd frame for his nervous, thin body. Flowers kept falling down around him, floating like snowflakes and landing in his thinning hair.

"When I met Apella, we were both at the Classes. She was a brilliant scientist, studying Medical. I was in the uppers also, training for Intelligence. We were lucky enough to be sent to the same town and were preparing for marriage and a child. But after years of trying, it was apparent that it was not going to happen for us. Apella left me." He paused, reliving some painful memory. I tried really hard not to say that he would have been better off. He would have. "She was pulled into a secret project for Superior Este and I was left to manage the archives in Ring Eight of Casuarina."

I wanted to stop him there. I could see where this was going.

He continued, "Apella was developing ways to help infertile couples conceive, working closely with Este and Semmez. At some point, she realized what they were really trying to do and that's when they took me." He stopped and engaged my eyes, slowly lifting up his shirt to reveal hundreds of tiny scars, burn marks. I winced and motioned for him to cover himself back up.

"They held me hostage for two years, threatening to kill me if she stopped making progress on the project. You see, she didn't want to do this to you, Rosa. It was never her intention for her research to be used in this way," he explained.

"But she let it happen. She didn't try and stop them. To preserve your life, hundreds have had to suffer." I couldn't abide her choice.

"I know you think she's selfish, but she really didn't know until it was too late. After they had impregnated the first round of girls, Apella dedicated all her time to caring for them, giving up her senior research role to become a nurse." I shuddered at the words 'first round'.

"After they let me go, we thought it would be over." Alexei sighed, showing his weariness. I did pity him.

"What? They let you go?" I was confused. I thought they had run away to save Alexei. Little bits of the truth kept getting lost. Their lies running through every conversation we'd ever had. "Why did you run, then?"

"We're not matched. We're too genetically similar and they were never going to allow us to use the technology to have a child together. If we were ever going to have a chance at a family, we had to escape," he admitted, the truth coming out at last. They ran just so they could have a baby.

"So Joseph and I…" I said, following a single blossom twirling to the ground.

"It is very rare for people from the same town to be matched, but the two of you are so genetically different, the computer selected you as an ideal match." He finished my thought for me. I laughed. It was not news to me that Joseph and I were different.

It didn't make much sense. Now that they were on the run, they would not have access to the technology needed to conceive that child they so desperately wanted—there was something missing from his story.

"So, what, the plan was to steal Clara's baby all along?" I could feel the rage boiling up inside me. How could this possibly make me sympathetic to her? I hated her even more. Had she let Clara die? I pushed Alexei and he fell backwards to the ground, jarring his arms to break his fall. The curtain of blossoms fell more rapidly to the earth as I pushed through them. I stood over him, considering calling for Joseph and Deshi to come help me, stalling as I watched him fumbling around, trying to find his glasses in the dirt.

"No, no. Apella loved Clara. She wanted to give her a chance with her baby. We knew it was a risk, but Clara was never going to leave your side," he stammered. It was slightly hilarious that this six-foot-two man was afraid of me. "Now that Clara's gone, she wants to try and make it up to her, care for Hessa as her own. Hessa would be a brother to our child."

"Apella's pregnant?" My voice ran high, coasting along a wave of disbelief and anger.

He just looked at me with his sickly blue eyes, so pale they were almost clear. He gave a diminutive nod, confirming my suspicions.

Ugh! I felt sick. Was I always to be surrounded by gooey-eyed pregnant women and expectant fathers? I put my foot to his chest, pushing down. It was unbelievable to me the things people were willing to sacrifice for a child. Lie, steal, risk lives. At the same time though, I knew I would have done anything to protect Hessa. I eased off, a little.

How many lives had she ruined so that she could have this child? Too many to count.

"So why aren't they scouring the wilderness to find you two traitors?" I asked. There were so many questions.

"Apella and I are inconsequential to the project now. They have everything they need to continue. My guess is, they don't believe us to be alive. Clara was on her fourth pregnancy, she was to be disposed of after this child and you...well."

I never got used to it. The way the Superiors treated us like we were nothing. Vessels to be used and disposed of. What was the purpose of all of this? Where was it leading?

"What about me?" I was afraid to ask.

His pale face twisted, his nose wiggling like a mouse. He ran his hand through his fair hair, coming up with a handful of flowers. Shaking them off, he told me, "Well, you were always considered slightly defective because of your extraordinary eyes. You were an experiment. The babies they are aiming for are more like Hessa, an interesting combination of characteristics, blue eyes, light brown skin. If your eye colors were passed to your child, you would no longer be useful." He put his head down, ashamed, as he should be.

I was defective, in the Superiors' minds. I stood taller. Out here, those things didn't matter. I searched myself. Letting my eyes follow one blossom, drowsily wandering to the earth, picking up minute winds and changing direction. I think I liked being defective.

"What about Joseph and Deshi? Won't they be looking for them?" I asked, thinking they must be missing us by now.

"I don't know," he said honestly.

I only had one more question. "What exactly is the Project?"

"The Project is the Woodlands way to become as they have always wanted," he wheezed. "To be All Kind. They use the samples to create the perfect race, a raceless race where every child will look almost the same. They have around four-hundred girls at the moment. Each girl can produce an indefinite amount of children."

I gulped. My mind was spinning.

"Do you remember when they took all the eldest children about eight or nine years ago?" I nodded. Of course I remembered. I drew a breath, which cut my lungs sharply.

"Well, that's where it started. Those children were the first test subjects."

I couldn't believe it. A lot of those kids were only well, kids.

"Apella worked very hard perfecting her methods. Her technology is flawless," he said. I tried to control my rolling stomach at the thought of what 'perfecting her methods' may have actually involved for those poor children. "And Este has taken that technology to another, dreadful level. There will be no need to continue interracial marriage or breeding. No need for breeding at all."

"I don't understand," I said, feeling like I was drowning in this information. I shook the droplets of horrible revelations from my hair.

"What about the children in towns now?" I thought of my mother and her baby.

Alexei, the bearer of bad tidings said, "They will be fine. But it is the end of families. Soon, they will announce no children can be conceived after a certain date. The one-child law was a way to wind things down and get the first test subjects. Now they will stop women having any babies outside of the Project." He paused, speculating, "Something in the water maybe…" His eyes wandered.

I guess they could. They had enough girls to produce the children required to make this work and they were always going to have a fresh supply.

I was reeling. Feeling faint. I dropped the apples and the nuts I'd collected. They fell with a dull thud in the dirt. I stepped off Alexei and he breathed a sigh of relief. I felt myself being sucked into a black hole, pulled backwards in time and space. Angered and frightened. The arrogance of the Superiors. It was insane. It was as I had always suspected. We were not protected—we were *controlled*. I felt a cloud of nausea hit me and I fell. Joseph caught me under my arms and sat me down on the ground.

They had come to find me.

I turned and vomited, physically purging myself of the information I had just heard. I wiped my mouth inelegantly.

"How long have you been standing there?" I asked.

"Long enough," Deshi replied, glaring in Alexei's direction. Joseph looked sympathetic, like he could see the two sides, his brows pulling together in consternation. So many lies. Part of me wished I hadn't heard the story. The thought of all those girls, walking in line like zombies. What a miserable future they had in front of them. I couldn't bear it.

"Where's Hessa?" I asked.

"He's with Apella," Deshi said.

My feelings for her were confused. She was weak and selfish, yes. But she was just a pawn in a much bigger and disturbing plan. I was not able to forgive her, I'm not sure I ever would, but I understood her better.

I said plainly, "I will think about what you asked."

Joseph handed Alexei his glasses, which he put on, dirt still clinging to the thin wire frames. He walked past me, without saying a word. I was tempted to say boo to his back, to see if he would scamper away.

Joseph lugged me to my feet. "I think you scared him," he said, lips crooked to the side, a wicked glint in his eye.

"Good."

I started to think that Joseph, Deshi, and I needed to make a plan—one that didn't involve Apella or Alexei.

31

A Couple

Lying with Joseph by the fire, it was hard to concentrate. I needed to ask him a question, but I kept forgetting my words. His lips on my neck, his hand running up and down my forearm, the gold took over and I lost my place. I grabbed his hand and stopped him, difficult as it was.

"I want to talk to you and Deshi." My eyes looked to Deshi and Hessa, sleeping peacefully, light snuffly snoring coming from the beautiful baby.

"Uhuh…" he managed, as he ran the tip of his nose along my earlobe, I shivered. "Stop it!" I whispered harshly, squeezing his wrist. He stopped.

"What is it?" he asked, unapologetic.

I looked over to make sure Apella and Alexei were asleep and whispered, "I think we should leave them."

I could feel him shaking his head behind me. "No, we can't. I know you don't like to think about it, but that baby is coming. We will need Apella's help when the day comes."

I thought about it. "But she pretty much left Clara to die. What makes you think she wouldn't let me die too?" If it came to that. I felt my body tensing.

Joseph loosened his hold on me and whispered, "You're not remembering things clearly. You were in shock. Think back to that morning." His voice was steady.

I didn't want to.

"I can't," I said, feeling my breathing getting quicker. It was a strangling feeling. The idea of remembering that day squeezed the air out of me.

He pulled me closer, warm arms encircling me, lulling me into a false sense of security. "I think you need to."

I closed my eyes. Memories of the darkness, the fire, the noise, filtered in. I remembered voices. They came back to me in snippets, pieces of time cut out and brought back to me, frayed and dirty.

"Come on, breathe."

Muffled thuds, compressions.

"What can I do?" A calm voice, strong. Joseph.

"Put your hand there," she said.

"Where?"

"Yes, there, push down. Hard. Harder than that. We need to slow the bleeding. Rub while you compress. There may be a clot."

"Thump, thump, thump."

The memory floated away, as did the voices, flying out the tunnel, softer and softer until there was silence.

"Oh!" I gasped. After I had given up and clung to the rails, disconnected. Apella had returned to try and save Clara.

Joseph was quiet for a while. He was stroking my arm. My eyes were heavy. I could feel myself drifting off. Then he stopped.

"You know, we had to pull her off Clara. She never gave up."

Sleep was yanked away from me, like losing a tug-o-war, burning the palms of my hands. "And you didn't either. But I did." I could feel the blade turning in on myself. I sat there and let it happen. I was useless.

"You can't do that. You can't blame yourself. You were in shock. You need to realize that maybe, no one was to blame," he said earnestly. It was so easy for him to see the best in people. I wasn't like that.

"You loved her too. You didn't go into shock." I sounded like I was accusing him, but that's not how I meant it to come out.

"I did. But, you...you loved her more. She was your sister."

I sighed. To me, that wasn't really good enough. And without Apella to blame, where could it go?

I felt this nasty, gulping feeling, like air going down the wrong hole.

Acid rising. Thinking about Clara was too painful. I turned my head, and whispered angrily, "Will you…just, please. Shut up!"

I was annoyed at him. He was stripping away my ammunition. My reasons. Apella still had a lot to answer for. I wasn't going to let her off the hook so easily.

"All right, easy," he said, "Just promise me you'll think about it."

I was silent. I knew he was right. I supposed being together also meant I should probably listen to him, at least some of the time. I didn't like the idea and I hardly slept thinking of ways around it, coming to no solution.

32.

The City

After days of walking though long grass and bendy saplings, the terrain changed. The line we were following sunk down like all of a sudden it was too heavy for the earth to shoulder it. We were between two raised platforms, running parallel to each other. Familiar concrete edged the platforms. I couldn't see over the top. It occurred to me that this was what it would be like for me. Loving Joseph would leave me stranded, stuck in the sunken part, both futures running parallel to each other, never touching, and me, never being able to see how it might play out. Jumping up, trying to look over the edge, never quite making it. Because the truth was, I didn't want either future.

I shook it out. *Just keep moving*, I thought, *don't be a coward now. Be stronger.*

We were approaching the ruins of a city.

The greenery still dominated, cascading up and over everything. But in between there was evidence of crumbling stone buildings. Rotted holes where the doors once were. Painted, metal window frames in yellow and peeling, aqua-painted walls. It was ghostly and dead.

The comforting sounds of the forest existed in the city, in a strange collision of what should and shouldn't be. So this was how our ancestors had lived. It was a confusing sprawl. There was no order to the layout of buildings. It was like people had built them wherever they pleased.

I was carrying Hessa on my back. He was gurgling, making little squeaking noises as we walked. Apella announced that she would like to scout around, see if there was anything useful left inside the buildings. I shrugged. *There was no harm,* I thought. Besides, I was curious to look around too. We decided to find a decent place to camp, make that our meeting place, and allow ourselves a couple of hours to explore.

We worked our way into the disintegrating city, the buildings getting higher as we went. After about half an hour of walking, we had pushed our way into several buildings, finding them all to be unsound, too dangerous to sleep in. I rolled my eyes as Alexei ran his hand over a doorframe, knocking in various places like he thought it would welcome him, tell him a secret and say you're safe here. I turned away. None of these building were safe. They were held together by the fact that no one had touched them in years. One sharp shove and they would collapse.

I scanned ahead and was shocked to see the silhouette of a man. My heart stopped. I tugged on Joseph's sleeve.

"Look over there," I whispered.

We both stared at it for a long time. The man never moved, never made a sound. He kept the same pose, one hand across his chest, the other outstretched as if asking for something. When we approached it slowly, we noticed there were plants growing up and around his legs. It was a statue.

I approached, sweeping back the vegetation from the iron man's feet to reveal a plaque. Vladimir Lenin. I guess he must have been an important man many years ago. Now, he was one of the only reminders that people had ever lived here, barely maintaining himself against the rule of nature.

The area around the statue was flat and sheltered by surrounding trees. Apella seemed anxious and readily agreed to making this the meeting place, before she and Alexei hurriedly disappeared between buildings.

With Hessa on my back and the two boys leading the way, we ventured forth. It was an eerie atmosphere and the stillness solicited silence. It felt like we were walking in a graveyard. Black windows stared at us like empty eyes, doorways opened like screaming mouths. I couldn't help wondering what had happened to all the people. Did they leave in a mass exodus, or did they suffer the fate of most of the ones left outside the

Rings? Bombed to bits.

Hessa's snuffling was the only sound to punctuate the silence. Gurgle, snuffle, breathe, stop breathing, breathe again. I kept timing my steps to his breath, walking in a sporadic, staccato motion, like I was stealing through the shadows on a secret mission.

"What's wrong with you?" Joseph looked down at me with a smirk. "Do you need to use the bathroom or something?" I must have looked funny, dancing around, fast step, slow step.

I rolled my eyes. "Nah, I'm just defective." They both looked at me like I was crazy. I swiped my arm at them. "I'll tell you later."

We seemed to be entering what was once a commercial area. There were remnants of signs with numbers on them, written in a language I didn't recognize, all loops and long lines, but some of the writing was numbers, prices. I stopped to investigate a light shining from within one of the openings. Joseph and Deshi were laughing at something up ahead, pointing through a broken window. Through what was left of a shop front, something sparkling caught my eye and I went to examine it more closely. Piles of gold and silver chains were tangled on the ground. Jewelry. There amongst them was a shiny white ball surrounded by sparkly crystals. I reached down to pick it up, mesmerized by its perfection, when weight hit me from above, followed by an unearthly shriek.

I screamed and saw Joseph and Deshi turn towards me in the corner of my panic, before something tore at my face. Then all I could see was blood. Hessa.

It was clawing at my back and I did the only thing I could think of. Stumbling backwards against a wall I tried to knock the thing off. It didn't work. It was caught in my hair, screeching and hissing, tearing chunks of it from my head. I reached my hands back, trying to punch it, finding fur and claws and teeth. Hessa was screaming. I fell to my knees disoriented. I couldn't see. The panic spread like a shock as I scrambled to protect my baby.

Somewhere in the chaos, I felt the weight lift and I was able to pull Hessa from my back and bring him to face me. I wiped my eyes, thankfully, it was only a cut above my eye that had blurred my vision. Hessa was mostly unscathed, with a few small scratches on his arms and face. The cradle had prevented the creature from getting to him with its teeth.

Joseph had pulled it from my back and now it was attacking him. It's muscled body frantically scratching and hissing as it tried to find a soft piece of flesh to bite into. Joseph had his hands around its hideous face, pulling back its open jaws.

"Do something!" I screamed to Deshi, who was standing there, mouth open wide in shock. He didn't move. I ran to Deshi and almost threw Hessa at him in my haste, scanning the area for some kind of weapon. There was nothing, just grass and rubble.

I decided I would just have to try to pull or kick it off. As I approached, Joseph yelled at me, "Get back!"

I wasn't going to watch him get mauled to death. I kept coming. I wasn't sure what I was going to do. I clenched my fists, ready to jump, when something flew past me and landed on the beast. It squealed, but kept snapping despite the stick protruding from its abdomen. I could see blood, but I couldn't tell whether it was Joseph's or the creatures, a mess of black spots and yellow fur, solid and really strong, with only a stump of a tail. I looked at the long, carved spear waggling around as Joseph wrestled with it. Where had it come from?

My question was answered as a tall girl with reddish blonde hair walked towards the cat-like beast, pulled the spear out, and stabbed it again, using the crude weapon as a lever to throw it off Joseph's body. I ran to him. He was alive but badly scratched and cut up. We both watched as she punctured the agonized creature again and again, blood oozing out of several wounds. It twitched and writhed one last time, a strangled yeow escaping its jaws as it died. Its tongue grotesquely hung out of its feral mouth.

She turned to face us and I recognized her immediately. I recalled her crazed face as she stabbed that poor White Coat through the eye. She didn't look hysterical or feral anymore but there was a wildness to her I didn't trust.

I noticed she was no longer pregnant. Her stomach was flat, as mine used to be. She was wearing tight, shiny pants and a low-cut top that barely contained her breasts. I suddenly felt conscious of my own appearance. Looking down at my round form sticking out of my grey cotton uniform I felt stumpy and ugly.

"Thank you," I managed to stammer. I envied her lithe body as she took quick steps towards us and introduced herself.

"I'm Careen." She shook her strawberry hair, the bloody spear still gripped tightly in one hand. We cringed away from her as she approached. "Sorry," she muttered as she dropped the spear with a clank.

"You're from the facility, right? I remember your face from the clearing. How'd you get here?" I said, trying to sound unthreatening.

Careen regarded me with a slow face, her mouth twisting into a broad smile. But I could tell she didn't recognize me. She bent down and pulled a knife from her hip. She talked as she worked, slowly carving the animal into small pieces, teasing the rough fur hide away from the muscle, and skillfully managing to keep it in one piece.

The knife scraped against bone, a sound that itched my teeth. "How was that purple smoke?" she said with her head down, "Weird, right?" I nodded. She tucked her hair behind her ear and paused, "Pretty colors though."

Joseph chuckled, "Yeah, we paid particular attention to making it look pretty."

I gave him a scornful look for mocking her and he put his arms up. "No really, that was all Desh."

Deshi grinned proudly. "Well, why create something that sophisticated and not make it aesthetically pleasing?"

Careen looked up from the carcass, narrowed her eyes for a second, and then blinked it away. "Anyway, I didn't know what was going on but, I guess, I must have known in my..." She pointed to the back of her head.

"Subconscious?" I volunteered.

She arched one perfect eyebrow at me. "If you say so."

"I saw you run into the forest...I..." I started to say but she cut me off.

"Yeah I ran. I ran forever, for miles and miles. The white coats were searching during the day so I climbed trees to avoid them and at night, I just kept running." She separated parts of the carcass into piles, her hands covered in dark blood. "I was like you," she pointed to my belly and shrugged, "but I didn't know." Her voice was light as air and she didn't seem upset when she said, "I buried it next to a nice tree. It was only this big," she indicated by pointing from her outstretched thumb to her finger how small it was.

I felt my stomach roll and my heart strain in sympathy at the thought of her delivering a baby on her own.

She leaned back on her heels and smiled. "So do you hunt? I hunt. I can help you," she said eagerly.

"You've already helped, Careen. You saved my life," Joseph said gratefully.

She stood and kicked her hip out, running her hand down his arm, she said, "Anytime, handsome."

Joseph regarded his arm with newfound fascination and then looked to me with his eyebrows raised.

I clenched my fists trying to get a handle on this odd girl. It was getting dark. I interrupted their little moment. "We'd better find the others; it's about time to meet."

Careen collected the meat and piled the dark flesh into the skinned hide. All that was left behind was a disgusting pile of guts and bones. I felt sick but I kept it down.

Hessa fell asleep despite his scratches. The cradle I built acted as a protective cage around his delicate body.

I helped Joseph to his feet and we made our way back to the statue, Careen walking next to Joseph, swinging the skin and meat by her side like she was carrying a shopping bag.

When we arrived, Apella and Alexei had already built a fire. Apella had her face buried in her hands. She was crying silently.

"I don't understand. They should be here," she said, unaware we were standing right there, listening.

"We are here," Joseph bellowed. He looked scary, crusted blood streaks across his face, blond hair matted. His shirt was torn to shreds and his arms were scratched.

Apella jumped. I got the feeling she wasn't talking about us. "Goodness! What happened to you two?" she exclaimed, quickly following it up with, "Where's Hessa? Is he all right?"

"He's fine," I said. Apella got out her pack and searched around for a suture kit.

"Wow! You've got your own doctor! Lucky," Careen said excitedly. She was weird. She said it like, *'Wow! You got the last piece of cake! Lucky.'* She seemed to get excited about the wrong things.

I introduced Careen to Apella and Alexei, explaining how she had saved us from the creature. Careen then dumped the remnants of the ugly cat by the fire. Apella left my face half-stitched up and turned to Careen, clasping both hands around the surprised girl's own dirty ones saying, "Are you one of them?" Apella's eyes were desperately hopeful. Careen looked at her, not confused exactly; her eyes were wide and mirroring Apella's excitement like she couldn't form her own reaction.

Joseph spoke before I could, "What are you on about, Apella? She's one of us; she came from the facility." Apella's mouth snapped shut but it was too late for her to cover herself with more lies. I've never seen Joseph so angry before, he held his face close to hers, his eyes intense as she leaned backwards in fear. We'd all had enough of them lying. Alexei went to assist, but Deshi held him back.

"I, I…" she stuttered, "I'm sorry. There were rumors that there were people here. Survivors from before the Woodlands were built. I was hoping we would find them and get some help."

Joseph released her from his gaze. "I didn't think you were that naive, Apella. There's no one here. There hasn't been anyone here for hundreds of years." He waved her off dismissively. She returned to stitching me up shakily and then Joseph reluctantly let her see to his wounds.

"What have you got there?" Alexei inquired, pointing at the pile of meat and fur. He used a stick to lift the hide, its hollowed-out face looking even scarier now than when it was alive. Its over-sized, pointed ears, no longer sitting upright, curled down over its forehead, looking like the top of them had been lightly dipped in black ink. Inspecting the pattern of the fur, he typed things into his reader. "A lynx, strong, cat-like animal, jumps down on its prey from above. Hunts alone." I didn't need a reader to tell me that.

Careen found a large, flat stone and placed it at the edge of the fire. She watched it closely as it heated up, touching it lightly every now and then. She then threw the cut-up meat on the stone. It sizzled, browning nicely and smelling good, but when she offered it to me, I couldn't eat it. The vision of her stabbing and disemboweling the foul cat was too fresh in my memory. She shrugged and moved on to the others. They all tried a piece. Joseph grinned, "Not bad, Careen," his mouth full of food. She smiled at him, her big blue eyes reflecting happiness at having pleased him.

After dinner, we talked, which we didn't usually do. Careen seemed to want fit several months' worth of talking into one breath. Never sitting down for very long, she jumped from topic to topic and then back again. Talking in circles.

"Yep, I'm from Iroko. I was one of the only American descendants in that town," she said proudly, bobbing her head up and down. I didn't understand her pride. In Pau, no one talked about their origins. She walked over to Apella and ran her fingers through the woman's straight blond hair. Apella recoiled. "Hmm, I like your hair. I wish mine would sit like that." I glared at her, her stupid hair looked perfect.

She stared at her fingers for a while and then started babbling again. I found her very hard to follow. She was like a puppet, animated and jerky. Her mouth moved too fast for her brain to catch up. Joseph indulged her, watching her, nodding his head like he understood her broken-word vomit. I only managed to pick out a few details. She was from Iroko and she had been in Classes for about a year when she was taken. She was going to be a Guardian.

Finally, late into the night, Deshi fed Hessa and put himself and the baby to bed. Careen cooed and fussed over the child and I prickled without meaning to. We offered her a sleeping bag but she said she was comfortable to lie by the fire. I wanted her covered up. Her body was everything I had been, and missed so much.

I made a pathetic show of climbing in with Joseph and snuggling extra close to his warm body. Unaware, he happily held me close as he drifted off. I couldn't sleep. My heavy eyes held open by imaginary matchsticks, a new person with disturbing talents making me uneasy.

I looked past the firelight; sure I could see yellow eyes floating in the distance. I propped myself up, peering into the darkness.

"It's ok," Careen said. "They won't come any closer to the fire, especially not with this many people here."

"What are they?" I asked

"Not sure, but there are a lot of them around the city," she replied, sitting back on her knees, bouncing up and down. "It's feels good not to be alone anymore," she admitted, showing a vulnerability unseen before now. "The forest, it's noisy and quiet at the same time, you know?" she said, covering her ears. I had to remind myself that she was just like me, but without Joseph, without anyone at all.

"You should try and get some rest. You're safe now," I said, trying to sound comforting.

I knew I wouldn't sleep very well. I felt less safe here than in the forest. I had fleeting dreams of yellow-eyed monsters chasing me, cornering me against a wall of stone, laughing and hissing, claws and fangs bared.

33

The Wall

I woke up to Hessa's 'knitting needles in my ears' scream. I dragged myself out of my bag, eyes half shut, and started preparing his bottle. Joseph was still dozing. I let him sleep. I walked to Deshi's rake-like form, but the baby was not there. Panic hit me, like a claw turning my heart sideways. The crying was coming from outside the circle of sleeping bodies. I kicked Deshi. He jumped up fast when he realized Hessa was missing.

"Where is he?" Deshi said, his normally smooth voice cracking around the edges. We followed the crying, sweeping our heads back and forth along the ground until we came upon a pair of long legs, attached to Careen, standing with her back to us, rocking on her heels, hushing the baby in her arms.

"What are you doing?" I asked accusingly.

She looked up from Hessa, eyes reproachful. "What? I just thought I would let you get some rest," she said as she handed Hessa to me.

"You can't just walk off with him like that without asking. You scared us to death!" I placed the teat of the bottle in Hessa's mouth, watching him eagerly drink the grey liquid, his unnaturally blue eyes peering over the rim.

"I don't see what the problem is," she snapped suddenly, clapping her hands on her toned thighs. "You know, he doesn't look much like you," she added, reaching out to touch his springy, black curls.

I pulled away. "That's because I'm not his mother," I said, handing Hessa to Deshi and standing side on to display my swollen middle.

"Oh, where is she?" Careen asked innocently, her mood swinging from aggression to sweetness in an instant.

"She's dead," I replied, wishing I didn't have to talk about it, feeling my heart tear a little at the memory of Clara.

"I'm so sorry," Careen said as she patted my arm gently. I stared down at her arm in confusion. I was starting to think she was a bit more than batty.

I shrugged her off and changed the subject. I needed some information from her anyway. I was thinking about the end of summer. We really needed to find or build shelter in that time, before winter hit. To do that, we needed some tools that I couldn't fashion from sticks. I asked her whether she had seen anything resembling a tool shed or shop.

"No, but there is a big building with different commercial sections. There might be something in there." Her eyes slid up my body with scrutiny. "We could get you some new clothes too."

I ignored her condescending assessment of my appearance and went back to tell the others my idea. There were arguments, of course. About one thing I was adamant—we *couldn't* stay in the city. We would get supplies and walk through to the other side, see what the terrain was like, and make a plan from there. For once, Alexei and Joseph agreed with me. Apella wasn't sure, still holding on to the ludicrous idea that there were people hiding somewhere in the rubble. There was no evidence that anyone had been here in hundreds of years. It was completely overrun by nature. Careen said she would go along with anything and Deshi pursed his mouth shrewdly and shrugged his shoulders. "It doesn't matter what I think."

I agreed to let Apella stay with Hessa by the fire. We took knives and Careen's spear with us. She said if we stuck to the more open parts, wider roads and lower buildings, the lynxes would not be a problem. The creatures with the yellow eyes only came out at night.

She led us back to the end of the railway line and over a bridge. It was a great stone and iron structure that had stood the test of time where other constructions had not. Its strong archways looped in and out of the water like a snake, reflecting against the water on this clear, sunny day. I stepped on tentatively, imagining it crumbling under my feet. Careen assured me it was safe. She had used it several times. Joseph took my hand and I relaxed a little.

Alexei was enthusiastic, to say the least, talking about the history of the town, a name I couldn't pronounce.

"Iratusk…what?" I said crankily.

"Irkutsk," Alexei corrected me. "Yes, apparently this bridge took ten years to build in 1950, quite impressive really given the technology of the time." I felt sorry that I had engaged him. He prattled on and Deshi and Joseph humored him, pretending to listen. Careen was bounding ahead like an excitable toddler. Peering over the edge every now and then, beckoning with her hands, "Hurry up, fellas. We're nearly there."

When we arrived at the other side, Careen stopped, trying to remember which direction to go. Like she flipped a coin in her head, she picked a street randomly and skipped off.

I found it hard to keep up, waddling like I was carrying several balloons full of water under my shirt. Thankfully, Joseph stayed with me. He curled his fingers in mine and we walked peacefully, forgetting, for a moment, where we were. If you didn't think about the death and destruction, the yellow-eyed creatures and the feral, attacking cats, the city was quite beautiful. On this side of the bridge, the buildings were larger. They climbed up to the sky, all carved stone and metal, with pillowy, rounded roofs made of copper turned green with age. These buildings bordered a wide, stone-paved street that had lanterns attached to iron poles sticking out of the footpath.

The other three rounded a corner ahead of us and for a few minutes we were alone. I stopped for a breath. Putting my hands in the small of my back, I stretched backwards, staring at the sky, watching the clouds blow south with speed. When I straightened, he swiftly bent down and put his lips to mine, transferring the heat of gold and electricity through my mouth and down my spine. I kissed him back briefly, smiling as I extricated myself from his arms.

"You know, with all this romance, I'm liable to faint," I said, rolling my eyes as I put the back of my hand to my forehead.

"I'll always catch you," Joseph said with a wink.

I fanned my face. "Oh, sir, you're too much!" and I succumbed to giggling. Joseph laughed, slipping his hand around my waist and giving me a gentle squeeze. The sun was high and the city looked less frightening, more like a scenic ruin in this light.

A dark face poked out from behind the corner. Squinting in the sunlight, Deshi said, "Guys, you need to see this," and then his head disappeared. I would have run, but in my current state the most I could manage was a brisk walk. We rounded the corner and were faced with a towering structure of latticed metal and broken glass. On the top of the building were six-foot-high letters, spelling out words I didn't understand. We caught up to the others as Careen was climbing up the concrete stairs that led into the building.

"Are you sure it's safe?" Deshi asked nervously. His voice echoed around the tall entrance foyer we were standing in.

"It's fine, I've been in a couple of times. It's well worth it, come on." Careen tugged on Deshi's shirt and pulled him toward some grated metal stairs, her long legs making easy work of them. She bounded up, her short hair swaying softly as she jumped from stair to stair. They led onto one another in a zigzag, reaching at least six or seven stories high.

We climbed two sets and then Careen dragged us down a dusty hallway. Shady entrances were cluttered with rubbish on every side. She grabbed Joseph's hand, pulled him through a gap in the rubbish, and they disappeared into the darkness. Deshi turned on his torch. The light cut a line through the dark, illuminating metal racks from which strange items of clothing were hanging: shiny plastic bodices, shimmering pants, revealing tops, and underwear in plastic packets. What provocative clothes the people wore back then. Careen held up a black plastic top on a hanger, tight and low cut. "Here, try this on," she said blithely.

I gagged, "There is no way I would fit into that!" Nor would I want to. It looked more like underwear than clothes to wear in public.

"What about this?" Careen suggested, holding up what looked like a see-through nightdress. All made of nylon and plastic. It seemed it was the only material that had held together. Then it hit me, what kind of shop this was. I had been in one back in Pau, when I turned twelve and my mother took me to buy a bra. That shop was more dainty cotton and lace but the idea was the same.

"Let's save that kind of thing for after the baby's born," Joseph said, grinning his stupid head off.

I froze. I had thought a lot about how our relationship would change after I had the baby but I hadn't even considered the physical side of things. I could feel the blood racing to my face.

Deshi and Joseph were chuckling away. Alexei looked extremely uncomfortable, propping and then re-propping his elbow against the doorway. Careen looked oblivious to the underlying implications of what Joseph had said.

"It's all right, Rosa," Joseph said between fits of laughter. "I was only joking." I stormed passed them both, pushing their shoulders, hard. I wanted to knock their heads together but it would only make them laugh more. I stood in the cluttered hall, looking back and forth. Surely, there had to be something more useful in here other than plastic sex clothes.

Picking up a pack of underwear wrapped in plastic off the dusty floor, I realized that was what I needed to be looking for. I rummaged through other shop openings and found some cotton, button-down, shirts sealed in plastic. I grabbed one for each of us and kept looking. I found leather bags that were still mostly intact, some socks, and even some leather gloves. I searched around for something for Hessa and found a few packets of socks, a jumpsuit that looked way too big and some singlets. It would be good to give him some clothes so he didn't have to be swaddled in cut-up blankets all the time. It seemed the people of yesterday were big on wrapping their clothes in plastic.

I shoved it all in the leather bags I had found. I could see the boys had calmed down and were doing the same thing, tossing clothes and other useful items into shiny nylon bags slung over their shoulders. But I couldn't find any tools.

I worked my way right to the back of one of the stores, wading my way through a sea of over-turned racks and rubbish. It smelled like dust, like old death. Right at the back, behind a filthy, laminated counter covered in paper and metal coins, I found what I was looking for, a red metal door with a plastic plaque on the front that said 'Utulidad.' It was locked. I called for the boys and they worked at kicking it in. Booted bangs, the only noise this place had entertained in a long time.

We were rewarded for our persistence. Inside was a small room with a toolbox full of useful items. Mounted on the wall was another red box. Inside was exactly what I wanted. I smashed the glass with my hand wrapped inside a leather bag and pulled the shiny axe head from the box. The handle disintegrated as soon as I touched it, but I could make a new one.

We made our way out, looking ridiculous, like over-burdened mules. Wearing some things, and strapping the bags around ourselves as best we could. Careen emerged last, twirling a tight, hot pink top on her finger and gripping a large hunting knife in her other hand.

She leaped down the stairs like a gazelle, shoved her serrated knife in her pocket, and peeled off her top in front of everyone. She dropped the grimy, bloodstained one on the ground with distaste and stood bare chested in front of us. Her pale face showed not even a flicker of awareness that her nakedness might make us uncomfortable. I stared wide-eyed at her while the boys averted their eyes. She shimmied into her new top and adjusted her cleavage. She looked and behaved so differently to me that I couldn't quite digest what I was looking at.

We walked back to the campsite, our progress slowed by our new possessions. Along the way, I dropped some of the less important things, sparkly hair ties and clips, a thin silk scarf wrapped in plastic, all useless. Joseph carried the small toolbox; I carried the treasured axe head.

Again, we lagged behind the others by a few hundred meters. I bumped hips with Joseph's affectionately, folding my hands inside my shirt anxiously. I wanted to ask him something but I was afraid of how it would come out.

"What do you think of Careen?" I asked nervously.

Joseph paused and rubbed his chin. "She's all right, why?"

"I mean, what do you think of her, really?"

He stopped walking and turned to face me, "Rosa, what is this about?"

"Well, she's quite attractive, isn't she?" I said, staring at my stomach, my feet imagined, as they hid under my enormousness.

He chuckled, a deep vibration that I wished I could jump into, a pool of sound. "I suppose..."

"Yeah, I thought so," I said, disappointed. I wanted him to say she was hideous, or that he didn't even notice her looks at all.

"Is this about the nightdress? I was being stupid, just joking," he assured me.

"No. It's not that. Believe me, I'm used to you being stupid," I teased.

"Then, what are you worried about?" he said, smiling irresistibly. My heart swelled and skipped.

"Just that," I said, touching his mouth, tracing the smile on his lips.

"Rosa, I rescued you from underground, I fought a lynx for you, tried to wrestle a bear for you. How can you possibly doubt my feelings for you now?" He laughed.

"I'm glad you find it so funny," I said as I punched his arm.

"Ouch!"

He calmed down and took my hand, trying to be serious, "Rosa, you are the only one for me, and whether you see it or not, you are beautiful, pregnant or not, ok?"

"Ok," I said dubiously.

He shifted uneasily, not sure how to approach. "Can I ask you something?" he asked, his beautiful eyes gazing into my own 'defective' ones.

"Anything."

He reached out his hand, hovering it over my bulging stomach. I had been afraid he would want to do this. I was surprised it had taken him so long to ask. I urged the leech not to kick. "Can I...?"

I sighed and nodded.

His warm hand circled the top of my belly. I allowed it for a few seconds and then I asked him to stop. It made something tighten in my chest, a guilty feeling I couldn't explain. He did stop, but I could tell it made him sad.

We had enough problems to worry about, without me adding jealousy to the list.

34

The Plan

Iwas deep in thought as we wound our way back to the campsite, barely noticing the leaning buildings, barely hearing Careen's inane chatter. The details of the city melted away like running paint colors.

My hand swung absently in Joseph's as I contemplated our situation. We'd been following Apella and Alexei blindly, partly because they were the adults and they had a plan. But I was starting to learn that age did not automatically mean someone was wiser. After the ridiculous revelation that they'd been searching for people living in the ruins of the city, I doubted their ability to lead, to make good decisions.

We were now close to the border between old Russia and Mongolia. We could keep walking but to what end? If we went on indefinitely, the seasons would change and winter would kill us. With no shelter or stocks of food, we wouldn't survive. There had to be a better plan than this.

I tapped my belly, feeling the hardness of it, the unbreakable shell that kept a barrier between Joseph and me, between my feelings for him and my feelings about our instant little family. In two months' time, I would be having this baby whether I liked it or not. I didn't want to do that on the side of a cliff or in a cave, half-frozen and starving. I shook my head, my hair falling in a curtain around my face. No. We needed to sit down and work it out together.

It was dusk when we arrived back at the camp. The grey light was greyer still for the disappointing fact that Apella had not lit the fire. She sat huddled under a blanket, her blonde hair shining like a vague, dusty halo, rocking Hessa. I rolled my eyes at her incompetence. One of our biggest concerns should be that Hessa wouldn't survive a journey through snow and ice.

We threw our new belongings in a pile just outside the circle of logs. The shiny stack of new possessions made us ragged and grimy by comparison. If I'd had the energy I would have changed, but all five of us collapsed on the logs, food the only thing on our minds. Deshi coaxed a fire from the dying coals and I scrounged for food. I couldn't find much in the way of edible plants. I screwed up my nose, it would be grey sludge tonight.

After we ate, I announced my concerns.

Clearing my throat of the grey slime that seemed to cling to the inside of my mouth like candle wax, I said, "What happens after tonight? I mean, what's the plan for the next part of our journey?"

Alexei held up his map and traced his finger along the route we had already travelled. We had walked so far. "I think we have another couple of weeks of walking left to do and then we will be in Mongolia, or what used to be Mongolia," he said.

My legs ached at the thought of it. "And then what?" I asked. "What's in Mongolia? Is there something there you're not telling us about?" I searched their eyes, looking for the lie. Apella kept her eyes on Hessa; Alexei leaned away from my gaze. "We haven't seen the choppers in weeks. No one's looking for us. Why should we keep going? Why not prepare ourselves for winter near here?"

Joseph and Deshi nodded in agreement. We were so weary and it would only get harder as the weather changed. Careen looked confused, her pale face serenely blank. Her eyes flicked to the nodding boys and she mimicked their movements. I had a feeling she would go along with anything if it meant she wouldn't be alone.

"We can't be sure they are not still looking for the boys," Alexei argued. "Deshi in particular was very valuable to the Classes."

Deshi ran one hand over his arm smoothly. "I'm willing to take the risk," he said plainly.

"Me too," Joseph chimed in. "Rosa's right. We can't keep walking, hoping that someone will save us, or that we'll find decent shelter before winter comes. We need to start preparing now."

Apella looked desperate, she was going to lose, her rounded eyes begging someone to agree, her voice on edge, "I'm sure they are close. If we keep looking, we might find a settlement."

I scoffed. "You need to give up on this idea. No one is coming to save us." I squeezed my hands into fists. I wished I was wrong. I wished there was a humble settlement right around the corner where welcoming strangers would invite us in, but we were alone. We couldn't follow an old map or hold onto the crazy idea that someone was coming to help us anymore. We had to think about survival.

I stood up, the chill in the air hinting at what was to come. I knew this was what needed to be done. "Tomorrow morning we will walk out of this ruin and search for a good place to make our own settlement."

There was silence and the clawed hand of doubt scratched its way along the dirt towards me. Apella and Alexei could go on without us. I wasn't sure I cared what they did. Remembering Clara's labor, she pretty much did it all on her own anyway. Until the end anyway. I shuddered.

Joseph put his arm around me, instantly warming my shivering body. "You're making big plans. You really think we can do it?" he challenged.

A sense of purpose was blooming in me, like so much blood it seeped and spread. I honestly didn't know if this would work, but of the two choices, this made more sense to me.

35

Yellow Eyes

Sometime in the night, I felt a strong chill. I shuffled around in my sleeping bag, thinking I had rolled to far from the fire. Joseph stirred but did not wake. He muttered something and put his hand on my waist. I looked to the center and saw nothing but the spotted orange glow that clung to ash. The fire was out. I heard scratching, or something being dragged across the other side of the campsite. I breathed in slowly, trying not to make any noise. As I exhaled, a glowing light just past the fire froze, yellow eyes shining in the moonlight. I jabbed Joseph sharply in the ribs. He made a startled, snorting noise as he awoke and, whatever it was, became smaller as it retreated but didn't disappear.

"Joseph," I whispered, "there's a yellow-eyed thing out there." I pointed to the eyes, grabbing his head and aiming it in the creature's direction. "The fire, Careen said it scared them." Joseph's body went rigid and he jumped out of the sleeping bag like a spring.

We woke the others and together we stoked the coals, throwing kindling and logs on until it was roaring, our skin looking golden in the flames. Behind the statue of the man with the outstretched hand, I saw the flick of a long tail and black and white stripes. I heard scuffling. I drew breath in slowly, weighing up the threat. My eyes searched the darkness anxiously and found several pairs of yellow eyes floating like a disturbing set of stringed lights about fifty meters from where we were.

"Can you see that?" I pointed in their direction.

Joseph nodded, jaw tight, looking unnaturally magnificent in his shredded shirt. The fire glazed his skin gold, his muscles tensed and ready to fight.

The eyes were joining with other eyes, forming a semi-circle, closing in slowly from the western side of our campsite, like a ring of candles, flickering as they blinked. Apella panicked and darted behind Alexei, the whip of her grey shirt the only evidence she was there. I watched her in disgust, the desire to throw her to them was hard to suppress. We burned everything in sight, watching the flames climb higher and higher. Our faces and hands charred red from the heat but we couldn't step back. Deshi and Joseph armed themselves with the knives. I waited to see Careen striding forward, spear in hand, but she wasn't there. I gulped, horrific visions of her torn-up body sprawled somewhere clawed at my mind. Where the hell was she?

The eyes stalled at the sight of the fire, there was a faint cry like a 'whoop' and then a chorus of whoops filtered through the air above our heads. Slowly the eyes edged away from sight. Whatever they were, there were at least thirty of them and my guess was there were probably more. Joseph's hand curled over my shoulder and I set my head down on it. "We can't stay here," I whispered, feeling the panic ease with his touch. He squeezed his hand and nodded, eyes distant.

As the grey morning approached, we were shocked to discover how close they had come while we were sleeping. All around us were the remnants of our belongings, things dropped as they were dragged off into the night. These elusive creatures seemed intelligent and organized. Unlike the wolves, they hadn't just destroyed things; they had taken items of interest and discarded others.

I was just about to start searching for the grisly remains of Careen, when I heard a loud thump and she came strolling out of the wooded area to the east of our campsite, eyes bright. Her attitude was casual, unfettered, and she was surprised that we were angry at her, or even that we worried about her safety.

She admitted she had seen the creatures approaching and had jumped up into the closest tree, spending the night there.

"Thanks a lot for the warning," I said, glaring at her.

She shrugged, unconcerned. She was used to looking after herself. It seemed a very foreign idea that she should assist anyone else. I thought back to her behavior when we first met, suspecting it was less about heroics and more just the fact we were between her and her kill.

"Next time, it would be good if you could let us know there are animals stalking us before you scale the nearest tree." I tried to say it calmly but it came out sounding more biting.

She looked at me, her eyebrows drawn together like I had just snatched a sweet from her hand. Tucking her hair behind her ear and cocking her head to the side, she chirpily replied, "Sure thing!"

I looked at her like she was something other than human. She was so strange. I didn't like the idea of being holed up with her over winter.

As we packed up, we noticed Alexei had lost his reader. The grey box was missing as well. I wondered why the animals would want with that. I imagined them preparing meals and it made my hairs stands on end. This place was starting to really give me the creeps. It was definitely time to leave.

Hessa cried out and I felt a pang of anxiety, wondering how we were going to feed him.

Deshi searched frantically for the box, with Hessa tucked under one arm, the baby screaming until his face went ashen and his lips were purple.

Careen turned around and retrieved the box from under a flat, grey rock at the base of the tree she had dropped down from. "Are you looking for this?" I took a step towards her, my feet pressed hard against the earth, ready to tear her throat out. But Joseph's arm was in front of me, blocking my path. "Let it go," he muttered through his teeth.

I did, just this once, noting she was someone to watch closely.

Deshi snatched the box from a baffled Careen and quickly prepared a bottle for the screaming child.

As Deshi fed Hessa, I took up the capsule and made some adjustments.

Attaching one-foot long, pointed spears to the top part that encased his head. It made him look like he was wearing a crown, but it would protect him from any animal jumping down on him.

Sadly, we had lost most of the clothes we had found and I didn't want to go back to get more. There was one shirt left which I offered to Joseph. It was too big for me. He thanked me and removed his torn t-shirt. I made an idiot of myself, swallowing a gasp at his well-muscled chest. When he pulled the shirt over his head, I turned my back to him. I didn't want him to see me blushing.

"All right, Jo," Deshi smirked, as Joseph did up the remaining buttons. "We all know you're gorgeous. Stop showing off and start moving." He clapped his hands together smartly and flicked his head away from the campsite.

We made our way back to where we had left the train tracks two nights ago. We moved quickly, the urge to explore was gone. Apella was still unsure and Alexei had to half-drag her as she continually swiveled her head around, looking in doors and searching rooftops for evidence of people.

We followed the tracks out of the city and headed south-east, deciding to put at least a day's walk between us and the yellow-eyed beasts before looking for a place to shelter. Joseph scooped me up in his arms before I had time to argue.

"You look tired," he said

"Gee, thanks. You know? So do you," I said, poking at the dark circles under his eyes.

He pulled his head away from my touch and grinned. "Yeah well I'm bigger and stronger. I can cope better."

"The way I'm going I'll be bigger than you by mid-summer!" I joked.

He laughed. "Hmmm, you are getting a bit heavy." He pretended to drop me, catching me at the last second.

I squirmed unenthusiastically. "Well then, put me down."

He paused and shook his head, blond curls settling into their delicate weave. "Nope," he said as he took big strides, leading the way.

I put my head on his chest, the pressure of the last few days squeezing me like a concertina, making the air around me soft and dozy. I was pleased with my decision. It was going to be hard. *Hard, hard work*, Mr. Gomez would say. But it felt better knowing we had a purpose, a strategy. I knew my knowledge of building was going to be useful. I could help. I could do something other than grow fatter and more uncomfortable every day. I listened to Joseph's heartbeat, deep in his chest, and I pushed the doubt down with it. Pushed down the feeling I could be wrong, that it would be too hard. We had to keep moving forward. We had to try.

I let the dozy feeling wrap around me like a loose bandage and daydreamed about what it might be like to have a home. A home with Joseph and, of course, Hessa and Deshi. Could I make room for another in our little family? For the first time, I opened my mind to the possibility. It was a hazy dream. I could see the four of us; the fifth member was a sketchy grey cloud I couldn't quite put a face to. Up until now, the leech was not even allowed to exist in my dreams. But it was pushing away at them now, infringing on the edges. Making it presence known.

36

Build

After a couple of days walking, we started scouting for a position for a hut and store. I put together a rough house plan, using the surrounding timbers as a starting point. We needed somewhere flat, which possibly backed onto a hill, and hopefully faced the morning sun.

Low, grass-covered mounds dominated the scenery like a voluptuous woman had laid down and pulled a green blanket over her body. Small patches of woods sprouted up like green-brown birthmarks on the land. It was a gentle and inviting, although I could imagine it was very different once covered in snow.

We chose to build against the shelter of a low hill. It was stupidly idyllic, with a creek running through the valley and plenty of well-shaped adolescent pines that would make perfect logs for a cabin. The construction would be simple. The boys would cut the trees and drag them to the site. I would carve the notches in the logs and shape wooden pegs to secure each log to another. Apella and Careen would pack every crevice with mud and collect stones for a fireplace. At this, Apella's smooth as silk face scrunched up unappealingly. I smirked at her and rubbed my hands together. Hands that were itching to get dirty.

Once we started, we quickly got into a rhythm, working in unison to achieve this one goal. Apella stopped talking about survivors and settlements. Deshi, Joseph, and I took turns caring for Hessa while working and Alexei flapped about, occasionally being useful, but more often than not just getting in the way.

Hessa was changing daily. Changing from a baby to a little person. As we worked, he would lie on a rug and happily gaze at the sky, kicking his chubby little legs in excitement. He had his mother's temperament, always smiling, hardly ever crying. He adapted easily.

We walked into the forest every day. It was wonderful not to be trudging down the same line. We meandered down different paths, stopping whenever we pleased to examine something or collect some food. I started to teach Joseph about the different fruits and nuts we needed to store. He wasn't a very good student, listening to half of what I had to say before pinning me against a tree, burying his face in my hair and kissing my neck. Driving me crazy. He was very good at this, and I was very good at being distracted. To a point. There always seemed to be a moment where something would clamp down inside me and I had to stop him.

The cabin was nearly finished. It had been two and a half weeks and the basic structure was done. I stood back and appraised it, casting my eyes over the dark wood and dripping mud. It was a bit wonky, leaning into the wind like it was listening for a secret, but it was solid, strong. It had no shutters or a door yet, but it would be comfortable. The fireplace was half-finished, made of stones and clay mud. I tapped my finger on my chin absently; I needed to ask Careen to focus less on hunting and more on the fireplace. We needed that done if we were to stay warm over winter.

The sun pulled back like an eyelid over a blue iris, streaks of light skipping over the craggy bark of the pine log I was planing. I ran my hand over it, enjoying the splintering feeling, the coarseness. My arm tugged backwards and I lost balance. Joseph pressed his hands into my back and steadied me. I squinted up at his shadowed face. "Want to go for a walk?" I nodded eagerly. The time for us to be alone was coming to a close;

there would be no privacy when we were holed up in the cabin for days or weeks at a time.

I looked down as we walked, I couldn't see my feet anymore, but I noticed the leaves were starting to change color and drop to the forest floor. The seasons were changing. I scooped up various plants and seeds as we moved, examining them in my palm. Tossing some away and stuffing others in the brown leather bag I had brought with me from the ruined city. I found my knowledge was pretty limited. I would bring things back to the hut; we'd examined them, weigh up the risk of trying them, but most we threw away. We could do nothing if one of us was poisoned.

Joseph bent down and picked up a pinecone off the ground. He swung around, asking me the question he always asked, "Eat or don't eat?" His eyes glinting with mischief.

"Eat," I replied.

Joseph opened his mouth to bite the pinecone.

"Not like that," I laughed. I took it from his hand and showed him how to pull the edible nuts out of the woody, brown spikes. I handed him one. He ate it, screwing up his nose.

"I think I prefer the grey stuff," he said, scratching his arm unconsciously.

"Well, you better get used to it. If there's no light, it will be nuts and berries," I lectured, shaking my index finger at him.

He wrapped his hand around my finger and bent his head down to catch my eyes. I shivered under the intensity of his gaze. "Don't forget the dried meat," Joseph teased, knowing it would annoy me for him to talk about Careen's contribution to our food stores. She proved to be quite a good hunter, bringing back rabbits and birds, which she carved up with frighteningly good skill, drying strips of them over the fire. She also collected piles of pelts, which would be useful for warmth over winter. I appreciated everything she did, but I found her intimidating. In the back of my mind, I worried about how much she seemed to enjoy the killing. At least, she had stopped rubbing herself up against Joseph like a cat starved of attention. Mostly because he had told her, kindly but firmly, that he wasn't interested. I guess it was better than the solution I had played out in my head, where I jumped on her and scratched her eyes out. Joseph only found my irritation with her amusing and he seemed to enjoy bringing it up just to get a reaction out of me.

"You can't just eat meat all the time," I snapped.

"I know, I know," he said, arms up in surrender, the sleeves of his shirt pulling back to reveal his forearms.

"What's that?" I asked, grabbing his arm and inspecting it more closely. It was red and bumpy, the skin angry and raw. I ran my fingers lightly over the sore flesh and he sharply withdrew, wincing in pain.

"It's nothing. I think my skin's just irritated from all the sawdust. My boss is such a slave driver, you know," he said with a smirk, jerking his sleeve down and pulling me towards him.

I was concerned, but as soon as he started tiptoeing his fingers up my arm, I forgot what I was thinking. Joseph had become very good at avoiding my huge stomach as his fingers meandered up my arm and found their way to my hair. Pulling my head gently to the side, he parted my lips with his own. My head filled with gold, pushing logical thoughts out of my head like loose slips of paper.

After a while, he pulled his head back and I felt his lips gently brushing my ear. "I'm so impressed with you," he whispered.

"Really, why?" I asked, not really caring for the answer, just craving his lips on my ear again.

"You've come so far."

I froze, no longer moving towards him. Feeling my body reluctantly, but instinctively, pulling away from his touch. A beautiful oak tree leaned down to hear us, its orange and yellow leaves lighting the branches up like flame.

"What does that mean?" I asked defensively, clenching my fists.

Joseph eyes fell. He scratched his arm again and let his arms fall to his sides. "I'm sorry. I didn't mean anything by it. Rosa, I don't want to fight."

I took another step back, my feet crunching and then squelching into the dirt as I stomped, vibrating with anger. "Just explain to me what

I have done to impress you so much?" I spat.

"I just meant, you've changed, you're more open, you've let me in."

He stumbled over his words, trying to diffuse me. He held out his hand but I smacked it away. I hated when he tried to 'manage' me like this. It made it even harder to control my anger. It rose in me like an over boiling pot, bubbles surging up and burning me with hot steam. I was of two minds, one part of me trying to calm down but the other, overwhelming part, held onto the anger and pushed it forward.

"I didn't realize I was so behind before," I said sarcastically, knowing I was taking it too far, but unable to stop myself. As I grew in size, so did the strength of my changing emotions. I was fuming, although not entirely sure why. "You can't change me, you know, this is it." I was stamping the earth like a child having a tantrum, smattering the colored leaves with dirt.

Joseph's expression changed from apologetic and calm to angry, his mouth pursed, eyebrows knotted, a temper starting to boil up to join mine.

"Believe me, I know that," he said loudly, his deep voice booming through the forest. I leaned away, shocked; he had never really raised his voice to me. I knew I had gone too far, I knew it, so why didn't I stop? I pushed his chest. He didn't move. So I turned my back to him and uttered, "You need to leave, now," even though I didn't want him to go anywhere. I was desperate for him to stay.

"Fine, you get your way." He walked away from me, his boots thumping through the forest loudly. But as his furious form retreated through the trees, I caught him mutter, "You always do."

My face fell and tears brimmed over, splashing down my face. I willed him to turn around, to see my sorry face, but he never did. He just stormed through the soft undergrowth, trampling plants and scratching his arm furiously as he went, until he disappeared from sight.

I looked through the spaces between the branches of the oak tree. Little framed windows of white light sparked and shot down to the forest floor. *What's wrong with me, Clara? Why can't I be happy? Why am I always pushing him away?*

I thought back to the day when I was eavesdropping on Joseph and Clara's conversation. "She trusts you, she just doesn't trust herself," she'd said. She was right. The closer it got to my due date, the more I worried about my feelings. I didn't trust that I could make it work. I didn't understand why he had faith in me, when everything I loved turned to dust. I fell to my knees, placing my hands in the dirt. This was what came of loving me. I picked up a handful and watched it trickle to the ground. Dust. Tears turning to mud as they merged with the ground.

I found Joseph stacking stones for the fireplace, the clink of rock on rock interrupted by his slight heaves. I touched his arm and he swung around, startled. When he saw it was me he relaxed a little, but I could see he was still hurt.

"I'm sorry," I admitted, drawing the apology out of my mouth like a heavy bucket from a well. It was difficult, but I didn't want him leaving without trying to work this out. In truth, I wanted to convince him not to go.

His surprise was hurtful and obvious. "Wow, ok, I thought it would take a little longer than that," he laughed, that familiar smile returning to his face.

I moved closer, pressing my fingers to his chest. "I'm just a mess. The hormones make me crazy. I think, as we get closer to the leech…I mean, the baby being born, the more I worry about how things will change," I confessed, heart jumping. I was wracked with uncertainty, feeling stupid to have put myself in this situation in the first place.

Joseph put his hands on my shoulders and looked me in the eye. "I'm scared too, Rosa. Don't you get it? I don't want to lose you. I don't know what will happen when the baby comes. I'm not sure how I will feel, or how you will feel." His eyes left mine and he looked past me. "Sometimes I worry this was a mistake." I went cold, sharp shivers shooting through me.

I hated how desperate I sounded when I said, "It's not. Whatever happens later, I will always be glad that I had this, no matter how painful the rest might be. Don't give up on me yet, Joseph. You know, you can't always predict what I might do," I said, smiling sadly.

"Oh, I know that!" he laughed as his arms slipped from my shoulders to my waist and he pulled me to his chest.

"So, it's not a mistake?" I asked, looking up into his eyes.

"Oh, it definitely is!" he said, grinning, "But I don't care."

I wanted to say, *then don't go*, but I knew it wouldn't change his mind. He wasn't as stubborn as me, but he was pretty close. I thought of going with him but I would only make them take longer. Instead, we climbed the hill that rose from behind our little cabin to watch the sunset. Joseph had to push me up the hill, but it was worth it to get to the top. We could see the mounds of grassy hills; rocky patches sliding into creeks and wooded forests. It felt like we were the only humans that had been here in hundreds of years. We probably were.

The sky was cloudy, which made for a more spectacular sunset. Colors of purple pierced bright oranges and deep dark reds the color of blood. We sat in the wet grass and watched the sun slip below the hills. I leaned into his chest, his warm arms wrapped around my shoulders, his shirt, uncharacteristically, buttoned at the wrist. His legs sprawled on either side of me and I felt cocooned, safe in my space between his chest and his worn, dirt-caked boots. I sighed at the state of them. All that walking. We had both come so far.

I placed a hand on his knee and he shifted slightly. "Don't go," I said, feeling tears welling. Panic and hope mixed together. I was annoyed that I said it. I didn't want to be this person. This pathetic wreck, so tied to him. I was angry too. He opened me up, and now he was leaving, again. I felt like I would stay open until he returned, a throbbing wound bound together loosely by dirty string. I could have been happy before, but he changed what happiness meant.

"Rosa, don't worry. I won't be gone long. It'll only be a couple of days. It will give you a chance to miss me," he said, but his cheek was unconvincing.

I closed my mouth. Anything I said would only sound like begging, and it wouldn't make any difference anyway. I was full of misgivings about this trip and I knew the next few days would be unbearable.

We stayed there for hours, talking and laughing. He held my hand and I kissed his fingers one by one. He nuzzled his now scruffy face in my hair and caressed my neck. We were determined to enjoy this last night together. Somewhere, the panic lifted and I floated away on a cloud of happiness and tiredness.

I only had a slight awareness I was moving, my head fuzzy from sleep. He lowered me into my bed, now propped up off the floor by fur and dried grass. It was warm and comfortable. I sunk into it, awaiting the extra warmth of his body beside my own, the comforting sound of his slow, even breathing. But all I could hear was a faint clattering. I opened my eyes drowsily to see him stuffing things into his backpack. I opened my mouth but he beat me to it, whispering, "The sooner I leave, the sooner I will be back."

"No," I begged, finding my voice. I pulled myself up, fighting sleep. "Please. At least leave in the morning." My voice stripped down, withering and pathetic.

"All right," he sighed, placing his pack against the wall. He climbed into the bag with me and I snuggled into his chest. I wished I could hide his pack or find some other way to stop him or delay his leaving. I fell asleep, concocting ideas of how I would convince him to stay in the morning.

When I opened my eyes to the beginning of morning, Joseph and Careen were gone.

37

Break

There are so many things I didn't understand. Needs and wants I didn't even know I had. Not until it was too late.

The next two days were absolute agony. When I realized he'd left, I was furious, throwing things around in a fit of anger. When I calmed down, I found a scrawled note on a scrap of wood.

'Sorry I left without saying goodbye. Knew you would make me stay. Back soon. I love you. Joseph.'

I threw it out the window, the scrap slicing through the air like a saw blade. Feeling tethered to it like it was my last shred of hope, I ran outside and retrieved it. I held it close to my heart while the others watched, feeling like an idiot, but having no other tangible thing to hold onto. I was so worried. There were so many dangerous things out there. I thought about the wolves, the yellow-eyed animals. I shuddered. It was terrifying to think of him being attacked again.

I turned my focus on Hessa and finishing shutters for the window. Distraction was the key. The fireplace was finished and drying. I laid Hessa next to me as I used the axe to plane down planks of wood ready to attach to each other for window shutters. He watched me with his perfect blue eyes, squinting as the sun grabbed around my shadow. He held his hands in front of his face, mesmerized by them one second and sucking on them the next. I handed him his doll and let him suck on that. Sometimes it was like his mother was staring back at me. It calmed me. I felt her invisible arm link with mine. I played with his tiny feet, tickled his toes, and watched his delighted face when I held them up for him to see, like they were not his own. He made me laugh and brought me out of my miserable state, for a little while.

Towards the end of the day, the sky darkened. Hessa's face was shrouded in shadows. I worked on, until the first splashes of water hit his little face.

I pulled myself up slowly and brought Hessa out of the rain. This would be a good test for our cabin. The clay had been drying for about a week. I hoped it was enough time. I pick Hessa up and walked towards the dark wood shelter, the need for a door very evident as rain cascaded down the gap, creating a curtain of water to pass through. The others filtered in from the forest with various handfuls of nuts and fruit, tumbling them into a blanket by the fireplace. I laid Hessa on my bed and made a fire. The sudden chill in the air was hurting my lungs. It had changed so quickly.

I thought of Joseph and Careen and prayed they'd found shelter somewhere.

I struggled to light the fire. Damp wood, damp matches. I blew on it, trying to persuade a flame. Slowly sparks crept up around the timber. But once I had it going, the room filled with smoke; dark grey smoke, pushing forward and pouring out the windows. Hessa was coughing. Our eyes were stinging. The chimney must have been blocked, or had collapsed outside. I smothered the fire, then, using the water that was pouring from where the door should be, I completely extinguished it.

The cabin was only leaking in one corner of the room. But rain was streaming through the uncovered windows. We moved all our stuff into the dry corner and stayed close to each other for warmth. I used some of our only nails to hammer a blanket over the windows, which helped a little. The rain had certainly pointed out some things that needed to be fixed. It was going to be a damp, miserable night.

I couldn't sleep. I was too concerned for Joseph and Careen. Listening to the wind blowing outside, it sounded devilish, howling and whipping the trees. I worried about the strength of our cabin. If it fell down on us, we would be crushed by the trunks on the roof. It held strong. I pictured

Careen and Joseph huddling together in the cold, as we were. At least I started to, until my imagination had them crawling all over each other and I felt sick to my stomach. It wasn't going to happen, I convinced myself. I held Hessa close and concentrated on keeping him warm.

Deshi was awake too. Apella and Alexei were intertwined with one another and had fallen asleep in a tangle.

"Don't worry, I'm sure they're fine," Deshi said unconvincingly. He held out his hands out for Hessa, but I wasn't giving him up tonight.

I shook my head. "Don't you worry—there is no way I'll sleep tonight. You try and get some rest."

"You forget, I worry about Joseph the same way you do," he said, annoyed. I nodded. There were no words for him.

Changing the subject, I asked, "What do you think of Careen?"

He laughed. "If you're asking—do I think she'll have a go with Joseph, absolutely!"

My heart stopped.

"Just ask me if you think he would rise to the bait," he said, leading. I didn't say anything and he answered himself, "Absolutely not."

He put his hand on my arm and patted it awkwardly. "You have nothing to worry about."

"Yeah, except them freezing to death, or being attacked by an animal, or not having enough to eat," I said bitingly.

"Ha, yeah, except for that."

I laughed despite myself.

"Rosa, I don't think you understand just how much he loves you."

I squirmed uncomfortably. A cloud of memories rustled up, like shaking a blanket full of dust. Bits billowing out, some floating away, others getting stuck up your nose; a choking feeling, making you want to sneeze.

"I do," I said quietly, but I sounded unsure. I knew how I felt, but his feelings had always seemed a bit confused in my mind. There was the *before* and the *after*. *Before*, when we were in Pau, when he wanted to be close and then pushed me away, the *after* when he told me to leave him alone at the Classes. Then there was the *before* that I didn't know about, those four months I was missing, where he said he never stopped looking for me. The next *after*, was yet to come. After the baby was born.

Deshi laughed, but there was a bitter edge to it. "No, you don't." He looked to the door, watching the water streaming down the entrance, almost solid. "When you were at the Classes, did you ever see how much pain he was in?"

Most of my memories were of him joking around and talking to his friends. There were only a couple of times that he gave the impression that he was less than happy. I held my heart, feeling like if I didn't, it would fall out of my chest. These memories were too painful. They brought with them visions of Rash, Henri, blood and broken faces. I just shook my head.

"He was in agony. He wanted to talk to you, but he knew you had no future together; he was trying to do the right thing. But by the time he had decided to tell you how he felt, it was too late, you were gone." Deshi's hands fell flatly on his crossed legs. "When you disappeared, so did Joseph. He was tormented. He barely ate or slept. I don't know why, but I think he blamed himself, like he could have stopped it." Deshi shook his head. I knew Deshi blamed me; he probably blamed me for a lot of things.

"Anyway, what I'm trying to say is, he would never jeopardize the delicate 'thing' you have, not in a million years." He said it with distaste. He didn't get it. I'm not sure I really did either. All I knew was how it felt.

He looked at me, eyes tracking up and down, narrowing. I knew he didn't think I was worth it. Our relationship always tipped back and forth like this. Talking about Joseph was a mistake for us. It hurt.

I tried hard not to sound jealous when I said, "Do you think he is safe with her?"

"I don't know."

I rolled my eyes, "Well, that's comforting"

"She's a bit crazy, but I don't think she'd hurt him. I think she's just traumatized or something."

I stared into my lap, Hessa folded neatly into the crook of my arm. Was I traumatized? Probably.

The Woodlands

At some point in our conversation, the rain started to ease. A damp, dreary morning peeked through the doorway, mist rising off the grass. We roused ourselves and surveyed the damage. The top of the fireplace had collapsed, dark grey stones and clay scattered on the ground. But apart from that, everything looked ok. The cabin had held up remarkably well through the storm. We identified the holes and started working to fix the problems. The fireplace needed to be shorter and wider to make it more stable. Once it was repaired, we lit a fire and let it burn all day, baking the stonework and drying the cabin out.

Apella and Alexei went into the forest to search for food. I tried following them once but I felt I could barely walk two steps without feeling the weight of the leech pushing down. I needed to go to the toilet all the time and I felt quite sure, if I walked too far, the child would fall out. *Bang!* Like a chicken dropping an egg.

Apella asked me to lie down and she poked and prodded my stomach. Squeezing me like an orange. She informed me that the baby was engaged. I giggled, "What? Already? When's the wedding?" Apella almost smiled. Almost. She explained the head was down and that's why I felt pressure. So, it was standing on its head and bouncing up and down on my bladder. Great. She also said not to worry, this could happen weeks before the baby was actually born but I should try not to push myself.

Every time someone went past the tree line and returned, my heart cartwheeled. I could always hear them coming before I saw them and I hoped against hope that it was Joseph, stomping through the forest. It never was.

The forest was looking sparser now, more leaves on the ground than the branches, looking like stark, straggly fingers reaching to the sky, calling the snow. The colors of the leaves reminded me of the sunset we had viewed from the top of our hill. I could almost feel him breathing into my neck, his strong arms holding me. Almost, but not quite. I knew he had probably reached the city by now but there was no way he would be back today unless he ran all the way. I dreaded another night alone but at least the rain had moved on. With the fireplace repaired, hopefully we would get some sleep.

Deshi helped me drag the heavy shutters inside. We leaned them in the windows, leaving a crack for ventilation. Deshi settled Hessa and gave him a bottle. We ate in silence, chewing on Careen's dried rabbit. All of us wondering where they were, whether they had found anything, and when they would be back.

Apella parted the silence with her wispy voice. "Rosa, I have been meaning to say thank you."

I looked at her incredulously. Thank me for what? I had been nothing but mean to her from the moment we left the facility.

"Without your knowledge and persistence, we never would have built this home. We would have kept walking and ended up freezing to death. This was a good idea," she finished.

I felt myself blushing, unused to the attention, the adulation. "Well, I guess I should thank you too. For rescuing me, I mean." I only half-meant it but I attempted to smile. She was trying. She leaned over to me and hugged me. My body stiffened in reply.

She composed herself, tightening her face, straightening her clothing, reminding me of my mother; unable to really show emotion. Uncomfortable that she had displayed vulnerability. I knew deep down that was why I found Apella so hard to deal with.

"Aw, well, isn't that sweet," Deshi cooed, shaking his head from side to side, slowly. I shot him a dark look.

Alexei stuttered as he patted me on the back, "I'm sure they'll be back tomorrow, try and get some sleep, dear."

We curled up around the fire. The cabin was warm and felt secure and safe. Surprisingly, I fell asleep quickly, the stress of the last two days stripping me of the will to keep my eyes open.

I dreamed I was in the ruins of the city again. I felt different. Looking down at my stomach, it was smooth and flat. I touched it, panicked. My hands coasting over a tight blue top and shiny pants. I was screaming. 'Where's my baby? Where's my baby?' as I searched frantically, overturning whatever was in my way. Hearing a cry, I changed direction. I kept searching as yellow eyes closed in on me. Laughing as their tails curled and whipped. In the distance, I could see Joseph holding a child. He looked at me for a second, smiling, then returned his gaze to the baby in his arms and walked away. The yellow eyes pounced on me, tearing my flesh with their claws as I kept screaming, 'My baby, my baby,' over and over again. One of them cupped its hand over my mouth, speaking. 'You can't scream, no one screams here'.

I woke up sweating and cold. It was still dark and the fire was out. I heard birds calling and knew it must not be far from morning. I dragged myself up and brought my knees to my chest, well, as close as I could anyway. My dream was echoing in my head. Something was wrong and, for the first time, I was fearful for my baby.

I put a dry log on the fire, watching the coals brighten and begin the dance of sparks to flames. I leaned down and blew, anxious to feel the heat. "Joseph, come home." I wished into the coals. I sat there and waited for the others to wake. They were taking too long, so I grabbed a blanket and made my way outside in the darkness. I scrambled up the hill. It was much harder without Joseph's hands on my back but I got to the top in time to see the sunrise.

It was grey and then suddenly a flourish of color. The blood red sending shivers down my spine. It spread over the hills like a great hand. Lighting the darkness and stirring the wildlife.

I sent my love out over the hills and through the valley, willing it to reach him and pull him back to me. I prayed he would burst through the trees at any second. I sat and stared at the place where I thought he would return. Nothing. Soon the others would be wondering where I was, so I made my way down the hill, slipping several times on the dewy grass.

No one ate breakfast. Everyone kept staring off in the distance waiting, watching. If they came back now it would be miraculously fast but logic had no place in our thoughts. Like it or not we had created a little family and right now two of its members were missing. None of us would feel right until they returned.

The cabin was about two-hundred meters from the edge of the forest. None of us wanted to go far, so we all sat outside, trying to keep busy by packing extra mud into the cabin walls or playing with Hessa, all of us watching the edge of the forest diligently. I started fashioning a broom to sweep the floor with. Initially, we thought we wouldn't have time to make a proper floor, but now it seemed we could lay some stones. I spoke to Deshi and we spent some time finding nice flat ones we could use. By lunchtime, we had a decent-sized pile. Time was passing so slowly it was painful.

We stacked the stones inside and I crouched down and started digging holes to match their shapes. It was therapeutic, assessing their shape, size, and thickness and fitting them together like a jigsaw puzzle. We didn't talk, both too anxious to make conversation, so we worked silently. We'd laid about five stones when Deshi picked one up to hand to me and then stopped, smiling as he glanced out the window. He put the stone down and held out his hand, pulling me to my feet.

There he was, walking casually out of the woods. He moved slowly and deliberately. Almost mechanically. I ran outside. He was less than one hundred and fifty meters away. I ran towards him, the joy coursing through my veins, the gold running over me like rain. I would have skipped if I could.

Where was Careen?

He put his hand up as if to wave and then stopped, clutching his chest. Something was wrong. I started running, gold turning to slick black oil. If I could get there, maybe I could stop it. My face stung with tears, as I ran as fast as my body would allow, feeling the weight of the baby pulling me down.

One-hundred meters.

He looked at me, confused, and he fell to his knees. His hands braced his body for a second before they crumpled under his weight and he was lying face first in the dirt. Careen appeared from the forest, running as fast as she could. Her face fierce and concentrated. She didn't even stop as she passed Joseph and headed for the cabin.

"They're coming!" she screamed.

I didn't listen. I was nearly there. I could hear the others running towards us. Frantic footfalls sounding like a stampede.

Twenty meters.

I approached him slowly. When I reached his twisted body I leaned down, afraid to touch him. I reached out a trembling hand and stroked his blond curls. I whispered, "Joseph?"

He moaned. I eased him onto his side. His right arm was soaked in blood. I carefully peeled back his shirtsleeve. What I saw was beyond description. The red rawness was replaced with a gaping wound, blood and pus mangling his perfect skin. Tiny blue veins tracked up his arm. I followed them and pulled open his shirt, buttons diving from his chest like crickets. Tiny spider web veins spun their way grotesquely towards his heart.

He looked at me but right through me. He blinked once and then he exhaled slowly. I watched his parted lips, waiting for him to inhale. One second, two seconds, three seconds…Hysteria rising, my own breathing fast and uneven. I shook him. He lay limp. The others had reached me.

"No!" I screamed. "Do something. Help him!" My voice was alien, panicked and high pitched.

I threw myself across his body and wailed. I kept screaming, "Wake up, wake up. I can't do this without you. Wake up."

The pain was immense, like someone had stuck a live wire to my body and jolted me with electricity. My skin prickled and vibrated, tiny needles jabbing me all over. I put my head down to kiss his cold lips, shaking uncontrollably, hardly able to connect. This wasn't happening. It had to be a dream. "Wake up!" I screamed again. His eyes were vacant and terrifying.

Wind whipped my hair around, like a tornado had come from nowhere to pluck me from this place. I held onto him tightly. They would have to tear me from him.

More pain. It started in my back and crept around to the front of my stomach, hardening as it went. Like fingers reaching around me from behind, it clasped tightly around my belly and locked like a stone vault. Wind and buzzing filled my ears. Careen screamed over the noise, "They're here!"

Arms dragged me backwards. Someone whispered, "Let go," impatiently as they wrenched me from Joseph. My eyes focused on the crescent-shaped wounds on Joseph's good arm, filling with blood from where my fingernails had been digging into his flesh.

"No, no, no, no!" I screamed, until I was suddenly rendered silent as more pain shot through me, making my legs spasm and my head cloudy. I watched my deadened feet plowing the ground. Leaving a path of dug-up dirt back to where my heart lay.

Apella was kneeling over Joseph, pumping his chest with her folded hands. Leaning down and blowing into his mouth. I craned my head, waiting for his hand to move. Waiting for him to sit up and laugh, telling Apella to stop kissing him, he was spoken for.

Nothing.

Above her a chopper was hovering, a man climbed down a ladder a rope ladder that was swinging uncontrollably. Shots rang out, splitting the air like a whip crack. The man fell dead from the ladder but another was descending after him. More shots, this time ringing out from two different locations. Joseph and the others were getting farther and farther away. I couldn't put the two scenarios together. It was a jumble of images. Was he dead?

I heard a massive explosion, booming thunder. The ground shook. Alexei and Apella were running, dragging Joseph across the ground, slipping and struggling under his weight. Deshi was running with Hessa, towards me, covering the baby's face with his hand. Then a mass of people seemed to come out of nowhere, surrounding us. The burning helicopter, blades still turning slowly, whipped up the dirt behind them. I couldn't make sense of anything I was seeing.

The dragging stopped. People ran past me. Two men had Joseph under the arms and someone was holding his feet. He was grey and lifeless. His body didn't respond to being jerked up and down as they carried him.

He was dead.

I felt myself spinning out of control. I was trying to breath but I couldn't suck in any air, it was too painful, it burned, crushing me under an invisible weight. I was drowning. The despair was more than I could stand.

I heard voices but the words were nonsensical.

"The monkeys must have turned it on."

"They followed the signal."

"Yes, six of them."

"One fatality."

Was I going mad? I clawed my way out but the pain was dragging me back under, working its way into my ribs, trying to part them and pry me open like a can of beans. Where was Joseph? I needed to see him now. I grasped at imaginary fingers, craving his touch like it was the only thing that would stop me from sinking into the dark forever.

"Joseph!" I shrieked one last time as a door shut in my face. The green of the hills disappeared. The smell of damp dirt filled my nostrils. There was no air here.

I was underground.

38

Birth

How can I do this alone? Everything has been turned around and I no longer know where I am or what I am supposed to be doing. The guiding light is gone. The gold has turned to lead. I'm sinking and I have no will to fight it. I hate you for leaving me here. I hate you both.

The impatient voice was speaking to me. Less impatient and more irritated. Asking me to get up, could I walk? I didn't want to walk. I didn't want to move. The ground was hard and cool. It felt like as good a place as any to give up. I lay with my cheek pressed to it, waiting for the next onslaught of pain to attack me. Hoping it would tear me open and kill me right there.

But it wouldn't leave me alone. I wanted to sink under water, drown in my grief, but it wouldn't let me. It pulled me to sitting and tore at my arms. *Get up!* It rumbled and tightened until I couldn't stand to lie there anymore. *Get up!*

Apella approached me, her perfect face shadowed with concern. She seemed far away, turning her head and muttering quietly to these strange people dressed in greens and browns. "We need to move her; she'll be safer further underground."

No.

"No!" I cried. "I'm not going anywhere."

I tried to stand but my legs strained and more pain hit me like a sledgehammer. My body vibrated, as if struck like a bell.

They whispered to each other and then Apella nodded minutely.

Strange, covered feet were in my vision, white canvas shoes with dark stars on them, muddy and worn, one lace untied. The wearer leaned down, a dark shadow of a face, and squeezed my neck between his thumb and forefinger. Everything went dim, muffled voices, a sharp intake of breath, and then it was black.

I half-hoped I was dead, but the intensity of the pain that woke me was so strong I actually started scrambling backwards to escape it. I hit my head on the back of a bed. Apella and Deshi were both there, looking at me with pity or fear, I wasn't sure. Apella placed a cool hand on my forehead.

"You're in labor, Rosa, it won't be long now," she said calmly.

I hated her. I focused all my anger on her tiny, pale face. Willing it to crack and crumble like a shattered plate. How could she be so calm? Joseph was dead. We were captured. I surveyed the room quickly. There were things I recognized, like the hospital bed and the white sheets but there were other things I didn't get, like the roof of the room was carved rock. And why was Deshi allowed to be in here with me? There was one other person in the room, a tall man with blondish hair. He walked over to me and held my wrist. He was wearing tan pants and a colorful check shirt with the familiar white coat over the top. He looked to be in his late thirties. He smiled at me. I just stared blankly back. Things didn't fit. Where the hell was I?

I was about to ask when the pain and hardening began again. I held my stomach as it rippled across my body and cried softly. A small whimper. Closing my eyes, I tried to dig right inside the pain. Any distraction to stop me from thinking about Joseph's lifeless body, or kissing his cold, cold lips.

Someone took my hand. It was cool and damp. I didn't open my eyes. I clenched them closed. I would pretend it was him. If I didn't look, I could hold onto him for just a little bit longer. I gripped onto the hand tightly. I can do this, I'll get it out, and then I can leave.

"You're doing great, Rosa, keep going. I know it's hard...But Joseph..." Deshi couldn't finish his sentence. I could hear him sniffling.

"No one speak, please," I ordered, waving my hand around the room threateningly.

I imagined he was next to me, rubbing my back and pulling my hair out of my face. 'You're a mess,' he would whisper, grinning. Sweat dripped over my brow and into my eyes, I swiped it away. If he was here, I could do this. If he was here, I could do this better.

Trembling, I could feel it coming on stronger now. So close together, I couldn't breathe between them. Like an assault, with no way to counter. It felt like I was being stretched, a crowbar between every bone in my spine pulling me open, breaking me apart, piece by piece.

I screamed. An unnatural howling scream that came from deep within, carrying with it the physical and emotional suffering I was enduring at that moment. I heard glass shattering, metal trays hitting the ground, and people crying out, close by. "Stop, wait!" a woman yelled.

Something was telling me I had to get up. Get up. Move, now.

Eyes still closed, I dragged myself off the bed, stopping to bow over every thirty seconds, as the contractions hit and then passed. I opened my eyes and steadied myself against the wall, inching myself slowly towards the door.

The man with the tan pants walked towards me. I put my hands up, ready to push him away, "Don't touch me. Please, I need to..." I pleaded through quivering lips. I didn't know what I needed to do but I had to move. He didn't try and stop me, he didn't speak, he just gently pulled my arm around his neck and supported me as I walked. Apella walked next to me, "There's not much time," she whispered, telling me, or him I wasn't sure. He nodded. I ignored her. I wasn't sure where I was going, but I pushed through my pain, breathing and timing my steps between. I was propelled forward by an invisible force and, with nothing left to lead me, no hope to hold onto to, I abandoned myself to it. I got to the door and Deshi pushed it open for me.

A metal bar came straight at my face and I fell backwards onto the floor, blood gushing from a cut across my cheek. The pain of the cut was barely noticeable compared to the contractions. A sticky, cold, liquid spilled all over my front. My legs buckled, I knew that was it, I could go no further. I closed my eyes.

"Oh God, I'm sorry. Rosa, Rosa, are you all right?" Someone was shaking me.

A hand was at my face, warm and familiar. Was I dead?

I daren't open my eyes. I kept them shut as the hand attached to a strong arm pulled me into a lap.

Unfortunately, I couldn't be dead as the sudden and acute need to push was upon me. Someone steadied me as I pulled my legs up and pushed for all I was worth. I opened my eyes narrowly. Apella was facing me. Her eyes were focused as she looked into mine and said, "Rosa, try not to push." Something was wrong.

"What? What is it?" A frantic voice whispered as I held my breath.

"The cord is wrapped around the baby's neck."

It hit me and the urge to push again was so strong I wasn't sure I could fight it, it felt wrong. Then that voice uttered deep and low in my ear. "Hold on. Just hold on." If I was imagining it, I didn't want to know. I just closed my eyes and listened. Letting the words wash over me, sprinkling gold dust over my eyelashes. Panting and clenching my fists, I kept fighting. I was always fighting.

After what seemed like forever, Apella said, "Ok, next one you can push."

I couldn't keep going. If this ended, would my delusion disappear? I would be alone again. My energy was gone. *Let it kill me*, I thought.

"I can't," I replied, listless, I let my arms fall to the floor. My legs relaxed. I gave up. "He's gone," I said and I wanted to go with him.

"What's wrong with her?" I heard Deshi say, confused.

"She's under too much stress," Apella replied.

I felt warm hands take up my bleeding face.

"Open your eyes," he said

I shook my head, "No."

"You are so stubborn," he said with a weak laugh. I felt warm breath on my face and anticipated his lips touching mine. The kiss was unlike anything I had felt before, intense and sweet, painful and almost frightening. The lips pulled away. "Open your eyes," he asked again.

I opened one eye briefly. I saw a flash of blond curls. His scruffy face was as grey as breakfast but the smile on his face was real and full of smashing color.

"One more push, Rosa, then it's over," the man in the white coat said kindly, but urgently.

Joseph put his arms under my own and entwined his fingers with mine. I summoned what I could, sure it would not be enough, and pushed.

It was out.

Finally.

The release was tangible. The flood of relief overwhelming.

I waited to hear a cry. With Clara, Hessa had cried almost immediately. Apella was holding it in her arms, rubbing its body down fervently with a towel. We were all silent, watching, waiting. She concentrated her fingers on its chest, rubbing gently in small, circular motions.

"Waaaaa!" it cried and announced itself to the world. An unearthly caterwaul that hurt my ears. I turned away.

I shivered, feeling cold, my body retreating from the trauma. They covered us both in a thick, fur-lined blanket. I lay there in his arms on the corridor floor.

"You did it," he whispered, his chin resting on my shoulder. I turned. He looked sick, his face pasty and pale, but he was alive. My brain gave up trying to understand how this was possible. Questions could be answered in time. "You look beautiful," he said, not taking his eyes off me, despite the commotion going on around us.

He was attached to several machines that he had dragged down the corridor with him. The metal bar that had hit my face was lying next to us, a stand for a fluid bag.

"Ha, I was sure you would tell me I was a mess!" I laughed.

"You are," he said, "but a beautiful one."

I rolled my eyes, looking over to the others, all smiling down on us. Apella held a child swaddled in cotton. I raised my eyebrows, questioning.

She understood. "He's fine."

The leech was a boy.

39

Ties

F ive minutes after the birth of our son, Joseph's heart stopped. As he had before, outside, he clutched his chest in pain, tried to breathe but couldn't, and then he fell to the side of me.

I sat there in shock and watched as they dragged him away. His usually large form looked oddly small. They put metal pads to his chest and yelled 'clear!'. His body pulsed unnaturally, rising as if attached to the pads by magnets. They did this again and again. His heart would start and then it would stop, over and over. I sat there shrouded in a blanket, an onlooker to the chaos, barely noticing the people fussing around me.

Now I sit in my room. Pieces of the puzzle slowly filter through as visitors come and go, feeding me small bits of information. They had me in with the baby to start with, but after two days, I asked them to take him away.

One thing I knew, Apella was right all along. These people were the survivors. They were not from the Woodlands and, as of yet, I didn't exactly know where they came from.

Joseph lay in the bed next to mine, breathing with the aid of a machine. It pumped air in and out of his lungs for him, squeezing in and out like a concertina. The blip of the heart monitor, a comforting noise, let me know, for now, he was alive. How had it come to this, so quickly, so violently?

The kind doctor, who introduced himself as Matthew after all the confusion had subsided, explained it to me carefully, repeating it several times, as it took a while to sink in. Joseph had been bitten by a spider.

"A spider?" I raised my eyebrows dubiously.

"Yes," he said running his hand through his hair casually. "Think of it as a tiny, microscopic killer with eight legs, smaller than a grain of sand."

"Is this supposed to make me feel better?" I asked, scowling.

A warm smile spread across his face and I felt my temper calm. He tipped his chin, "You asked me, remember?" His voice was the timbre of honey, slow, deliberate. Sure. I crossed my arms and listened. "Joseph would never have seen it. They are translucent and live inside the rings of the tree trunks." Guilt stabbed me, jagged and pulsing. It must have come out of one of the trees I had asked the boys to fell for the cabin.

Matthew moved to Joseph and pointed to his ragged arm. "The venom started here, eroding the skin as it went." I covered my mouth, feeling the heave of a cry creeping up my throat. They had left it open so the wound could breathe. The muscle was gone and it was a concave mash of red flesh. It hurt me so much to see him this way.

Matthew returned to me. I watched his lips moving, the way his mouth turned up on one side as he spoke, "The poison worked its way through his system, arriving at his heart. Usually it takes a long time to get to the heart, but because he ran so far, the blood was pumping faster around his body. It sped the whole process up."

"So he should have died," I said, feeling deadened myself.

Matthew nodded, his hands clasped across his lap. He lifted his hand and I thought he was going to touch me but he just rearranged the covers around my knees. "We got to him in time," he said.

While I was in labor, Joseph was in the other room, close to death but fighting. They administered the anti-venom and began the process of cleansing his blood of the poison. He was awake. He had asked for me and they had told him I was safe. They didn't tell him I was in labor.

Then I'd screamed.

"They tried to hold him down. The nurses were swinging from his arms like pendulums," Matthew said with humor in his eyes, "but he's strong. He was too strong."

I winced as I heard how Joseph followed my screams; unaware of how sick he was or what damage he was doing to himself, dragging monitors and bags of blood and fluid with him. It was so hard to hear. If I had just kept my mouth shut, maybe he would have been ok. It made me feel sick to think of the choices I had made and what they had done to the people I loved.

Matthew moved to check Joseph's monitor, putting a stethoscope in his ears and listening to Joseph's heart. "Adrenalin makes the heart pump blood faster," he said with his hands on Joseph's chest. "It pushed the leftover poison straight to his heart, causing the second heart attack."

Heart attack. He was nineteen, strong and healthy. He shouldn't have had a heart attack. He never would have if he hadn't met me.

Matthew put his hand on mine. "So now we just need to wait. His body needs time to repair."

I looked over at what was left of my Joseph. His strong jaw looked hollowed, his sun-kissed skin was now pale and yellow. He looked ten years older than he was. All the same, he was beautiful.

"But he will wake up?" I asked, although it sounded like pleading.

"I don't know, but there is hope," Matthew said with a reassuring smile. He made me feel comfortable. His ease of talking, the way he planted himself on the end of the bed without asking, was unlike any doctor I'd ever met.

"What can I do?" I leaned in, my eyes exploding out of my head with desperation.

He smiled gently and patted my hand. "Just look after yourself and your baby. Joseph's going to want to see you both happy and well when he wakes up."

I sunk into my pillow, which smelled like mildewed feathers. Was that all? I had tried. But for me, the overwhelming feeling I'd had after giving birth was release. I'd spent the last four months dreaming of having the thing out of me. Now that it was, it was hard to feel anything other than relief. My worry for Joseph took up most of my time—there was little room in my head or my heart for the baby.

"Have you thought of a name?" Matthew asked as he paused in the doorway, his hand wrapped around the scuffed yellow doorframe.

I shook my head. I'd always thought Joseph would name it. He was the one who wanted the baby. I reached over and touched Joseph's hand. It was warm. I wondered if that was all we were going to be allowed. Just those short two months together. It had gone so fast. I wish I had taken the time to appreciate it while I was there. But then I didn't know it was going to be ripped out of my shaking arms.

I pulled myself back in time and dreamed of his hands touching my face, his lips caressing my neck. Where did it go? It disappeared like a wisp of smoke disturbed. I reached out to grab it but it was nothing and slipped through my fingers. I rocked back and forth, hugging my knees. I ached, thinking I might never get it back.

Every day they brought the baby in to feed. Which I did. I wasn't a monster; I didn't want him to starve. Feeding was a strange feeling and I wasn't entirely sure how I felt about it. I imagined Joseph would laugh at my awkwardness, my shyness about people seeing me with my shirt up. The baby fed well but screamed every time they took him away. I closed my ears to it. I couldn't be what they wanted me to be.

I focused on connecting the floating puzzle pieces I had garnered so far. But it was difficult, the people never stayed too long, they always seemed bustled and busy. They were cagey. When I asked them questions, they quickly made excuses and left. They didn't seem dangerous but there was a silent threat in their aloofness.

When Careen bounced into my room, I was surprised. I hadn't seen her since the day the baby was born and I thought maybe she'd left. She swept her hair behind her ears, the fluorescent lights streaking it the color of autumn leaves, and said flatly, "Where's your baby?"

I sighed, my own hair swung like a ragged curtain in front of my eyes, the color of dull dirt. "I don't know."

Her eyebrow arched, but for once she didn't blurt out whatever she was thinking. I waited for it to return to its normal position over her stunning blue eyes before I asked, "Careen, what happened?" My arms splayed open, palms up, like I was asking the heavens, "How did it all go so wrong?"

She flinched at my emotional tone and moved away. Seeming unaware of Joseph in a coma next to my bed, she plonked herself at his feet and put her hand on his leg. I resisted the urge to slap her because I wanted to hear what she had to say.

She paused, her eyes dancing about in her head like she was searching for the answer up there. When she finally opened her mouth, I jumped. "The trip there was pretty boring," she said lightly, "Your Joseph was a complete gentleman."

"He always is," I snapped.

She smiled to herself, twirling a strand of hair around her finger. "On that rainy night, he gave me his blanket." I gathered the sheets in my fists, trying not to turn her from a strawberry blond to a patchy bald girl. "He was scratching his arm a lot but I just thought he was nervous." I rolled my eyes, wondering how someone who'd survived on her own for so long could be so blind to her surroundings. I cursed myself again for not being there. I would've known something was wrong. I squeezed my fists tighter, my nails digging into my palms. It was a good pain, a distracting one, but it wasn't enough. I knew something was wrong before he left but I let him go.

Careen's eyes swept over my hands, which were attempting to turn my sheets to dust, and said, "The place was swarming with soldiers. We nearly walked straight into some but Joseph saw them and pulled me behind a wall. They were talking about us." She stood up straight, imitating the conversation they'd overheard. "Stupid kids. They must have switched it from reader to communicator."

"Well, they must be here somewhere and we are not to leave until we find the two boys and Apella. The rest don't matter."

She giggled, covering her mouth. "You know, they were monkeys."

I ran my hand through my tangle of hair and leaned my cheek into it.

"What were monkeys?" I asked, exasperated.

"The yellow eyes, dopey," she said through her perfectly shaped lips, like it was obvious. "The survivors said the monkeys were playing with the reader and made the switch. It set off a signal, which was easy enough for the soldiers to follow." That wasn't funny. It was frightening to know they were looking for us and they knew our last location.

"Careen, focus."

She waved me off dismissively. "Anyway, once Joseph heard that, he started running. Yelling at me that we had to warn you guys." She frowned, her delicate nose pinched in concentration. "I guess they heard us or something because halfway back, we heard the choppers." She put her hand to her heart. "I'm sorry. I didn't know he was sick. I think I would have helped him if I'd known." I stared down at my fingers, still splintered from working on the cabin. I was scared of what I might say if I looked at her. "When he fell down, that's when I knew something was wrong, but by then, well, you know," her eyes flicked to the monitors. I shuddered at the memory of him walking towards us. The way happiness had swelled inside me and then was quickly replaced with fear and throat-closing panic.

She patted his leg. So she did notice he was there. "That's all I know really. The green hills all around here are hollowed out. The survivors don't live here; they send people up to keep tabs on the Superiors. They seem nice, don't you think?"

She tilted her head, waiting for me to respond. I just stared at her hand on Joseph's leg, boring holes in her long, slender fingers with my narrowed eyes. Finally, she became uncomfortable and said her goodbyes. She was going to explore the rest of the mounds that day. She skipped out the door, without a care in the world.

Apella and Deshi visited me more than anyone else. Apella, ever hopeful, brought the baby in to see me as often as she could. I knew she was caring for him, but I can't say it bothered me. She was capable.

Deshi brought Hessa to see me as well. I laid him on the bed in front of me, sitting cross-legged on the mattress. His big blue eyes stared at the light above my head. I stroked his dark skin and smiled. Something hummed in my chest, an uncomfortable squeezing. *I know you're disappointed in me, Clara.* I thought of her clear eyes, everything about her was clear and pure. That was something Joseph and her shared. I snapped my head to Apella. "Can you bring the baby in here?" I asked. She darted off quickly, returning five minutes later with the boy.

I handed Hessa to Deshi and took the baby, cradling him in my arms. I peered into his face, wondering how something that had been inside me for nine months could feel so far away. He blinked at me and scratched his cheek accidentally with his fingernail, pulling at his skin like he didn't know it was his own.

His eyelashes were dark, like mine, but his skin and hair were fair like Joseph's. I traced the tips of my fingers through his wavy blonde hair, touching him as lightly as I could.

"Why are his eyes grey?" I asked Apella as I handed him back to her. She sighed, obviously disappointed.

"Sometimes it takes time for babies to develop eye color. Maybe in a few weeks-" she started.

"Thanks, you can take him back now." That beautiful green with flecks of gold I was searching for was not there. I wanted to see Joseph's eyes again, so very much.

Deshi glared at me with raw irritation. "If Jo saw you now, he'd be devastated. It would break his heart to see you treat his son this way."

I crumpled. I was upset too. I wanted to be better but I couldn't seem to claw my way back out of the fog this time. It pegged me to the ground as I whipped and struggled. I was in a stasis of hell I didn't know how to escape.

"His heart's already broken," I whispered. And mine? I wasn't sure where it was, floating somewhere out in the atmosphere, between the lines of blood red and purple of the sunset. It wasn't here with me.

"You have to try, Rosa, try harder than you're trying. If not for yourself, try for Joseph," Deshi pleaded.

"That's a lot of trying," I sneered sarcastically.

I could feel the anger rising up in me. I knew I should stop but of course I didn't. I screamed at him. "And how is it that you're so fine? You're supposed to love him too! What would you do if we took Hessa away from you—how would you feel then?" I took it too far, as I always did. Deshi sighed and took Hessa away; his straight posture and upward glance snubbed my wretchedness. He was suffering but he didn't let it drag him down to uselessness like me. I didn't see him again for two weeks.

Joseph, wake up. I knew I couldn't do this. I told you I couldn't, but you didn't believe me. Your faith in me was foolish and misplaced.

Blip. Blip. Blip. Breathe in, breathe out, breathe in, breathe out.

I couldn't stand the noise anymore. I'd been in here four weeks now, and I'd never left this room. The machine's humming and Joseph's mechanical breathing was suddenly too much. It squeezed my head and tore at my ears. Air. I needed air.

He had to be close by. I pulled on the clothes they'd provided. Blue cotton pants, odd-looking white shoes with a red star sewn onto the side, and a white cotton t-shirt. I grabbed a jacket as an afterthought, I hadn't been outside for a while and the weather may have changed.

I walked down the hall, peering in doorways. It reminded me, chillingly, of being underground in the facility. My heart beat irregularly.

Three doors down, I peered in to find Apella rocking the baby to sleep in a wooden chair. Colorful curtains hung from fake windows, pictures of toy bears were painted on the wall. A small handmade rabbit sat in the corner of his cot. When she saw my dark face, Apella startled.

I walked in quietly. "Can I have him?" I asked, holding my hands out like I was asking for a sandwich.

"Of course." She handed the tiny child to me wrapped in a yellow blanket.

"I want to go outside," I said, hunched over the sleeping child.

"Um, ok, I'll have to ask..." she stuttered, pushing a red button behind her again and again, without breaking eye contact.

Matthew appeared in the door, flanked by two nurses.

"Rosa wants to go outside—is that permitted?" Apella asked.

Matthew watched me as I held the baby uneasily, considering my request. "Can't see why not. You've been sitting in that room four weeks now. It might do you some good to get some fresh air. Come with me," he beckoned with a tanned finger. The nurses entered the baby's room as we left, pretending they hadn't been called by the emergency button, fluffing pillows and straightening sheets.

I followed Matthew. Apella tagged along behind us. We walked in silence. Every now and then he stopped to turn lights on, a chain reaction of fluorescence pushing out the darkness. As I swept my eyes around, it was obvious that most of this vast catacomb was devoid of people.

We descended down a slope, and then it flattened out for a while. We climbed steeply. Several steps led to a big metal door. Matthew unwound a giant metal cog and the door creaked open.

"We'll wait here," he said with an unperturbed smile.

"But..." Apella objected. Matthew was standing in front of her and she was on her tiptoes, poking her head over his shoulder, straining to catch my eyes and tell me she thought it was a bad idea.

"We'll wait here. Come back before it gets too dark and push here," Matthew said as he revealed a tiny button hidden under a flap of grass, "when you're ready to come in." Then he shut the door and they disappeared. I ran my hand over where the door had been. Remarkable. You couldn't feel a lump or bump or anything.

We'd come out on the other side of the valley. I could see our little cabin in the distance, planted sloppily in the landscape. I couldn't see the chopper. They must have moved it. The baby snored and snuffled in my arms. He was peaceful, unaware.

With quick steps I made my way to the place I wanted to go, enjoying how light my body felt. If I wanted, I could run. I jumped lithely across the stream and quickly made it to the cabin. It looked tiny and sad now.

After four weeks, you'd never know I'd been pregnant. My smooth skin had bounced back perfectly. The only reminder to me was my belly button, once a perfect round dimple; it now looked like a frown, a downward facing indent in my dark brown skin.

The air clung to me like tiny icicles as I started climbing hill. I picked my way up the incline carefully, holding the baby in one arm and steadying myself with the other. It was slow and cumbersome. The sun followed me up over the hill. Fresh smells of grass and pine filled my nose.

I reached the top and sat down. Bringing my knees up, I laid the baby down on my legs so he was facing me. I wondered what Apella thought I was going to do. I suppressed a wicked giggle at the thought of her worrying about me throwing the baby in the stream, or tossing him off the hillside. Matthew had only known me a short time but he knew me well enough to realize I was not murderous. I was struggling but I didn't want to hurt him. I wasn't sure what I wanted to do with him.

I examined the baby carefully. He was still sleeping, his little eyes rolling under his eyelids. I wondered what babies dreamed about. What memories did they have of their life within the womb?

"You've been with me this whole time," I said. "Your dreams are probably filled with wolves howling and chopper blades grinding into the ground. Your father talking and laughing."

Tears came easily.

"You heard Aunt Clara screaming when she brought your cousin Hessa into the world." I frowned, wondering if that was the right word, cousin. "You heard me crying when she slipped away. You probably even felt my heart beating so fast every time your father kissed me or even touched my hand."

I stroked his tiny, blonde head. He looked nothing like me. What part of him was me?

"What should I do?" I asked the sky. The sun was setting, a muted, streaky sunset, mostly yellows and oranges. I imagined Joseph was here, but he was standing back from me, waiting. This decision was mine to make.

I unwrapped the baby, inspecting him closely. A tiny, scooped nose, a heart-shaped mouth, I shrugged. These were features I'd seen on every other baby. He was defenseless, small, but strong. He kicked his leg inadvertently.

"You're a fighter like me, aren't you?" I cooed, tapping his bare belly lightly, something stirring in me I couldn't identify.

He opened one eye lazily. So there it was—his eyes were blue. I was disappointed, I was hoping for that beautiful green of his father's eyes.

"How about this? I'll make a deal with you," I said as I let him grab my finger, curling and uncurling. "I'll try. I'll try harder."

He opened the other eye, yawning and showing me his gummy mouth and milk-stained tongue.

I gasped, my heart beating strangely. Steady but fast. Warmth creeping in. Not a surge of it, not an instant flood, more like a slow drip, edging its way in softly and certainly.

One blue eye and one brown.

Acknowledgements

Firstly I'd like to thank my husband Michael for being ever patient and supportive of probably the craziest thing I've ever attempted. Even though the only feedback you ever gave me was, 'it's good', it kept me going when I doubted myself, because you never did. My children Lennox, Rosalie and Emaline deserve special credit for putting up with a somewhat absent mother and really, you three were the inspiration for this story in so many ways.

Thanks to my sister Kristen for being the guinea pig who had to read to first version of this book. And for answering all my annoying texts in the middle of the night, asking you unreasonably for feedback on each chapter immediately after you'd read them.

Chloe Lim you are a legend. Thank you for editing The Woodlands so thoroughly, removing all my unnecessary commas and adding all the ones I missed. Your support and gentle pushing in the right direction helped make it what it is now.

To the members of Clean Teen Publishing: I never thought publishing a book could be this fun! Thank you Rebecca Gober, Courtney Nuckels, Marya Heiman, Dyan Brown and Cynthia Shepp for believing in The Woodlands and taking on this first time Aussie author who decided to write about a post apocalyptic Russia.

Finally, I am eternally grateful to my Beta readers. Your amazing support, generous feedback and honesty gave me the confidence to pursue publishing The Woodlands and now, here we are!

About the Author

Daughter of a Malaysian nuclear physicist father and an Australian doctor mother, Lauren Nicolle Taylor was expected to follow the science career path. And she did, for a while, completing a Health Science degree with Honors in obstetrics and gynecology. But there was always a niggling need to create which led to many artistic adventures.

When Lauren hit her thirties, she started throwing herself into artistic endeavors, but was not entirely satisfied. The solution: Complete a massive renovation and sell their house so they could buy their dream block of land and build. After selling the house, buying the block and getting the plans ready, the couple discovered they had been misled and the block was undevelopable. This left her family of five homeless.

Taken in by Lauren's parents, with no home to renovate and faced with a stressful problem with no solution, Lauren found herself drawn to the computer. She sat down and poured all of her emotions and pent up creative energy into writing The Woodlands.

Family, a multicultural background and a dab of medical intrigue are all strong themes in her writing. Lauren took the advice of 'write what you know' and twisted it into a romantic, dystopian adventure! Visit Lauren at her website: www.LaurenNicolleTaylor.com.

CPSIA information can be obtained at www.ICGtesting.com
Printed in the USA
BVOW04s2000010914

365071BV00004B/106/P